Slump

By Kevin Waltman

Cinco Puntos Press
El Paso ✹ Texas

FIRST EDITION

10 9 8 7 6 5 4 3 2 1

Library of Congress Cataloging-in-Publication Data

Waltman, Kevin.
Slump / by Kevin Waltman. — First edition.
pages cm — (D-Bow's high school hoops ; [2])
  Summary: Derrick "D-Bow" Bowman thought sophomore year would be easier, but his girlfriend Jasmine leaves him for putting too much focus on basketball, the jump shot he worked on all summer is not working, and his father has an accident, forcing Derrick to accept that basketball cannot be his only priority.
  ISBN 978-1-941026-00-7 (hardback); ISBN 978-1-941026-01-4 (paper); ISBN 978-1-941026-02-1 (eBook)
  [1. Basketball—Fiction. 2. High schools—Fiction. 3. Schools—Fiction. 4. African Americans—Fiction.] I. Title.
  PZ7.W1728Slu 2014
  [Fic]—dc23
                            2014007657

Book and cover design by Anne M. Giangiulio
with b-ball advice from Bubba, Lulu and John Jacob.

Many thanks to Ben Osborne, editor of *SLAM* Magazine,
for connecting Cinco Puntos to Kevin Waltman.

For Royce Waltman, who always did his dirty best.

PART I

1.

Any other sixteeen-year-old gets invited over to his girl's place to watch a movie and it doesn't mean they're going to "watch a movie." But with Jasmine, it actually means that's what we're doing—sitting on the couch in her living room, her tablet between us, checking out Jackie Robinson and *42*. She chose it with me in mind, I know, because otherwise no way does Jasmine get a sports movie. But I'm not feeling it. Baseball. History. Whatever.

What I'd feel is some alone time with my girl. Maybe hit *pause* and see what happens live-action on this couch. But it would be easier to uproot Roy Hibbert in the post than to get Mr. and Mrs. Winters to leave their precious Jasmine alone with me on a Saturday night. Her dad in particular doesn't seem to trust me. Every time I glance his way, he lifts his eyes from the book he's reading and gives me this dead stare, like he can see right into my heart and tease out all my desires. Every time I come to the house, he says, "Hello, Derrick," like he's greeting his sworn enemy, and then he just watches me in silence the rest of the time. Jasmine's mom, at least, asks me how I'm doing, even has

Kevin Waltman

the courtesy to talk to me about the upcoming season. But every time I answer her questions, she gets this strange look on her face, the way a teacher listens to an answer that's not quite right. Then maybe she'll wonder aloud if the city should be shelling out millions of dollars just to keep the Pacers here.

What it means right now is I have to sit inches from Jasmine—hear her soft breaths, smell that wild scent that always seems to cling to her—and *behave*. Once, when her dad got up to answer the phone, I dared so much as put my hand on her knee. She swatted at it with the back of her hand like there was a bug on her, said, "Come *on*, Derrick," and tilted her head toward her mom.

My mind drifts. I gaze around the living room. There's nice sturdy furniture all facing inward toward an area rug. Hardwood floors without a speck of dust. No television to be found, but three heavy bookshelves stacked with serious-looking literature. They live in an old two-story just off Fall Creek. From the looks of it, they've pumped some money into the place. Around them, the other houses and apartments show years of neglect, structures that must have been prizes way back when, now sagging into city decay. Sometimes I come here, and I think Jasmine's parents are single-handedly trying to lift up the neighborhood. Other times I think they're just trying to show off how much better they are. I also wonder what they thought of her last boyfriend—Nick Starks, the point guard before me for Marion East. If they think so little of basketball, I bet they're confused about why Jasmine keeps bringing home ballers.

Jasmine must sense me drifting because she glances up at me, then back down to the screen. So again I try to invest myself in the

Slump   9

movie. Oh, it's good. I guess it even *matters*. But what really gets me invested again is that Jasmine edges just a centimeter my way, enough so our legs touch. Then she leans into me. It's a soft, slow movement. I can almost feel her muscles easing one by one. I loop my arm around her and pull her in as tight as we can dare with her parents watching. She nestles her head against my shoulder and chest, and her curls brush just for a second against my mouth and chin. *Damn.* I'm surprised she can hear the movie over my heart.

The thing is, I know that's kind of pathetic—getting all heated up just by sitting so close. I mean, my boy Wes has been hitting it with Iesha for months. All summer. All fall. I know he runs game about it like any other guy—an exaggeration here, a little lie there—but if half of what he says is true, he's way past getting sprung over this kind of thing.

Jasmine's dad clears his throat and says something to her mom about a school board election. It's just a little noise to remind his precious girl he's still watching. And it works. She straightens back up, and we watch the rest of the movie like we're nothing more than good friends.

They underestimate their girl though. In truth, it wouldn't matter if we had the house to ourselves for a whole weekend. No way Jasmine's letting me get very far. Even later when we're in her car, she's not taking me anywhere but straight back to my house. As we approach, I try to drum up some conversation just to keep the night from ending.

"Movie was good," I say.

"Mm-hmm."

"You know all that stuff? Like, before watching the movie?" I ask.

"Most of it." She comes to a full stop at Patton, probably the only person in the city who doesn't just roll on through here. I always get tensed up when she's driving me around. I got so wrapped up in hoops this summer—running on the blacktop with Moose, then with my AAU team so I could play against organized competition, the best of the best—that I didn't have time to get my license. She rolls up to our house and then hits me with it again. "Be nice if I didn't have to be your chauffeur *and* your girlfriend," she says.

"Aww," I say, starting to protest. "You know how it is."

Jasmine laughs. Just tilts her head back like she thinks she's hilarious. "Oh, Derrick," she says. "I love how you've known me for a year, and you still don't know when I'm putting you on."

I smile back at her. "It's not like you make it easy."

"Where's the fun in easy?" Then we sit there, the night silent except for her running engine. "Besides," she says, "I've got to keep you on your toes about it with the season coming." Then she leans over and kisses me. It's a brush of a kiss, so brief it seems almost accidental, but even in that split second there's a jolt. "Go on," she says, motioning toward my door. "I'll see you tomorrow."

Then, in a blink of an eye, I'm on the sidewalk watching her go. It makes me feel played, all of it—the teasing, the relenting, the tempting little send-off—as played as if I'm on the court trying to guard some jitterbug point, the kind who's all zig and zag, faking and faking until you're turned in circles and jumping at phantoms.

Soon. That's all I can think. Soon with Jasmine.

And soon, a season to dig into. A slate of games. A shot at Hamilton Academy and Vasco Lorbner, the team and the player that bumped us last year. If I close my eyes I can still see his shot that sent us home. And I can see him from the AAU circuit, where he showed

Slump 11

out—not just the best big in Indiana, but in the whole country. He seemed even cockier this summer, telling me every time we crossed paths that he was looking forward to beating us again come winter. The player, his legend, his ego, growing and growing into some giant I've got to knock down.

Jasmine's taillights flash as she stops again at the corner. Then she's gone.

I'm a coiled spring.

Kevin Waltman

2.

We hit those boards in our practice unis, and I feel the jump in my legs. Been too long. I see Moose getting his hammies loose at mid-court, then Devin takes a break from knocking down Js to come over to me. It's his senior year. If we had a little static last year, it's gone for real now. We know that together we can form one of the top backcourts in Indiana.

"You ready for this, Bowen?" he asks.

"Born ready," I say.

AAU in the summer just isn't the same. I know that it matters, that scouts get all over it because it's the best against the best. But aside from bumping into Vasco and hearing him talk trash—something I seem to mind in everyone but him—it felt like I was just going through the motions. Real basketball is here. In the gym. With my boys.

Stanford busts out of the locker room at a near sprint, then joins Moose in his stretches. With those two, Coach Bolden's dream has come true—Moose shed a good fifteen pounds over the summer. It's like every ounce of it turned into muscle on Stanford's frame. Stanford's shaved his head for the dawn of the season. It makes him look a little younger somehow, like it shows off how lanky he is, but there's a little more rip in those arms this time around.

I nod toward Moose. "It's here," I say. All those blazing July days we ran at the Fall Creek court, we kept telling each other we were sweating to be stronger for November.

Finally, the doors to the locker room swing open and Bolden comes striding out, looking like a man who means business. Murphy's on his heels. When he hits the court, he jogs to the center, clapping his hands. "Let's go, let's go, let's *go!*" he shouts. The freshmen straggle in behind him, one of them without his kicks even laced yet.

I try not to laugh, but I steal another peek at Moose. He just grins and shakes his head—*freshmen*. Always the same. One of them, a wire named Josh Reynolds who's got a chance at finding some perimeter minutes, sidles up next to me. Maybe he thinks standing next to me will make him look good by association or something. He's got this naïve smile that makes him look even younger than he is. He's all eagerness, a little sheen of sweat on his face. I just give him a quick elbow. "Freshmen on the end, Reynolds," I say. His face sags into a mope and he looks like a ten-year-old who lost his lunch money, never mind he's 6'1".

No time for pity. "Down and back!" Bolden shouts, and he blows that whistle like an angry sergeant. *Boom!* We're off. Already loose, I go full tilt and get out in front. Behind me, I hear the thunder of a dozen pairs of shoes pounding hardwood. I feel this rush in my chest. That sound means I'm back with the team. It means the season's in swing again. It means in a couple weeks Bolden will have us worked into a frenzy, ready to tear apart Bowman Academy when they step between these lines.

Kevin Waltman

We get back to the baseline and Bolden doesn't even pause. "Down and back!" he shouts again. Then again. And again. And again. He follows this up with a few sets of suicides. I watch the eyes on the freshmen grow wide, like they're trying to ask *How long is this crazy man gonna run us?* They've heard the stories about Bolden, but the reality of the man is bigger than the myth.

After the second suicide, Murphy walks over to Moose. He's got a basketball in hand and bounces it to the big man. He nods to a side bucket. "Free throws?"

"Naw, Coach," Moose says. He zips the ball back at Murphy, a little pepper on the pass to let him know he means it. "I didn't bust ass all summer so I could ease off now."

"Atta boy, Moose," Bolden says. He loves it. It's not like anyone's going to confuse Moose with a long distance runner. He's still built more like Glen Davis than Blake Griffin, and his chest is heaving with the effort. My man's gassed. But when Bolden blows that whistle again, Moose is off, digging hard. Better than can be said for some of the freshmen who are dragging like they've ruptured an Achilles.

Bolden puts us through more suicides, then has us go down and back a few times in a defensive slide. By the time we're into the third one of those, even my thighs are burning. I see Moose start to straighten up when he thinks the coaches aren't looking. And, at last, a freshman bows out. As I turn at the baseline, I see him at mid-court. It's Reynolds. He just raises up and puts his hands on his lower back. He takes a couple steps off to the side and doubles over. I see Bolden approach so quickly his whistle bounces off his chest as he walks.

We finish the drill leisurely, everyone easing off now that

Slump 15

Bolden's locked in on Reynolds. Coach works on him, daring him to quit, shouting to make an example of him. Reynolds has a lighter complexion, almost amber. It makes it easy to see the blush rising in his cheeks. He tries to make eye contact at first, but soon that head just sags, sags, sags, until his chin's down on his chest. "You think this is bad?" Bolden shouts. "If you hang your head at this, how are you gonna react when things get tough in a *game*?" We're all on the baseline now, catching our breath. Now Bolden just stares at him, trying to decide whether he's made his point enough yet. It's a brutal silence for a few seconds before Coach just says, "Go on," like a father finally letting a kid go out to play even though his chores aren't done. Reynolds trots back but doesn't look at anyone, his head still down. I feel for him—something about the way he looks reminds me of my little brother Jayson—but I'm not here to hold some freshman's hand every time Bolden gets mad.

"All right," Coach barks. "Let's see what we've got. Bigs down here with me. Perimeter guys stay there with Coach Murphy."

First drill we do with Murphy is just a catch and shoot. We jab baseline and then flare to the wing for his pass. Devin goes first, since he's a senior, and he drains his.

"One!" Murphy yells.

Then me—a splash from range with the form I worked on all summer.

"Nice motion, D," Murphy says. "Two!"

Murphy keeps counting out how many we've made in a row. We make it up to six.

Then it's Reynolds. Maybe his legs are still a little wobbly from

Kevin Waltman

the sprints—as soon as he releases, you can tell the thing's short. It barely scratches iron, and Murphy yells out, "Start over at zero!"

We hit the opposite wing. That rhythm of kicks cutting on hardwood, of leather finding bottom, of Murphy keeping track of our makes—it all clips along at a cracking pace. But this time, Reynolds misses even worse. It hits glass first and then bangs off the rim toward the opposite sideline. He runs after it with his head down, and I can see it happening. The kid's coming undone right in front of us.

When we shift to the baseline, I bury my J and then hurry to the back of the line to get in his ear. "You're good, man. It's all good. Just keep with it here."

Reynolds nods real quick, but he doesn't look at me. He takes a deep breath. When it's his turn, I can see the doubt on his face even before he catches Murphy's pass. Sure enough, his shot sails long—an air ball—and he mutters to himself and shakes his head as he chases it down.

Reynolds is going to have to get it straightened out on his own, I decide. I know I've got to use every possible moment to get better if I'm going to close that gap between me and Vasco. The J stays true for me on both baselines, then the top of the key. On the last one, I bottom it out so true it draws a long, impressed whistle from Murphy.

"Way to stroke it," Devin tells me.

"It's on this year," I tell him. "We get someone to step up at the three, and we'll run fools off."

"Might be a big if," Devin says. He nods toward our teammates, and I see what he means. Reynolds has potential, but he's a disaster so far. Then there's a sophomore who moved in at the end of last school

Slump 17

year, J.J. Fuller. But he's hard to read. Nice stroke. Some bullish bulk to him. Except he has no burst as far as I can tell. That's about it.

When we finally start running sets, that problem becomes apparent. Fuller gets first crack, but it seems like the only move he's got is to lower his head and go straight to the rim. Once in a while it works out, but more often he gets pinned deep with nowhere to go. He looks mad all the time too. The more he struggles to make plays, the deeper his brow pinches down. If Reynolds looks like a fourth-grader, Fuller looks like he's forty—a stocky build with a big, blockish head. He's darker-skinned too—it all makes him look like some severe old man who's going to yell at you for playing your music too loud.

Meanwhile, Reynolds is running at the two spot with the second team—a tough draw. That means he's trying to check Devin, who just turns him inside-out. One possession Devin drives past Reynolds to set up an easy dunk for Moose. Next time Reynolds gets pinned in the lane, and Devin calmly buries a three. Next time Reynolds darts to the passing lane, only for me to drop a back-door to Devin who lays one in.

On that one, Reynolds doesn't even try to recover. He just stands there, his heels on the three-point stripe and watches his man score. "You better work harder than that!" Bolden yells. "Your man's scoring, and you're out there feeling sorry for yourself. You can't let one mistake turn into two!"

And then it happens. I see Reynolds break, right there. This horrible pained look crosses his face, and he hangs his head again. He juts out his lower lip, and his eyes get wide and glassy. It looks like he's going to cry. I'd be embarrassed for him if he did that. Instead, he just

Kevin Waltman

turns and starts for the locker room. He peels his jersey off and lets it hit the floor behind him.

We all look around, like someone ought to stop him. Bolden's not one to let off the gas. He doesn't even look at Reynolds. Just starts the next drill. Ruthless.

But that's the way it has to be. Practice clips along, drill to drill. Nobody so much as mentions Josh Reynolds. His exit does cool our fire a little bit, like it's cast a curse over us. It just seems wrong that less than an hour into the season, we're already down a man.

Coach Murphy feeds me as I rotate around the arc. This will be our after-practice ritual same as last year, only this time Coach Bolden is down on the other end feeding Moose in the post. We're determined to make this year the one.

I rattle one home from the wing, but my shot from the baseline skims off the back rim.

"One more," I shout to Murphy. I keep my hands out, waiting for the pass. He zips it to me, but runs at me with his hand up. I shoot fake and go. One dribble to the short baseline for a pull-up. Long again.

I rebound it and lay it in, then grab the ball again and back up. I knock in a short J just to end on a make. Still, those two misses leave a sour taste.

"You'll get it," Murphy says. He knows it's that pull-up jumper that's the real key. Nobody's going to confuse my shot with Stephen Curry's, but people will have to respect it this year. And if I can get all the way into the paint, I know I can finish near the rim. It's the

Slump

intermediate game that I need to work on, and it's coming as slowly as the long-range jumper did last year. I get that down though, and nobody will check me. Only thing left, I guess, would be to work on hitting jumpers coming off of screens, but Bolden wants me working on one thing at a time.

"I know," I say. After last year, I trust Bolden and Murphy a little more, so even if I'm frustrated at missing the pull-up, I'm not letting it get to me. I catch my breath in the lane. I see sweat stream off my face and fall on the ball, streaking the leather. It's been a good first day. Except for Reynolds. Something about watching him wilt was hard to handle.

"You okay?" Murphy asks.

"Yeah," I say. I don't want to gripe on the first day. But then I figure it's just Murphy. You can tell him whatever you want, and he won't go telling Bolden if he doesn't need to. So I jersey some sweat off my face and say, "Bolden got after Reynolds pretty hard."

Murphy glances down to the other end of the court, where Bolden's still working with Moose. We keep our voices low. "What are you trying to say?"

"Just—" I falter. It feels wrong criticizing Bolden right here in the gym. It's like swearing in church or something. "I don't know. I didn't think he needed to run him off. He could have told Reynolds to stop before he just gave in."

Murphy narrows his eyes at me. It's not an angry expression, just him trying to figure out how to respond. "Derrick, I didn't want to see the kid quit either, but what's Coach supposed to do? He can't go beg a freshman to stay just because the kid's feelings got hurt. He does that

Kevin Waltman

and how is he supposed to come down on Moose if he has to sometime? Or on Devin or you?"

I nod. He's right. I figure that's that, so I tell him I'll catch him tomorrow, and I head for the showers.

"Derrick!" Murphy calls. I turn and see that he's got this half-smile on his face and he's shaking his head at me. "You're not hearing me. Someone should have stopped Reynolds, but that was *your job*." I stare back at him. "If you want to take charge, then you need to be a leader. You should have been talking Reynolds back onto the court before he got halfway to the locker room."

"All right," I say, but I don't buy it. It's not until later—after my walk home and a quick text to Wes to tell him what went down and a short conversation with Jasmine who doesn't want to hear a word about it and after I eat dinner and hear my dad and Jayson get into some nonsense, when I crack the books and stare down at the page—that I finally have to admit it—Murphy's right. That one was on me.

3.

The days are getting colder so Uncle Kid and I are both in sweatshirts when I meet him at the court. Bolden had us practice early—six a.m.—so the women's team could use the court right after school. At least that's what he says. I think he really just wants to push us harder. Anyway, it's an afternoon off so I hit the blacktop with Uncle Kid before dinner.

"Who's Bolden gonna put at that three spot this year?" Kid asks. He's corralled a rebound from one of my shots and is spinning in lay ups on alternating sides of the rim. Even at his age and even without taking great care of himself, he's an agile guy. Give him a month to get in shape, and he could still crack any starting five in this state.

"That's the question," I say. "It's trouble no matter what."

"Shoot," Kid says. "Ain't gonna matter." He zips a behind-the-back pass my way. I loft up a deep fade that falls short. Not exactly a game shot, but this is time to just kick it with Kid. "You got the core. You, Devin, and Moose. Bolden's half as smart as he thinks he is, you'll rip right through Regionals."

I almost say, *At least Sectionals*, but I stop myself. I know that's messed up thinking. The only reason I'd say that is because I know Vasco and Hamilton Academy are lurking in Regionals. But if I don't at least believe we can take them down, then there's no way we'll actually do it. "I feel you," I say, trying to act confident. When Kid rifles me another pass, I grab it and rip it to the rim, just to shake off that touch of doubt.

Nobody else is at the park this time of day. It's near dusk in the second week of November so you're only on a court if you're a hoops junkie. When the wind kicks up, you can feel the full bitterness of winter lurking in it. If you don't keep moving, it's like you can feel that temperature dip down a little bit more by the minute. The trees just have a few dirt-brown leaves clinging to them so you can see across Fall Creek toward downtown. For most people, these are depressing days. Just a hard stretch until the holidays. But for me, all of this means live action—*real basketball*—is just over a week away.

"All right, Derrick," Kid says. "Level with me. Is Bolden still as much of a hard-ass as he always was? I hear the guy's softened up a little."

I smile at Kid. I can't tell if he's just messing with me or not. "All I can tell you is if Bolden's softened, I'd hate to have played for him before." I think about Reynolds. "I mean, you should have seen Bolden the other day. Just made some freshman quit."

"No shit," Kid says. He swipes the ball out of my hands and chucks up a quick jumper.

I realize I've touched a sore spot. Nobody besides Kid really knows all the details of why Bolden ran him off all those years ago, but that's because nobody talks about it. I chase down his rebound and

Slump 23

figure I better change the subject quick. "Game of *Horse*?" I ask. I'm deep in the corner, one foot out of bounds, so when Kid nods *Yes*, I say, "This starts it." I fire, a rainbow to clear the backboard, and it just scrapes off the iron.

Kid chases it down. "Ahh, little nephew," he says, "you should know better than to give me a freebie. That's all I need." He squares up from the shallow wing. "Bank," he says, then kisses one home. Just like that, it's all good again.

We match each other shot-for-shot, getting a letter here and there. Soon we revert back to trick shots, over-the-shoulder flips and long hooks, the kind of things you'd try when you were a kid. And that's what a session at the Fall Creek park with my uncle does—takes me right back to being ten, working up a sweat with him while he teaches me the game.

My mom's wary of me hanging with Kid. Always has been. But she squints just a little more after the whole drama with Hamilton Academy last year and how Kid tried to squeeze a job out of it. I don't care. Kid's my man, and he hasn't said squat about Hamilton since last year.

"Now tell me, D," he says while knocking home a twenty-footer, "how come a baller like you is hanging with your uncle. You don't have some honey hanging on you? Where's that girl? What's her name? Jayden?"

"Jasmine," I say. "She's busy." I square up from Kid's spot, but just the thought of Jasmine rattles me. I miss to the left, bad.

Kid senses my weak spot and stays after it. "Man, when I was your age I was drowning in girls. And, remember, girls were tighter with it back then. Not like now."

I try not to let it get to me, but it does. I know Kid's talking nonsense like every other guy who's ever yapped about how much he's getting. Same as Wes talking noise about him and Iesha. My next shot still rattles out, and Kid has me at S.

He scoops up the board, steps to the deep corner, buries a J. He doesn't say anything this time, not while I dribble over to the spot, not while I take a rhythm dribble, not while I set my feet. But just as I'm about to release, he leans over. "Don't think about the girl," he says.

I barely scrape iron. I wheel toward Kid to protest—it's just *wrong* to heckle a guy like that—but he's too busy laughing to even hear me if I did. "Ah, D," he says. "You can't let a girl in your head that easy."

It makes me mad at first, but when Kid sees that, he starts laughing even harder. I have no choice, I guess, but to let it go. I relax, let him have his fun. "Two out of three," I say.

"You're on," he says, then sprints over to scoop up the rock.

As he does, out of the corner of my eye I see a figure approaching the court. When I turn, I see it's someone on a bike, a basketball pinned in one elbow. Reynolds. On his bike, he seems oversized, like he's stolen it from a younger kid. His elbows and knees stick out awkwardly, and he looks every second like he's about to fall. He recognizes me too and hangs a quick u-turn. I'm almost offended. First I think, *Let him go. Let him just ride his sorry ass right back across Fall Creek Parkway if he's gonna be that way.* I turn back to see Kid bank home a J from the wing, and I chase down the rock and head to his spot. Then I stop. I check back toward Reynolds, who's waiting for traffic to clear so he can make his getaway, and I remember what Murphy said to me after that first practice.

I bounce the ball back to Kid. "Reynolds," I holler. "Come on, man."

Slump   25

He doesn't even turn around, just keeps swiveling his head to check traffic. I sprint to catch him before he has a chance to cross. I grab onto the back of his seat just before he starts to move. He pedals a couple times, dragging me forward with him, but at last he gives in. He gets off the bike and turns to me. "What?!" he shouts.

"I just want to talk to you, man."

He refuses to meet my eyes, looking down at his shoes. That amber face of his looks almost tender, like a little kid's or a girl's. "Nothin' to talk about."

The kid makes it hard. But I stick with it. "You gotta come back to practice," I say. "You had a rough start, but you can't just quit."

He gives this expression like he just tasted something rotten. "Come on, Derrick! I don't even want back at this point."

"That's not true," I tell him. I've seen him at this court enough to know he wants to suit up for Marion East.

"Well, it doesn't matter. Bolden won't ever take me back now," he says.

"Look, man, I'm trying to be solid with you. Bolden will take you back. I swear it." I steal a peek back at Uncle Kid who buries a twenty-footer, easy as waking up, and I wonder how true my promise is. I mean, if Bolden didn't make any exceptions for Kid back in the day, he's not cutting slack for Reynolds.

He snorts at that, aware that I'm laying it on a little thick. "Whatever," he says. He turns to go again. He's still not going to share the court with me, not even here. Something about that *whatever* makes me burn.

"Fine," I shout at him. "If you're such a baby, we don't need you anyway."

Kevin Waltman

He doesn't turn around, but his shoulders sink just for a second. I know in my heart I shouldn't have said it, that it was the opposite of what I wanted to do. Then again, some people are hell to help.

He busts across Fall Creek, his back tire spitting up some loose dirt. I head back to Kid, who has questions written all over his face. "Don't ask," I say.

"Fine," Kid says. He bounces the ball back to me. "Quit messing around and step up to take another beating."

"Kid, I'm gonna run you off this time."

He laughs, acting like that's an impossibility, and we're right back in our groove.

When I get home, Jayson's got my parents in a fit. He's been testing them more and more lately, like he wants to see just how much he can get away with before Dad truly goes all old school and cracks him good. Of course, Dad will never do that. But when I walk in, he's standing over Jayson—who's stretched out on the couch like he's just relaxing at the beach—pointing to Jayson's room.

"I know you have homework."

Jayson doesn't budge. "I can finish it later," he says.

"Listen to your father," Mom shouts. She's in her chair, trying in vain to read a magazine. When she sees me she shakes her head, just tired of the static with Jayson.

The house has been more tense than ever for the last couple months. Dad lost hours again when one of the places he works security decided they could get by with one guard after hours. So now he's trying to make up for it by working late shifts at a convenience store on Central. It cuts into his sleep. But more than that, he knows it's beneath him to be ringing people up like some teenager. All of it makes me second-guess my decision not to transfer to Hamilton Academy—it would have been like treason to transfer to Vasco's team, but they would've given my dad a full-time job. I try not to think about that. What's done is done.

I side-step the whole scene. I walk into my room and flop on my bed, stare up at my poster of LeBron. The League seems a *long* way off, but I just keep focusing on it. Work, work, work. Get better, get better, get better. And someday I'll be the poster on some other kid's wall, and I sure won't be dealing with an uptight girlfriend or stress from my folks.

That's when I hear it. "Thomas?" my mom says, then again real sharp: "Thomas!" I sprint back to the living room to see my dad leaning against the wall with a confused look on his face. Mom is beside him, and even Jayson is sitting up now.

"Dad?" I say. "You okay?"

He straightens up slowly and shakes his head like a dazed fighter. He raises up his hand and motions for my mom to leave him. "F-f-fine," he mutters. He starts to talk again, but it's like he can't get the words out. Then he shakes it off, says it again. "F-f-fine. I'm okay." But it's garbled again.

My mom's eyebrows pinch down in concern. "You need to go to the doctor," she says. "That's the second time."

Something about my mom snapping at him helps him regain the power of speech. "I don't need a doctor, Kaylene. I just lost my balance."

Mom spins away and storms back to the couch, gone from concerned to angry in a split second. She opens her magazine like she's trying to rip it in two. "You just don't want to spend the money!" she shouts at him.

"Sick people go to doctors, and I'm fine," he says. He tries to shout it after her, but there's not much breath behind it. Then he looks at us, tries to put that calm Dad-look on his face, but there's a trace of worry behind his glasses. "I'm fine, boys. Don't worry. You—" he motions at me— "go on back and relax." Then he points at Jayson. "You go do some homework."

This time Jayson obeys, slinking off the couch and slipping into his room. He doesn't even look at me, like he's ashamed of how he's acted.

4.

A year ago, Wes would have taken the desk right next to me. He would have leaned over every time Mrs. Hulsey turned to the board, making some crack to try to get me to laugh. And he would have been bugging me all week before every test, wanting to compare notes—just to come over and blow a few hours messing around instead of studying.

Instead, I've got to ride out American History solo, and it's not going well—a string of Cs and C+s so far. Wes is in the back, so close to Iesha I wouldn't be surprised to see her crawl into his lap. I should be happy for him. In some ways I am, but it's like my friend is just gone. Vanished into some fog of love.

Right now, Mrs. Hulsey is trying to drive home a point. "It changed everything," she says. "It was called 'The War to End All Wars.' Every facet of American life—literature, politics, religion—was touched by it. That's what happens when more than 300,000 men in a single generation are killed or wounded. In Russia, that was more like two million."

As she says that, there's an audible yawn somewhere in the

Kevin Waltman

classroom. Hulsey's excited expression drops into one of disappointment. She's always shocked and saddened that we're not all as amped as she is about things that happened a century ago. Every so often Marion East gets some young, white teacher who's seen one too many movies about going to an inner city school and saving everyone. The ones who've been here a while end up sneaking cigarettes behind the track between classes. Mrs. Hulsey isn't there yet, but give her a few years.

She puts one hand on her hip and gestures to the class with the other. "Who was that? I'm sorry if one of the most important events in American history bores you. Maybe you won't be bored when you see these things on the next exam."

A brave soul raises his hand. It's Martin Germain, a football player, who takes pride in how little he cares about this class. "Well, I get the American stuff," he says, "but why should we care about the Russians? Didn't we, like, hate them?"

Just like that, Mrs. Hulsey brightens again. Her eyes widen and her mouth pops open like she's about to gasp. Even a jaded question is enough for her. "That's the interesting thing, Martin," she says. "We did end up hating them, but during World War I, we were on the same side. That's how strange and intriguing history is."

She floats that comment out to us like she's fully expecting us to buy in all of a sudden. It's no go. The only response she gets is a muffled laugh from the back of the room. I turn, see it's from Wes, who's leaned over to whisper something into Iesha's ear.

For the first time, real anger flashes on Mrs. Hulsey's face. Her cheeks redden and her lips pinch together like she's trying to hold something back. When she does speak, her words are as measured as

Slump 31

when Coach Bolden's trying to hold back his rage during a timeout. "You think you know everything," she says. "Sophomores in high school, and you think you know it all. But do you know what sophomore means?" She pauses just for a second, but she doesn't really want us to answer. "The *soph* part is where we get *philosophy* and *sophisticated*. It means *wise*. But the other part is where we get the word *moron*. The word *sophomore* means *wise fool*. Next time you think you've got it all figured out, remember that."

The only sound in the classroom now is the hum of the heater. Mrs. Hulsey stands there for a few seconds, like she's surprised she got that angry. Then she tells us pages to read. She retreats behind her desk and marks up old assignments.

When the bell finally rings, I hang back for Wes. He and Iesha are still whispering to each other, like they're all alone on an island instead of in the middle of a classroom in the middle of the week in the middle of the city. I have to call his name to get his attention, and even then Iesha takes a few more steps with her hand in his, so it looks like he's about to drift away at any minute.

"What up, D?" he asks, still leaning in Iesha's direction.

"We hanging later?" I ask. "We can maybe hit up Ty's Tower."

His eyes light up for a second, but then he glances over at Iesha. She just gives him this knowing look, and he turns back to me. "Nah, D. Can't tonight. Maybe next week?"

I want to call bullshit on him. I mean, for years Wes clung to me like I was a life preserver. And he always jumped my case if I blew him off for hoops. Now he gets action with a girl and it's *Nah, D. Maybe next week.* "Sure," I say. I try to let the word slide out slow, to let him know this isn't cool, but he doesn't seem to notice. Soon as it's out of my mouth, he's turned back to Iesha, and they're out the door. Just me and Mrs. Hulsey, who's still not looked up from her desk.

Practice was ugly. Being stuck with Fuller at the three is starting to turn Josh Reynolds into Lance Stephenson in our minds. And if I weren't so mad at the kid, I'd make another appeal for him to come back.

The truth is though, we can make do with Fuller. Tonight was just one of those sluggish practices. The shine is off things, and now we're just slogging until the regular season starts.

I make the mistake about bringing it up to Jasmine. Now, she gets grief from her parents or gets something less than a perfect grade on a quiz, and I'm all ears. I'll listen to her vent all night if it means I get to spend time with her. But let me mention one thing about Bolden being the biggest pain-in-the-ass to ever blow a whistle, and I get the sigh. It's that long, frustrated sigh she gives when I've done something intolerable. She looks away as she does it, like it causes her physical pain.

"What?" I ask.

"Basketball," she says. "Again."

We're sitting on Massachusetts Avenue at some place you can get coffee and sweets and frozen yogurt. Not my speed, but I've never been one to say no to Jasmine. I mean, there have been maybe three other black people in here the whole time. The place is filled with people who scream money—thirtysomethings with their bratty kids, college-aged kids in their stupid band t-shirts and caps. I feel like there should be a sign at the Northeast end of Mass Ave telling people from my blocks that they're not invited down here. Sometimes I think this is the Indianapolis

Slump 33

Jasmine wants to belong to, but I give her the benefit of the doubt—there aren't really any decent places open late in our part of town.

"It's not like I'm making you memorize our offense," I tell her.

She gives a half-smile at this. "Fair enough." She takes a sip of her hot chocolate.

I push my luck a little. "And be honest, girl. You were into it last year when we got on that tear. We make it to State and you'll be as amped as anyone."

She sets her drink down and gives me a long stare. For a second I think I've crossed some line with her, but then, slowly, she lets her mouth curl into a grin. "Oh, Derrick," she says, "you are a funny guy."

After that she starts telling me about things she's learning in her Honors English class. Stuff about the Harlem Renaissance, stuff about W.E.B. DuBois, things I know I should care about. But I can't get worked up about what happened to poets a century ago, no matter how much she insists it's still important today. I don't let on though. I ask questions, nod along, be a good boyfriend. When she's done, she starts window shopping, making a huge deal out of some vintage handmade scarf she sees across the street. I want to get on her for liking white people things, but I know better. Besides, I also know she'll look good in that scarf if she ever gets it.

Later, we're parked down the street from my house. I don't want to go in—not because it'll be the same noise of Dad and Jayson arguing, but because this is as close as I've been to Jasmine all night. I lean over and kiss her, and she doesn't pull away. That's all it takes to set me racing. I lean in closer and take her hand in mine, feel the heat flowing from her. When I kiss her again, our bodies press together, and I can feel her heart pounding. I slide my free hand along her knee and up to her thigh. I pull back for just a second and look at her—her eyes are half-open, and her lips are still formed into a kiss. She shifts her hand in mine, then places her other one over it. Looking at our hands, her skin tone a couple shades lighter than mine, I think about more of our skin touching. I imagine rolling back to her house, sneaking up into her room—maybe her parents are out—and getting down to it for real.

But just as I go in for another kiss, images of where this could go zipping through my head, Jasmine squeezes my hand and pushes it back against my chest.

"You have to go," she says. She sounds out of breath and distracted, like she's afraid of what will happen if I don't get out of the car.

"Jasmine," I say and lean back in.

She stiffens and turns her head away. "No, Derrick. You've got to go. It's late and I need to get home." There's no sense in trying for more. It feels like someone just elbowed me in the stomach and my breath comes out fast as I sink back in my seat. "Don't be that way," she snaps. "Don't make me feel guilty, Derrick."

"I'm not, I just—" but I don't know where that's going. We look at each other for a while longer. We've been down this road before, and she's made it pretty clear that we're not going further any time soon. Still, I could feel how hot she was getting. Up the walk, the porch light at my house snaps on. If there was any chance before, it's gone now.

Jasmine leans over and kisses me on the cheek, like some aunt telling a child how sweet they are. "I had a great night, Derrick. Let's not mess it up. I'll talk to you tomorrow."

Slump 35

"Okay," I say, and I try to sound upbeat about it. "I'll see you at school."

Then it's up the walk to home, the crisp night air hitting me like a splash of cold water.

5.

Moose goes first. He's a coin toss from the stripe, so it's one of Reynolds' best chances. Moose takes a few slow dribbles, then lets fly with his awkward form. The free throw comes out flat, but zips through cleanly.

"That's one," Bolden says. Reynolds nods at him.

Devin's next and there's no doubt on his. It sings through the net and Bolden raises two fingers to Reynolds. He nods again. No choice, really, because he's got no room to complain. Coach Bolden let him back on, just two nights before our first game, but the deal is Reynolds has to run for it. And he's got to do the stairs in the gym while we practice below him. A set of stairs isn't that bad, but Bolden lined the rest of us up at the stripe—for each one we knock down it's a set for Reynolds.

Maybe Reynolds thought we'd take it easy on him, try to miss a few without being too obvious about it. No way. I want Reynolds back for his sake, but we've been busting it for weeks while he's been coasting. Personally, after the way he turned me down at the park and then strolled in now? I'd like to see him run until his feet bleed.

Stanford's up now and even he knocks one down, thanks to

Slump

a friendly roll. After that one falls, you can feel this little ripple pass through us all—everyone's gonna knock theirs down, one after the other. Jones knocks down his, then I bury one. A couple more and we're into the freshmen. I figure if anyone gets the yips and breaks the string, it'll be one of them, but they toe the line—one after the other—and it's bucket, bucket, bucket. When the last one falls, a few of us clap. Murphy whistles in approval and retrieves the ball. He pops it to Coach Bolden who catches it and tucks it under his elbow. "That's eleven," he says to Reynolds.

This time Reynolds does hang his head, but only for a second. When he looks back up, he has a sheepish little grin. His eyes are wide and glassy again, but he just looks fearful about the running in front of him, not like he's going to break down. "I figure I deserve that," he says.

We laugh then, even Bolden, and that's the first step toward Reynolds becoming part of the team again—a bigger step than all those he's about to take on the arena stairs. It means something that he's going to take his punishment with a smile. Well, we'll see if that lasts.

"All right," Bolden shouts. "Enough fun and games. Reynolds, you hit the stairs, and the rest of you hit the baseline."

We stand there, stunned.

"What?" Bolden shouts. "You thought I was just gonna run Reynolds? That's eleven down-and-backs for the rest of you. Now move!"

We're working half-court sets, ones against twos. With just two days before our first game, we look a little rough. It's that three spot that's killing us.

The twos just sag back in, with one guy chasing Devin. I feed

Moose down low and it's like the whole damn world collapses on him. He fires it back out to me. When my man runs to recover, I leave him chasing a ghost. But I hit all that traffic in the lane, and there's no look. Maybe a pull-up from fifteen, but that's still not flowing for me. I look to kick, and the one with the look is J.J. Fuller. His eyes widen, almost filling up that blockish face. But then he does it again—lowers his head and drives. Head down so that Coach Bolden could jump in from out of bounds, and he wouldn't see it. He settles for a tough baseline fade that barely grazes rim.

"Reset!" Bolden shouts. "We can get a better look than that for God's sake!"

"Come on, guys," Murphy encourages, "look alive now."

We run another possession, but it's more of the same. No looks to be had. Finally, instead of driving, I decide to do what I've been working on all off-season. I catch a reversal pass and rip it into the lane. I know I could get to the rim, but that's easy against our twos. Instead, I rise for the pull-up. Feels good coming off, but it's *juuust* a millimeter shy.

"That's okay," Bolden says. "Good look. That's what we want out of our offense. Just get good looks. The rest will take care of itself."

Murphy chimes in with more encouragement. "Keep firing, D. They'll fall, baby." But a look around at my other starters reveals some doubt that we'll ever score again. It seems like the only buckets we've had all practice have been put-backs by Moose and Stanford. Stanford's starting to talk more trash than he can back up. He gets this tough squint to his face, like something he's practiced after watching too many gang movies. It doesn't work for him. He's got those high cheekbones in his thin face, making him look almost feminine no matter how much

Slump 39

he scowls. But when Bowman Academy gets here Friday night, it will be good to have Stanford thinking he's a bad-ass.

Bolden tries Chris Jones at the three now. Jones is basically our first man off the pine for Moose or Stanford, but things are getting so bleak at the three it's worth a shot. Of course, first touch Jones gets, he freezes up. He dribbles once, then gets in a tangle in the lane, and the ball gets slapped loose. A few bodies hit the floor, but the rock gets knocked into Stanford's hands. He's off-balance, but hears the sharp "Ball! Ball!" from the corner. It's Devin. More open than he's been all practice. Stanford sends him the pass, but there's not much zip on it. That gives Reynolds just enough time to race back outside, trying to challenge the shot.

Everyone watches the smooth arc of the shot, following the orange until it finds home. But just as it rips through the net, I hear a pained yelp from the corner. There, in a heap, is Devin. He's clutching his ankle with both hands and writhing in pain.

Reynolds is standing over him with his hand still raised from challenging the shot, the way a big man will leave his hands up to show he didn't do anything wrong after getting whistled for a foul. Finally, he lowers his hand and extends it to Devin, a late offering to help him up. That's like giving a Band-aid to a man with a gunshot wound though—Devin's not getting up anytime soon. He cries out a few more times, just animal sounds that aren't even words, while Murphy and Bolden rush over to him.

Bolden is the world's biggest hard-ass, but let one of his boys get banged up and he's as protective as anyone. He kneels next to Devin and puts his hand on his forehead, like some nurse comforting a patient. He talks to him quietly so nobody else can hear, and Devin starts to calm down. "Ice," Bolden says, and our manager Darius sprints off the floor to get some.

Devin finally lets go of his ankle. Bolden and Murphy help him up. He keeps that right foot a few inches off the floor though, while the coaches help him hop toward the locker room, one of them under each shoulder like they're carrying a wounded soldier.

"What happened?" Stanford finally asks. He's got that scowl working hard, one eyebrow pinched down like he's taking sight behind a gun.

Devin speaks through gritted teeth. "Came down on Reynolds' foot," he says. "Rolled my ankle."

"Shit, Reynolds," Stanford snaps. "You've been back an hour and you've already hurt a starter." If his comment hurts Reynolds, there's no telling because he's still standing where it all happened, eyes down while he slowly shakes his head.

"We don't need that, Stanford!" This is Murphy, shouting over his shoulder while he's still helping Devin to the locker room. "It could have happened to anyone." They all pause, letting Devin stand on his one foot for a second while Bolden slips the whistle from around his neck and hands it to Murphy. Then Bolden turns back to Devin, giving Murphy the nod to take over practice for a while. Murphy claps his hands and points to me. "Come on, Derrick. Get 'em going. Next man up for Devin."

I check the ball and start the offense, but we're all just going through the motions. Everyone is wondering the same thing—how bad is Devin's injury? I try to keep the worst scenarios—a ruptured Achilles, a broken ankle—out of my mind. But even as I drive the lane and dish

Slump 41

to Moose, my thoughts are with Devin. I can see it playing out. The trip to the hospital. The MRI. The long wait for results. The bad news. The lost season.

Damn. If we had trouble scoring *with* Devin, our possessions are going to be as jammed up as rush hour traffic.

Two days and Bowman Academy comes calling. Usually, I can't wait. But right now, this season is starting to feel cursed.

5 – GREEN
4 – STANFORD
3 – JONES
2 – FULLER
1 – BOWEN

Seeing my name written at the point guard spot fills me with pride. I knew it was coming. Everyone knew it. I was this team's starting point guard the moment last season ended. But it's still good to see.

Problem is, I was counting on Devin Varney's name being up there too. Now I've got Fuller in the backcourt and Jones at small forward. That's a tough way to run.

I lace up my AdiZeros and glance over at Devin. High ankle sprain. Grade two. That was the word after the MRI. The doctor said three weeks before Devin's back at full speed. That, we could live with. He'd miss five games and be back in time for Franklin. The Pike game at worst. But everyone's seen the same kind of injury derail NBA seasons. We've watched guys miss a month just to come back too early, doomed for lousy play and a quick aggravation of the injury.

Devin looks back my way. He's sitting in his street clothes at his locker, right foot in an air cast and elevated on a folding chair. "You got this, D," he says. "I'll be back before you know it, but you can run these first few in your sleep."

"You got that straight," I say. I give him a fist bump. Before you know it, it's time to hit the floor.

The gym's packed. When that band hits full volume as our kicks hit the hardwood, my heart's about to burst out of my chest. Right now I don't care if the damn Spurs walk through that door, I'm ready to go. I get myself into a solid lather and try to get the other guys amped.

As I go through the layup line, I keep hearing people calling my name like I'm a star on stage. It's been a long time since someone with my potential has come up here. Everyone wants to be able to say they knew me way back when. I know it'll get crazier next year—recruiters, boosters, money men. But it's nice to get recognition. I hear a particularly high-pitched shout—*Hey, Derrick!*—and I turn to see Daniella Cole staring at me. She's not bad looking, but she spreads it around and everyone knows it. I nod to her, but I don't make any kind of big deal. Last thing I need is Jasmine thinking I'm trying to hook up with Daniella.

A deeper scan of the crowd shows that my people aren't in the house yet, which is strange for them. They usually like to set up camp early so they get prime seats. I do catch a glimpse of Jasmine—she still hits the games, no matter how much she badmouths sports. She's next to Iesha. They're too busy laughing at something to see me. At least I get a nod from Wes in the band.

"Let's just stay calm and focused," Bolden says in our last huddle before the tip. "Don't get all crazed 'cause it's the first game. Patient

Slump 43

offense, tenacious defense!" Then we all put our hands in together. Bolden smacks that top fist on the stack and we shout, "Team!"

Game time.

Now, I trust Coach Bolden. So I'm all for running offense and following orders. Learned that the hard way last year. But when that ball goes up and Moose taps it to me, I've got other plans. Bowman Academy can play, I know, but they're not getting guys like me every night out at 2A, so I take a couple rhythm dribbles into the frontcourt, nod toward Fuller to start into the offense—and then just rip it to the rim. I blow by my man and get to the rack before their bigs can even catch their breath. I have to angle around one of them, so I can't throw it down, but it's a quick deuce—not to mention a little wake-up call to Bowman that they're in for the real deal tonight.

My early bucket gets the Bowman players back on their heels a little bit. When they bring the ball up, their guards look a little shell-shocked. They've got a nice big, Alex Danks, who'll wrestle it out with Moose all night. But on the first trip, their perimeter guys seem almost scared to make a post entry. They reverse and reverse, then settle for a tough pull-up from the wing. It bangs back rim and falls to Stanford. He pivots and outlets to me at the hash, and I *push*—get right on top of their small point guard and get him off-balance. He has to reach late, and I just miss a chance at a hoop-and-harm.

The crowd's already into it, like sharks sensing blood in the water. I square up the first and knock it down, get a round of fives from my teammates, then set my toe on the stripe again. Ref bounces me the orange, and I go through my routine. Take another deep breath, let fly, and bury the second—4-0, and we've barely broken a sweat.

When they inbound, I jump into their point. Coach didn't call for a press, and I'm not really trying to turn him over, but I want him to know we're gonna defend every inch of hardwood. Maybe get in his head a little. It works. He gives it up to their two-guard. I wave for Fuller to come pick him up. He comes in too hot, and the two rips past him, but all that does is get him sped up past his comfort zone. He flies into the frontcourt, gets off balance, and then tries to throw cross-court. There's no zip on it and Jones snags it easily.

This time they get back, so no easy ones for us. But now it's time to follow Coach's instructions. We work it through our set a few times, everyone getting a touch. Fuller hits his man with a spin, then kicks it baseline for me. I square my feet, but see my man running at me—so I slip past him, then drop a dime to Moose for an easy deuce. On top of that, Danks takes a cheap swat at him and gets a late whistle.

Bowman's coach has seen enough and calls time. Not even two minutes in, and we've got a six-point lead with a chance to make it seven. Our crowd gets up, half cheering us and half jeering Bowman, reveling in exactly what they came here to see—total domination. I scan for my family again and see that they're just now squeezing into some seats in the next-to-last row behind our bench. There's Mom, Jay and Uncle Kid, all with their coats still on. Dad's nowhere though.

It doesn't last. Moose knocks in his freebie, and it feels like everything's going to be easy street. We even get a stop next time down. But with a chance to really stretch out a lead early, the offense grinds to a halt. Bowman just packs it in. I swear, every player has one heel in the paint. No room to drive, no chance to feed Moose on the blocks. Fuller and Jones have looks, but they hesitate and by then their man recovers.

Slump   45

I figure it's on me again, so first chance I get I flare out to the right wing, my favorite spot to shoot from. I get a clean bounce from Fuller and rip it to the lane for a nice, clean pull-up.

Front rim and off. Felt good too. I shake it off and hustle back on D, tell myself the next one will fall.

But it doesn't. The next one is right on line, but just a hair long.

Fuller and Jones both give it a go, but they fare no better, rattling out open looks.

Meanwhile, Bowman starts to chip away. A free throw here. A put-back there. By the end of the first quarter, that seven-point lead is down to three.

It's not like we go scoreless. If we turn them over, they don't have a prayer of stopping our break. And Moose keeps fighting on the blocks, getting looks when he can. But the whole flow of the game has stopped. It's like we went from the pace of the Indy 500 to a slow, slumping limp.

By halftime it's tied, and you can feel the anxiety in our crowd. There's this unsettled murmur, like they're at some concert and are getting impatient for the act to finally take the stage.

Front rim and off. Front rim, back rim, out. Back rim and off.

Three different times in the third quarter I get a wide open look and miss. Each one could have stretched out our slim lead too, given us some breathing room against these guys. And with each one I could feel the crowd hold its breath, ready to explode, only to simmer back down when it rattles off.

At the break before the fourth, Coach Bolden tells us all to calm down. "We've got a three-point lead on these guys," he shouts. "No need to get frustrated and force things. Just defend, then stay patient on our end."

We break. As we take the floor Murphy hollers after us, "Let's go now! Let's bury these guys."

Bolden looks at him like Murphy just spat on his mama's grave. "What did I just say?" he yells. "Don't go getting them all stirred up." Then he shouts to us again. "Patient! Be patient."

He's right, I guess, but it's easier said than done. We come out and Bowman Academy sinks back on defense again. Every touch on the perimeter gives someone a decent look—but we pass them up, both because of Bolden's instructions and because nobody's been able to buy a jumper all night. Every time the ball gets reversed my way and I pass up a shot—even open threes, looks I've worked on forever—I hear our crowd get a little more restless. Finally, Fuller makes a nifty little pass inside to Stanford, but the whole defense collapses so there's nowhere to go with the ball. I flash to the top of the key to bail out Stanford. When the leather hits my hands I look up to find I'm all alone. My feet are just an inch past the arc, and I start into my motion. Then I think better of it and reverse the ball to Jones on the opposite wing.

This brings out the frustration from the fans. Through the collective groan, I hear clear shouts of *Shoot the damn ball!* and *That's all you, Bowen, come on!* My cheeks grow hot and a bitter taste settles onto my tongue—getting heckled in our own gym! It's about more than I can take.

Obviously, it is more than Fuller can handle because he forces—drives baseline into traffic and floats up a weak runner. Danks corrals it for Bowman and they rip it back at us.

Slump 47

They're in no hurry on their end either, working and working until they get Danks on a flash in the lane. He misses, but Stanford gets a cheap whistle and sends him to the stripe for two.

I walk to the other end of the floor, head down, just trying to gather my thoughts. The crowd keeps murmuring, not just frustrated now but actually worried that we might lose this game. *That's just noise,* I tell myself. *Just static.* Play it one possession at a time and everything will be fine. The Bowman crowd cheers, and I know Danks made the first. That murmur in our crowd gets more anxious. When I glimpse at the bench I see Murphy gnawing on his fingernails. Tight all around. Then Danks knocks down the second. One point game.

We come down and face that same sagging defense. We reverse and reverse and reverse the ball to the same old results. Nothing. When Jones catches outside, they don't even bother giving false pressure. It seems to go on forever, and I feel like the only way we'll loosen up this defense is if Devin hops out here, air cast and all. Finally, Moose takes control. He spins on Danks and seals him right at the rim. It's a full-grown-man move. Before he can even holler *Ball,* I put the orange in his mitts.

Bucket. At last. Our crowd leaps up, voicing their pent up shouts. Our bench is up too, pumping their fists and urging us on. It's like just seeing the ball go through the hoop flared up a fire in us.

The Bowman guards try to look chill about it, like *We got this,* but when they finally hit the offensive end they act a little confused. They hesitate, ball fake, start to cut and then back out to the perimeter again. After about thirty seconds they get antsy and force one into Danks. It squirts away from him and Stanford grabs it. He outlets to me and I push it up the floor. Their guards race back, and I pull up on the wing. I fake once to a cutting Fuller, but that's just to give myself some rhythm for a wide open three.

When it leaves my hand, I know it's true. Backpedal with my right arm still raised. Only to see it spin out after being halfway in the hole.

Bowman Academy clears and then their coach calls time when they hit the frontcourt.

Bolden just stands over me in our huddle. "What the hell, Bowen?" he shouts. "What are you trying to do with that shot?"

Before my better instincts can stop me, I blurt an answer. "I was trying to end it!"

Bolden's eyes bulge, but he doesn't jump me. He just shakes his head and turns to Murphy. "I swear sometimes I like dealing with freshmen better than sophomores. At least freshmen don't act like they know better than me!"

After that he just stresses the same things again. Defend, rebound, work the offense. And I don't dare object to anything. It all makes for a tense final quarter, but we wear them down. Moose gets free for a lay-in, then uproots Danks for a put-back, and we string together a few stops until Bowman has no choice but to foul. We knock in a few and that's that. But as we shake hands with the Bowman players and the crowd files out, there's a bittersweet feeling to it. Anyone will tell you that a win is a win, but this one doesn't quite feel the same. An ugly 40-35 opener is not what anyone had in mind.

Slump

When I exit the locker room, Uncle Kid's waiting for me. There are mostly just other players and their families lingering now, and the big lights over the court are killed so everything is dim. It makes it look like a party where the host is trying to get people to leave, but nobody's taking the hint.

The other players and their folks don't seem too upset by the game. Moose and his people are laughing it up. Reynolds gets a big bear hug from his dad, congratulating him on his first varsity game, even if he didn't get but a minute or two of action.

Kid knows better, so he just gives me a firm handshake and says, "Better than a loss."

"Barely," I say.

He slings his arm around my shoulder and directs me toward the exit, out into the night. It's like someone guiding a child away from a disaster so they don't see too much. When we get out there, he anticipates my first question. "Your dad couldn't make it, Derrick." He says it toward the cars on 34th, like he's giving directions to a lost driver. "He got called to cover for someone at the last minute."

I shrug it off. No sense in acting hurt, but it's the first time my dad's ever missed a game. He doesn't get as juiced as the rest of my family, but since I started in youth leagues he's always been there, at least ten minutes before tip, every single time.

"Don't get upset at him," Kid says. "He's doing all a man can."

The thing Kid doesn't say is that he wouldn't be pulling these hours if I'd have bolted to Hamilton Academy. *Damn.* I know they wouldn't have had to fight tooth and nail to eke one out against Bowman. Things would be a whole lot easier up there. But there's no sense in wondering about what if. My mom tells us that all the time— *You get too busy worrying about what ifs, and you forget to take care of what is.*

And what is is that we're gonna have to scratch every night out. At least until Devin gets back.

We reach our walk and Kid pops me on the back. "Gonna be a lot better nights than this one, D. Maybe some worse ones too, but a lot better. Bank on it."

"Thanks, Kid," I say. Then I nod toward the door. "You coming in?"

"Nah," he says. "I got plans." He looks away, that anxious, antsy expression he gets when he's up to something he doesn't want us to know about. I don't bother asking, just tell him *Later* and head for my door.

Inside, Dad's racked out on the couch again. It's not even late, but my mom and Jayson have beat it back to their rooms. I see slivers of light under each of their doors. A quick stop at the fridge to pull out some leftover pizza, and I head for my room too.

On my dresser sits a stack of camp brochures, team logos on each one. Indiana, Purdue, Michigan, Illinois. They can't start sending me letters yet, so this is how the big boys let me know they're interested. I wonder how jacked they'd be about signing me if they saw my line for tonight: nine points and four assists, 4-13 from the field. I did get eight rips, but these people aren't sending me mailers because I can get some boards.

There's a rustling in the living room as Dad wakes from the couch. The floorboards give a few creaks under his weight and then

Slump 51

there's the sound of the fridge opening. I think about going out to join him, but somehow it's just comforting hearing him move about the house, listening to him turn on the TV and then quickly squelch the volume to a low murmur because he thinks he might wake someone.

I flip through the latest mail. Wisconsin, Cincinnati, Louisville. When I first started playing, the dream was to go to some powerhouse—Indiana or UCLA or Carolina. But now, as the mailbox fills up again each day, I consider how many options there are. Maybe a dark horse like Mississippi State or Clemson. Maybe a smaller school like Gonzaga or Wichita State. The dream at this point is to make it to the League—and you can do that from anywhere. I mean, George Hill went to IUPUI, and now he's running point for the Pacers and just tearing it up. If you're good enough, the NBA scouts will find you.

Then again, maybe I ought to just cool it. A good first step would be scoring double figures at Marion East.

6.

Tomorrow night we head to Gary to play King, a Chicago team. It's a chance for cross-state bragging rights. The game after us is Hamilton versus another legendary Chicago team, Simeon. Which means another chance for Vasco and company to steal the show. I've got to stay focused on King though. Always gotta remember—the only team you can beat is the next one on your schedule.

Uncle Kid has drilled into me all the famous King names from back in the day—Marcus Liberty, Jamie Brandon, Rashard Griffith. I let Kid tell his old war stories, but I know those guys aren't walking through the door. The guy who is hitting the hardwood tomorrow night is Martin Randle-El, the best player we'll see until Vasco. He's 6'11" and just a load down low. Got a little range to keep guys honest too. If you could still jump straight to the League, he'd be a lottery pick with that size, but instead he'll spend a year at Kansas before bolting.

"Where's your head at, Derrick?"

"Right here," I say.

We're upstairs in Jasmine's room, working through some

Slump 53

geometry problems. She's got this stuff down from last year, so she helps me out some. It's not like I'm some dumb jock getting his honey to write his papers for him, but this stuff is no joke. Besides, it's a good excuse to get close to Jasmine without her pushing me away.

We're sitting on her bed, the book between us like a little border. Even her room just seems so perfect. Always clean, never a stray sock on the floor, books all ordered on the shelves just so. But it's more than the order. It's her plush comforter on her big bed, her framed posters behind glass, her bookshelf—made of thick, solid wood instead of one of those throw-together things that break if you bump it hard. Her parents are dropping coin for stuff instead of scouring thrift stores. I know her folks well enough to know they have the same ongoing fight as mine—whether to keep on keeping on or save up to jump to some nicer neighborhood. From the looks of this place, I'd say Jasmine's folks have the money to leap if they want to.

"You've been staring at that problem for five minutes," she says. "You sure you're still working on it?"

"I'm *concentrating*," I say, but my smile gives me away.

She laughs at me. "I swear, Derrick, you can't keep your head clear of hoops for even ten minutes. You're obsessed!"

"Look, Coach Bolden always tells us it's a game of angles, so maybe it'll help me with geometry."

She rolls her eyes. "You go on thinking that. See how it works out for you." She sighs and rolls away from me, leaving me sitting up by her pillows while she stretches on her back across the bottom part of her bed. Her sweater rides up from her jeans, showing a little sliver of skin. My eyes trace from there up her body to those fine curves. Her parents are gone, and it's almost dusk outside.

I put the textbook over on her nightstand, then lean down to her. I behave, keeping my hand on her stomach and not trying for too much too fast, but when I kiss her she rises up to me. It's like somehow I turned on a switch in her. Jasmine pulls herself up by my shoulders and presses against me. Her tongue pushes into my mouth, and then she pulls back to kiss me down along my neck, peeling back my shirt a little to bite my shoulder. I try not to lose my cool. I know rushing things could kill it but as I hear her breaths get heavier and faster, all I can think is, *This is finally happening.*

Jasmine backs me up so my shoulders are against her headboard. Then she swings her right leg across me so she's straddling me. I can't take it. She's practically begging me. So I lower my head to kiss her neck. Then lower. Then lower again. I can't stop my hands.

"Derrick," she sighs. "What are you doing?"

I don't answer. Just keep moving my hands wherever they want to go.

"Derrick," she says again. "Don't."

My hands move away from her chest, but slide down to her waist to pull her tighter to me. She pulls her arms from around my shoulders and squeezes them in between us like two bars along my chest. "Derrick," she says one more time, her voice full of warning.

I know to stop. Anyone who's listened to my mother preach for years about the right way to treat women knows to stop. So I do. But I don't know how not to act upset. "Shit," I say. It's under my breath— same way I'd say it when I miss a free throw in practice—but Jasmine's right next to me.

"Don't be that way," she says.

Slump   55

I lace my fingers behind my head, like that's the one way to keep my hands still. "I know," I say. "But…"

Jasmine stares hard at me, the heat in her eyes that was lust just a minute ago turning quickly to anger. "What?" She cocks her head at an angle. "What, Derrick? Go ahead and say it."

"Nothing," I say.

That's it for a while. Both of us breathe heavily into the silence. Then we hear the front door unlock and her parents come in, calling for their daughter.

The gym in Gary is boiling. Like mid-summer hot. Even a minute into warm-ups and everyone's streaming sweat. When I check the stands, people are fanning themselves with programs and mopping their foreheads with whatever they can find.

This time my family—all of them—made it on time. I see Jayson waving to me. He and Kid are squeezed between my parents, who are looking in opposite directions, like there's some other game they want to check out on different ends of the gym.

Jasmine didn't make the trek to Gary, so the only other person to check for is Wes. He's in his usual spot in the middle of the band. I throw a look his way every time I go through the layup line. His head's down though. He's trying to be all subtle and text, something that would get his ass jumped by the band director if he gets caught. Would serve him right, I think, because I know he's just hitting up Iesha. Like if they go five minutes without checking in, they're both going to melt.

We step between the lines with the same starting five as the first game. It doesn't take long to realize we're in for the same kind of dog fight. King sinks back in around Moose and Stanford, but the tougher part is that when we finally do get Moose the rock, King doesn't have to double. With Randle-El down there, they've got a guy Moose can't uproot. First few trips we settle for jumpers from Fuller. He gets one to spin in, but it's just the kind of possessions King wants for us.

On their end, no hurry. It's pretty clear they like these kinds of games. Maybe try a drive here, a shot fake there. But it's all built around Randle-El. They get him in the post once and Fuller's late on the double, so Moose just goes for a ride to the rim. Next time down Randle-El catches shallow wing and drops in a little J. Third time down he posts again, we double hard, and he hits a cutter for a lay-in. All so easy.

It goes on like that the whole first half. We work forever to get an ugly look, and they stay patient and get a gimme. It's not a total runaway, but when that horn sounds to hit the locker room we're down eight. It feels like 28 though. With the heat in this gym, it feels like we've been running suicides all night long. The locker room is just as hot, and we can't catch our breath. Moose hangs his head and sweat just streams off his nose. Coach Bolden's shirt is so drenched it looks like he got caught in a rainstorm.

"Got to know who's doubling on Randle-El," he says. "They're killing us every time we get crossed up. And on offense—" he trails off. Maybe he doesn't have any answers either. Then he straightens his back, regains his form. "On offense, let's make their asses work. I mean it. We're going through the motions." Here he imitates us, lazily acting out a shot fake and slow, methodical pass. "Shit. It's five-hundred degrees in that gym, and we're not making them jump. Get some pace going." He pauses again, smiles. "I don't run your asses all pre-season for the fun of it. Let's wear these guys down! Now come on!"

That gives us enough of a boost to make a rush at the start of the third. We get the rock popping on the offensive end and get some results—I get a little leaner, Fuller buries a mid-range J, Moose gets a deuce off my drive.

But by midway through the quarter our legs are mush. The ball rotation slows down and our cuts lose their zip. "Move!" Bolden yells from the sideline. "Pick it up!" But even Coach Bolden's urging can't get us going again. Eventually, the ball swings back to me baseline, and I figure it's as good as any look we'll get. As soon as the three leaves my hand though, I know it's short. I sprint in to follow my shot, but Randle-El rips it down and outlets to my man—who's floated all the way out near mid-court for a run-out. He races ahead for an easy deuce. And just like that, whatever comeback momentum we had dies. We're back down six and you can feel our crowd deflate, spent in this sauna of a gym.

At the break between quarters, Bolden walks a few paces out from the sideline to meet me before the huddle. Instead of jumping me like I expect, he just puts his hand on my shoulder. "Stay with it, Derrick," he says. "We'll get some shots to fall. Don't get frustrated and impatient."

I nod, and he cuffs me on the back of the neck as we head to the huddle. He knows something has to give. Without another shooter, there's just no climbing back against these guys. Bolden scans down the bench, looking for answers. "Reynolds," he says. It takes Reynolds a second to register the news—he just sits there. Murphy slaps him on the shoulder, tells him that means he's supposed to shed those warm-ups and go check in. As he goes, a few guys shake their heads. The guy's only been with us a week and hasn't shown much yet. Seems like we'd be better off sending Devin in to play on one leg.

Bolden gets about an inch from my face. I can see the sweat beaded all over his forehead. "Tell Fuller to slide to the three. Then get Reynolds going," he tells me. Then, right into my ear like a secret, he says, "He's got as good a chance as stretching that defense as anyone."

It's a gamble, but it's not like the rest of us are setting the world on fire. Besides, Bolden's had weird lineups pay off before. I mean, just last year he had me running at the four, and that worked out, so I'll give the man the benefit of the doubt. When I glance at Reynolds, the kid looks shook. He keeps kicking his feet out like he's trying to loosen up his legs and flapping his hands out like he's trying to shake water off them.

"Easy," I tell him. "You get a look on these guys, bury it."

"I feel you," he says, but his body language tells a different story. He's still all twitch and fidget. I can't fix his head for him though.

The first trip down, I know better than to give him a touch right away. Let the guy get a sweat up at least. I kick it Fuller's way. When I get it back, I try a drive. There's nothing doing, so I kick to Fuller again. He feeds Moose, but Randle-El has him moved way off the block, so I swing over and get it back. This time when I drive middle, I get a little crease and the whole King defense jumps. I pull up with a choice—force it over two guys or kick it out again. There's Reynolds on the wing, hands outstretched. I zip it his way, hit him right on the money.

And he leaves the thing a good two feet short. Misses so bad it just falls to the floor and rolls out of bounds. Reynolds hangs his head and trots back on defense, but I know he can hear the laughs and jeers from the crowd.

Slump

Next deadball, it's back to the old lineup. So much for the Reynolds experiment.

We make a little run. I turn one of their guards and get a run-out jam to get our crowd on our feet. Then Fuller finally gets a trey to fall. But that's all we can do. Randle-El keeps banging away down low and they ice it at the line. Final: 49-40, King.

It's a long haul back to Indy. Lots of dark miles on I-65. Coach Bolden has Murphy up beside him in the front seat. They've got a light on and all you can see is the back of their heads bent down. They're going over plays, over notes, but it looks like they're praying.

Moose, usually one to get guys laughing on a bus ride—even after a loss—has been snoozing in the back seat since the exit for Crown Point. So the bus is stone quiet. We all expected better than this out of the gate, even with Devin hobbled. After the game, we hit the showers and made a straight line for the bus, but on the way I caught a peek of the early action in the second game. Hamilton was already up double figures, and the one play I saw was Vasco on the drive, whipping a behind-the-back pass to his teammate for a bucket. We don't improve before we step up to them and we'll get run out by 40.

In the darkness, that play by Vasco haunts me. I see it over and over. Smooth and efficient. It would be showboating if it weren't so effective. And, yeah, I see that bomb he dropped on us in Regionals last year over and over again. It stings just as much now as it did then, like we keep losing that game again with every mile.

It'll get better, I tell myself. We'll get Devin back and defenses will have to come out after him. Room to drive. Room to feed the post. Everything will be better. But, damn, we should be steamrolling teams anyway. Maybe instead of just staying patient like Coach says, I should be forcing the issue more. I could drop 20 on just about any team we play.

I try to check those thoughts, put my mind on something better. Problem is, there's nowhere for my mind to go that isn't trouble. My family? Friction. My dad looks more and more exhausted and my mom keeps sniping at him to go see the doctor. Wes? My best friend is AWOL with his girl 24-7. And Jasmine? That's the most frustrating thing of all. There are times when Jasmine's voice runs through my head—a nice little compliment she gave me, her laugh—and it fills me up, but anymore I just hear her saying, *No. Stop. I can't.* That's when my pulse starts racing, and I feel like I'm going to burst.

Coach Bolden clicks off the light in the front seat, and the bus goes dark. The only light is the glow up ahead—the exit for West Lafayette, home of the Boilermakers. At home, I've got a mailer from them crammed in a box with so many others. But right now I'm just another rider on another bus, an hour from home with a loss hanging over my head.

Slump   61

7.

Ty's Tower is covered up. Word is the city's about to get hammered with snow. It's like everyone's decided to get their Christmas shopping done now in case they're house-bound for a couple weeks. Wes turns over some Timberland New Market Slip Ons in his hands. They're real light blue, the kind of thing Russell Westbrook might wear if he's trying to look casual at a press conference. Wes lifts them up and down, marveling. He could probably use a reminder that last year his dad stood him up on Christmas—didn't visit and didn't get him his kicks—and I had to help him out. That would be cold though.

"I need to rock these," he says.

He looks at me for verification, but he knows I always bow to his shoe knowledge. I make one decision a year on shoes: kicks for the season. I've gone Adi Zeros again, because who cares if people are down on Derrick Rose. He gets healthy, and he's still the best point in the world. He comes back, and people will come around. That's how it'll be with me when we get this season kick-started. We're sitting 3-2 right now—a couple grind-it-outs around a heartbreaker at Cathedral—but Devin's back in the lineup tomorrow night against Franklin.

"Iesha's gonna die when she sees me in these," he says.

"All about Iesha, right?" There's a little edge to the way I say that, more than I meant. So I laugh it off. Truth is, it wears on me. Every other word out of his mouth is Iesha now. He was a lot more fun when he couldn't get any.

Maybe he senses it because he nods toward the other end of the store. "Let's check the jerseys," he says. This is for me. Neither of us are going to buy anything, but Wes likes to scan through those racks of shoes like he's mining for a diamond, and I like to try on the throwback jerseys.

I grab a handful—Pip's old Bulls 33, Nique's sweet Hawks 21, and an Alex English just because those old Nuggets jerseys are sick. Used to be when we did this, we'd get the hard stare from the manager, but now he knows who I am. My stat line is nothing to swagger about. But on these blocks everyone's always so hyped for hoops that if you show even a little promise, people recognize you.

Wes tells me I have to get the Dominique jersey until I go back into the dressing room one more time. When I come back out, I sport the one I didn't show him before I went in. It's old school Iverson, blue with red trim, just the *PHILA* over top the 3 in front.

As soon as he sees it, Wes just raises his hands in the air. "Amen, D. That's the bullet," he says. "It looks so good on you, I'm gonna start calling you The Answer if you wear it."

I laugh, then remind him that I've got a couple inches on Iverson. Plus hops he never had. It's a crazy boast, and Wes knows it. He just

Slump 63

shakes his head at me. But then his phone gets hit up, and he's gone—off to the other side of the store again, mashing out a text to Iesha.

Used to be our house was buzzing the hours before a game. Jayson would have his music cranked up and Mom would be pacing in anticipation. Dad got into it, even if he didn't want to admit it. He'd be egging Uncle Kid on, getting him to tell stories about his playing days until he got worked up.

Now, it's basically silent.

Jayson's back in his room. He's got his music going, but it's so low I just hear a muffled bass thump once in a while. Mom and Dad are each reading a book. They're on opposite ends of the living room, like they're trying to put the most possible space between them. Uncle Kid didn't even come over. He's probably hanging with his boy Brownlee somewhere because the most action here is that Dad's head about bumps into his book every few minutes because he's having trouble staying awake.

It's about ten minutes before I have to hoof it to the gym, and nobody's said a word to me. I'm just idling on the couch, gym bag beside me. Finally, my dad looks up.

"Derrick, you doing okay?" he asks.

"It's all good," I say. "We get Devin back on the floor tonight."

Dad rocks forward in his chair and sets his book down. He takes off his glasses and rubs his eyes, then looks at me with full attention. "I don't mean basketball," he says. He waves his hand in the air, dismissing the very topic. "That will work itself out. I mean *you*. You've been walking around this place looking pretty serious the last couple weeks. I just wanted to know how you're doing."

"For real, I'm good," I say.

Dad bites down on his lip, trying to decide whether to let it go at that. He picks his book back up, but glances over at me one last time. "Okay. It's just that we get so caught up in the day-to-day that I think sometimes your mom and I take it for granted that you're fine. You can tell us if you're not."

I don't respond, but I steal a glance at Mom, who's put her book down to check out our conversation. Her face is calm, patient, like she's open to anything I might have to say. I don't say a word. No need getting into some conversation about girl trouble or anything this close to tip. But it's nice to hear my dad talk to me like that. It feels like for the last month my only conversations with my parents have been the same-old. *Be back by ten*, I get from them. Or, *remember to help clean the kitchen*. And all I'm telling them is if they need to drop me somewhere or pick me up. I don't want to hash anything out with my parents, but it's a nice reminder that I can.

Right now, it's time to shake this place up a little. Get people's pulses going so they can make some noise when they hit the gym. I grab my bag and head to Jayson's room. He looks up at me as he's softly rapping along with a Kanye joint. I just raise my thumb toward the ceiling a few times, and he gets it. Jay cranks the volume as high as he can, and in an instant the beats are pounding so hard they're rattling my ribs. I turn and hit the door just as Mom and Dad rise in unison, hollering to Jayson to turn it down. I know he can't hear them, and I'm all the way to the street before the music cuts out.

Franklin's on tap. Another big test, especially because they got a forward in Chuck Nash who's a real beast. But the good news is Devin's back.

Slump 65

All through warm-ups, he's just stepping out to the stripe—bucket, bucket, bucket. There's not gonna be any packing it in on us tonight.

"How's the wheel?" I ask, motioning to his ankle.

"Good to go," he says, but I can tell he's still being careful every time he plants on it.

When we get to the huddle, Bolden senses that we're extra amped. The crowd's more juiced too. You can feel it in the way the gym's been buzzing since warmups.

"Just because Devin's back doesn't mean it's easy," Bolden says. "You still need to guard and stay patient on O. And keep Nash in check. That means helping down on him when he gets it on the blocks." He takes a look around. "Come on now," Bolden shouts. "Heads in the game."

That's all he's got before it's time to get between the lines. Doesn't matter. With Devin out there, we've got a little swagger for the first time. Nash controls the tip for Franklin. But when their point brings it across, I get into him hard. He tries to shake me with a crossover, but I get a piece and he's lucky just to pick it up. It all gets him off balance. When he tries to get the ball to the wing, it sails about three feet wide of his teammate for a quick turnover.

"There it is," I shout and pump my fist to Devin. The crowd noise swells. They've been aching for something—anything—to get excited about. When I bring it up, I figure there's no sense wasting time. Let's test out Devin's J. He comes off a screen from Stanford. I give a quick head-fake the other way to freeze the defense, then zip it to Devin in the corner. Wide open. He catches it clean and lets it fly. His stroke is so pure, that thing's wet as soon as it leaves his hands. When it

Kevin Waltman

finds bottom, our crowd goes insane. Our whole team does too. Seeing a long-range three find bottom is such a release, it feels like when you were a kid and got cut loose for summer vacation, free to run at last.

Their point is as shook as a boxer who's about to go down. I hound him over to the right wing and make him give it up. They're supposed to reverse the ball back to him. He claps for it, but he doesn't really want it. When it comes his way, he stays back on his heels rather than stepping to meet the ball and that's all the opening I need. I jump the pass and deflect the rock toward mid-court. I chase it down and would have a free run at the rim, but their off-guard hacks me to stop the run-out.

Even after the whistle, I push it ahead like I'm going to dunk it, holding up at the last instant. I dribble behind my back and then shake my head as I hand the rock to the ref. Our crowd boos. Coach Bolden starts screaming that it should be an intentional foul, but the ref just holds his hand up at Coach.

Turns out, I don't even need a run-out. This time down, they're too eager to jump at Devin. So when he comes off that Stanford screen, it's like the seas have parted. I get an easy entry to Stanford, and then I slice down the lane as soon as my man turns his head. Stanford pops it back for a quick give-and-go, and I catch it right in the heart of the lane. Out of the corner of my eye, I see Nash jumping toward me. I know I should dump it off to Moose, but it's too good a chance to pass up. I take one power dribble and get right on top of Nash. He keeps me away from the rim so I can't throw it down, but I get a finger-roll finish, plus a whistle.

My feet hit the floor and I arch back and shout at the ceiling, letting loose all that pent up frustration. Moose comes over and shoves

Slump

me so hard he almost knocks me into the second row. "That's what I'm talking about, D!" he shouts. "Let's run these bitches off."

That's enough woofing for the ref to step in and tell us to cool it. We do. We know he could whistle a T just for Moose cussing, so we behave. Turns out it was enough to get under Nash's skin, because he gives me a cheap bump as I walk to the free throw line. "That's a lot of noise for one bucket," he says.

"Gonna be plenty more," I say, stepping up to him. "You think you can keep pace?"

"Shit," he mutters. "I'll get mine."

By that time, all the refs are on top of us, telling us to ease off. Good thing too because Moose has his back up. One more word out of Nash and it might just get out of hand. The Franklin coach asks for time, maybe trying to get his team settled. As we walk back to our bench, I just nod my head, like *Yeah, we got them rattled already.*

When we get there, Coach Bolden isn't having it. He grabs me by the jersey and yanks me toward the bench. "What in the hell is wrong with you?" he shouts. I start to answer, but he cuts me off. "We're up five. Five! And you're acting like you've just won State." He shakes his head and looks at Murphy, like now he does want some kind of explanation, but Murphy knows better than to say a word. It's Moose's turn next. "And you!" Bolden shouts at the big man. "Lord, I might expect such foolishness from a sophomore, but you should know better!"

Darius, our equipment manager, offers me a towel, and I snatch it from him. I give a quick mop of my face and then angrily sling the towel down at my feet. Just once it would be nice if Coach Bolden didn't kill our momentum.

He takes a long look at me. He decides not to say anything, but when we hit the court again the vibe has changed. I go through my routine and let fly. The ball feels perfect coming out of my hands, and I start to back away from the line with the free throw already good in my head—*6-0*, I'm thinking, *keep it rolling*—so I don't even see how it misses. I just hear the groan from the crowd and then see Nash looking for his outlet man.

Nash does nothing flashy. No jams, no fadeaways, not even an up-and-under. He just keeps plodding along—a post move here, a short jumper there. Slowly, Franklin edges ahead. By the early fourth quarter they've got a six-point lead on us. Devin has only been able to go a few minutes at a time. Even when he's out there, he's not the same old Devin. He's knocked in a couple more from range, but he needs wide open looks so he can take his time. When he's out, it's the same story. Fuller, Reynolds, Jones—none of them can stretch the defense.

I bring the ball into the frontcourt and kick it to Fuller. He looks and looks, the ball high over his head, waiting for Moose to post. There's nothing. Fuller swings it back to me, and Moose claps his hands a few times angrily, like *Just get it to me*. The big man has a right to be frustrated, but they've practically got him doubled even before he touches it.

Our crowd urges us, but there's no longer that bloodthirsty buzz from early in the game. Now it's an agitated cry. They can feel the game slipping away with each tick of the clock.

I take a deep breath. Time to take over. I know my man can't check me, but I also know if I lower my head and drive, the only look I'll have is that pull-up. And it's like that thing's jinxed. So I set him

Slump 69

up. I give a bounce, then another to my right, then dip my shoulder and go. It's all show though. As soon as he bites—jumping back into the lane—I cross the orange back to my left and set my toes behind the stripe. The shot leaves my hand pure. I just know I've cut their lead in half and put this game back within reach. Except it's front-rim-back-rim and out. A killer.

Nash grabs the board and outlets. But this time their back-up point, who's been so steady all game, gets too full of himself. He decides to challenge me. He pushes into the frontcourt and drives toward the hole. I stay on his shoulder the whole way. When he offers up a little scoop—*Whap!*—I smack it off the backboard and then chase it down to control. That show pumps a little life back into our crowd. They rise again for one last run. It amps me a little too, like I needed to remind myself that I'm the best damn player on this floor.

Coach Bolden windmills his arm to tell me to push it up, but I don't need any telling. I zip it ahead to Fuller, who takes one dribble and then finds Stanford in the paint. Stanford gives a pump and a power dribble, then stops near the rim, not quite free for a look.

"Ball, ball, ball!" I shout. I'm standing all alone on the left wing, praying Stanford finds me. He does, and I let go of another three. Head still, follow-through high. It's picture-perfect form. Only this one is a tick long. The rebound kicks toward the top of the key, and Fuller dives to tip it away from Franklin. Stanford chases down the rock. When he looks up, he sees me still in the same spot, all alone again. He rifles it to me. I take my time, setting my feet. I can hear the crowd yelling for me to bury it, a clear shout of *Bucket!* coming from just behind me as I let it go.

Kevin Waltman

But this time, even I know it's off. A scraper that leads to a little fight for the board, which ends in the ball going out of bounds off Moose's knee.

The gym is dead. I glance over to see Coach sending Devin back in for one last charge. The game already feels over. We slouch back to get ready to defend, Moose shaking his head the whole way.

"Damn," I say, to nobody in particular. "Those were good looks too."

That's all Moose can take. "Hell with your looks, man," he snaps at me. He's never looked as big as he does at this moment, right up on top of me. "Get me the damn ball!"

The ref hears it and gives Moose a look, but Fuller jumps between us. "Come on!" he pleads. "When I transferred here I thought I was coming to a team that was gonna get after it. Not guys who were going to get after each other."

Moose is in no mood. "Shut up with that bullshit, Fuller," he says.

This time the ref won't let it slide. It doesn't matter that Moose was talking to his teammates instead of arguing a call, the ref jacks him up.

And that's that. Down six, Franklin at the stripe for two, plus their ball after. Moose comes out too, exiled to the bench on Bolden's principles—a T sends you to the bench, no exceptions.

While Franklin's best shooter toes the stripe and some people in our crowd start to gather their stuff to hit the exits, Nash slides up next to me. He bends over and puts his hands on his knees so it looks like he's just catching his breath. But I know what's coming, and I deserve it. He asks, just softly enough so the ref can't hear, "You wanna talk some shit now, Bowen?"

8.

There's a knock on the door in American History. When Mrs. Hulsey opens it she gets handed a note. She holds it up in the air like a police officer about to hand someone a ticket.

"Derrick," she says.

In that moment, it doesn't matter if I'm the best baller to walk those halls in years. I mean, I could already have inked a deal in the League, and I'd get the same treatment as anyone else. Everyone *Oohs* and laughs and says things like, *Oh, you're in for it now* as I grab my books and walk to the front of the class.

I take the hall pass from Mrs. Hulsey and see that it directs me straight to Coach Bolden's office. Maybe at some schools, teachers would get worked up over a coach pulling a student out of class, but at Marion East, every faculty member knows that time in Bolden's office is tougher than time in the classroom. And they also know that he'll put anyone on the pine if they let their grades slip.

The halls are empty during class. I can hear my footsteps reverberate down the corridor. It's almost the same sound you hear when you're the first one running out into an empty gym, just you and the ball and a court. Except I don't have that same feeling—that sense that all that matters is the moment right in front of you, the work and sweat and pain it takes to get better—not while I'm plodding down to Coach's office. I almost feel like turning and bolting, just racing down senior wing and out the doors into the cold December day. I could make it downtown, disappear into the crowd of Christmas shoppers before anyone could catch me. Anything instead of taking another lecture from Bolden.

When I get to his office, he's leaning back in his chair, his fingers laced behind his head like a man who's just easing back after a big meal, not a care in the world. Murphy's beside him, standing, his arms crossed.

"Come on in, Derrick," Bolden says. "Have a seat." He doesn't even move.

I pull the lone metal chair up to the other side of his desk. It feels flimsy beneath me, like some toddler's seat, and I can't help but fidget as I try to get comfortable.

"Take it easy," Coach says. "Just relax."

This doesn't sound like the Joe Bolden I know. Something in my face must signal my doubts, because Murphy unclenches his arms and nods at me. "Really," he says, "we're not calling you in here to give you the third degree."

"Then what's up?" I ask.

"To your mind, what happened in the fourth against Franklin?"

What am I supposed to say? That I got trigger happy? That Moose lost his cool? Against my own will, I look down at the floor and just say that I missed a few good looks.

Slump   73

"So why do you think I've you called in here, Derrick?" Coach asks. It's the kind of tactic I hate. Teachers, coaches, parents—they always want to make you explain their own motivations. I mean, just come out and lay it on me. I just shrug. "You think those were bad shots I took in the fourth?"

Coach sways his head back and forth like he could go either way on that question. "You can knock those shots down, Derrick," he says. "I know that. But you're too quick to take them. Why not work for a better shot when you're struggling from outside?"

"Coach, I know those are gonna start falling. I'm right there with it, and—"

It's Murphy who cuts me off, holding both hands up like he's apologizing. "We're not saying that, D. We know you're a better shooter now. You're just in a little sophomore—"

"Don't you dare say that word!" Bolden snaps. Murphy falls silent like a scolded child. What Murphy was about to say was *slump*, as in the dreaded *sophomore slump*, curse of so many players who ripped through their freshman season only to find the going tougher the next year. Bolden takes a deep breath and then speaks more evenly. "You say that and it makes it sound like this is all luck. Or like Derrick has some hex on him. It's not that. There's no such thing. The way to fix this is to work harder and play smarter." Then he grumbles, more to himself than anyone else, "Same damn solution to every other basketball problem."

"I know, Coach," I say. "It's just that I had those open looks. I kept thinking if I could just get one to fall, I'd get the crowd back in it."

Bolden nods, but it's not one of agreement, just a signal that he's heard this all before. "That's just it, Derrick. You're in such a rush to make the big play, to get everyone hyped. Forget that stuff. You're our point guard, for God's sake. You know, Nick could have scored twice as many points as he did, but he was a point guard first."

My teeth clench down so hard they could grind through steel. Coach invoking that name—*Nick Starks*—is a cold move, and he knows it. Sure, Nick and I made our peace toward the end of last year, but any suggestion that I can't run point better than Nick is a slap in the face.

Murphy pipes up again, trying to soothe things. "We're just saying a little patience could help," he says.

"Okay, Coach," I say, but I don't look at him.

Bolden stands up and walks to the door. He passes so close he almost bumps me with his hip. It's hard to tell if it's because of the cramped office or because the old man is trying to intimidate me. The door scrapes open and I stand, ready to go. Instead, there's Moose's frame filling up the doorway. Bolden backs away from him and gestures toward me. "Tell Derrick what you need to tell him," Coach says.

Moose takes a deep breath, that huge chest heaving up and down. He's got on a sweet checkered shirt that shows off his new cut-up frame, but his jeans hang loose even on a man his size. He tries to make eye contact with me, but he rests his gaze somewhere on the wall past me. Coach must have put him up to this. "First, I want to apologize," Moose says. He cocks his neck hard enough to pop it. "I shouldn't have hollered at you in the game Saturday night. It cost us a technical and it shows you up in front of everyone." He takes another deep breath, but then he manages to make eye contact. "I'm sorry, D."

"It's cool, Moose," I say.

"But!" he shouts, before I can say anything else. Now he stares at

Slump   75

me, a little fire in his eyes, some leftover heat from the other night. This is the part that he really wanted to say. "I didn't bust my ass all summer so I could watch you launch threes this winter." It's as restrained as he can be. He's a gentle giant—but when his temper turns he's a scary sight, and right now he's as prickly as barbed wire.

"I feel you," I say.

"We good?" Bolden asks, glancing first at me and then at Moose.

"Yeah," I say.

Moose waits a second like he's not sure. Then, suddenly, he unclenches. His shoulders go slack and that huge smile softens his face. "Ah, we're good," he says. He steps to me and shakes my hand with his massive grip. Then he pulls me into him and rests a paw on top of my head, shaking it back and forth once. "I'm not hard to please, D. I told you last year when we first met—I get open down low, you gotta get me the rock."

9.

Jasmine's lips taste sweeter than usual, some trace of berry flavor from her lip gloss. We're in her car, deep in the shadows of the parking deck where nobody can see us.

I tilt my head so I can kiss down her neck, then slide the straps of her shirt and bra down her shoulder so I can kiss her there. She moans. Frustrated by her arm banging into the steering wheel, she climbs out of her seat and almost launches herself onto me. She spreads her legs to straddle me and grinds her hips up against me.

"Jesus," I say.

"Keep kissing my neck," she says.

She doesn't have to ask twice. As I follow her lead, I get a deep breath of her perfume, only now it's mixed with her natural scent.

I've been on my best behavior. My mom spotted me some cash to take Jasmine to a nice place downtown, and I haven't even breathed a word about hoops. Even went on a walk around the Circle, then ducked into a shop for some chocolates. The snow just keeps on. It seems like we're getting five new inches every week. But that's fine—

Jasmine and I huddled up near the window to people-watch, everyone racing around with their bags full of Christmas presents. I watched their breaths turn to little clouds in front of them and looked forward to Christmas Eve tomorrow night. Church. Good times with my parents. Wes coming over.

Even when we made it back to her car, I didn't force things. Just leaned over for a quick kiss. It was like I'd tossed gasoline on a fire. She's the one who got it all moving. So now, in the third floor of a Circle Centre parking deck, I figure this is it.

I reach down and feel for the bottom of her shirt. For a second, I let my fingers stay against her stomach, feel her react to my touch. She presses her mouth against mine, pushes her tongue inside. I can't take it anymore. I start to pull up her shirt. She doesn't stop me, so I keep going. I can see the bottom of her bra, and my heart's beating so fast I can feel the thump in my ears.

"Easy, Derrick," she says.

"It's all good," I say, raising the shirt on up.

Like she can't stop herself, she lifts her arms over her head, and I slide the shirt off. As soon as it's off, though, she clamps her arms against her chest and looks away. I know just one more kiss, just the right word—something, some magical key—will unlock her arms and there will be no turning back. But when I lean in, she pulls away.

"I can't," she says.

"Jasmine."

She shakes her head. "Please. I want to go further, but…"

I can't believe it. Denied now? I flop back against my seat. "For real?"

"I'm just not ready, Derrick," she says. "Be patient."

Kevin Waltman

She climbs off me and squeezes back into the driver seat, her elbow hitting the horn as she does. The sound reverberates off the parking garage walls like a short, sharp alarm. She puts her shirt back on, angrily smoothing down its wrinkles. I shake my head and pull down my seatbelt. "It's okay," I say, but it comes out wrong, like an accusation.

Jasmine's back stiffens. "I know it's okay. You do realize that's not for you to decide, right? I don't have to, like, ask for your forgiveness." She turns away from me to stare out her window, but the only view is a parking garage column. She bangs her hand on the steering wheel. "I mean if you're in such a hurry just to get laid, there are plenty other girls who will let you do whatever you want."

It's a mean, spiteful comment. And the way she glares at me afterward tells me she meant to sting me with it. My pulse is still racing from having her damn near undressed. I feel unhinged. The impulse to hurt her right back is impossible to control, so I search for something to say that will sting her just as bad. "Shit," I say, "I bet you let Nick *hit that*."

As soon as I say it, I want to take it back, want the last few seconds to rewind so I can try again. Bringing up her ex is way over the line, like pulling a gun on someone because they gave you a shove. But it's that phrase—hit that—that's really wrong. Before I can even begin stammering out an apology, Jasmine's jaw drops, like my comment caused her actual physical pain. She just presses the button to unlock the doors and points past me. *Get out.*

"Jasmine," I start, but she just shakes her head.

She tries to say something, but all that comes out is a little moan. She clasps her hand over her mouth and keeps shaking her head. She glances away again. I wait, thinking she'll calm down, and there will be something I can say to fix this. After a few seconds though, she bangs on the wheel again and shouts *"Go!"* She refuses to look at me, but when I open the car door and the light pops on, I can see tears gathering in the corner of her eye.

As soon as I get both feet on the cement, she leans over and slams the passenger door shut, then cranks it up and is off. I stand alone in the parking garage, trying to shake the image of those tears. I'm in the dark until some other car wheels around the ramp, its lights washing across me and making me feel totally exposed.

His breath smells of liquor. Not bad, not like he's going to crash the car. But Uncle Kid's got himself loosened up. We ride up Illinois. He bobs his head to some music he's got on, rapping along every now and then.

Kid glances over and reads my expression. "Girl trouble," he says. "Man, I can smell it on you, D."

"It's nothing," I say. I just want to get home and text Jasmine, start putting things right.

"Shit," he says, "why else you calling me up for a ride home this time of night? Girl trouble. Probably worse 'cause you didn't get your license. That's your first problem. No honey wants someone doesn't have their own wheels."

"Come on, Kid. Just drive." He hits the gas, but we get a red light at the next intersection. We sit there in silence and watch the cross traffic. Then a black Jag rolls up next to us, packed front and back with some fine specimens. The driver is a white girl, but the other three are various shades of brown. College girls, I bet. They don't even look over at us, but one of them says something that cracks them all up. Watching them laugh, all those bright white teeth flashing in the night, makes you want to be in the middle of them.

"Not bad, right?" Kid says. I don't respond, so he pushes me on the shoulder. "Oh come on, D!" he shouts. "Don't let one girl make you blind to all the others. If I was your age, I'd have those girls fighting over me."

I still don't say anything. It's not like I didn't notice how hot they are, but admitting it out loud would seem like cheating on Jasmine somehow. I don't want to feed Kid's crazy notions anyway.

But he doesn't need any encouragement from me. When the light turns green, he mashes it, getting every last ounce of power out of his Nova so he can keep up with the Jag. It's not subtle. By the time we hit the next light, the girls are all looking at us. They're smiling, but mostly they just think we're being stupid. Kid rolls down my window. "Talk to them, D," he says. I just stare ahead, mortified. I can feel the bitter cold pouring into the car, getting into my bones. "Talk some game, D," he says, but I still don't say a word.

I glance over though. The blonde driver is watching us, waiting for whatever it is we want to say. She rolls down her window. "What?" she asks.

"You girls want to come out with a future NBA star?" Kid shouts.

The black girl riding shotgun laughs. "You look a little old for a baller," she says.

"Not me," Kid says. "My boy here." He slaps me on the chest, pumping me up. "Don't tell me you haven't heard of Derrick Bowen. Best young point guard in the whole country."

Slump 81

"Oh, yeah?" the driver says. She looks straight at me. "You got some game?"

There's an itch in me that wants to act all cocky, say *Hop in* and *I'll show you game*. But I can't do it. I can still see Jasmine's face in my mind, those tears welling in her eyes.

The girls get tired of waiting. When that light turns green, they leave us in the dust, laughing as they go. This time Kid doesn't even try to keep up. He just keeps idling at Illinois and 16th, disgusted with me. "Derrick, you just dying on me. I mean, if I were your age I'd be killin' it all over town. All you got to do is *talk*. You say *anything*, and girls are ready to put it on you."

He finally starts up the road again, but he creeps. Traffic rips around us, some people honking. Finally Uncle Kid sighs and digs out a different CD—I want to crack back at him, tell him anyone still rocking discs doesn't have the right to be giving any lectures, but I let it be. He puts it in and I hear the old school beats crackling out. "Listen up to this," he says. "I know you're feeling bad, but this is the best advice ever. Ex girl to the next girl, D. Ex girl to the next girl."

Then he starts rapping along with the song. Loud. And, finally, I can't help but smile. Kid just isn't going to stop until I lighten up. By the time he drops me off, he's got me feeling all right again. Say what you want about Kid—all he wants is for people to have a good time.

The mood doesn't last. When I text an apology to Jasmine, she bangs right back at me: *You think 'sorry' cuts it? That wasn't some fight, Derrick. That was a deal breaker.*

So that's it.

Kevin Waltman

I spend a few minutes on my phone trying to find the track Uncle Kid played for me, but when I finally land on it—old Gang Starr—it can't do the trick again. I just feel hollow. I keep turning my phone over in my hand, thinking of things to text Jasmine. But there's nothing left.

Slump   83

10.

Christmas is what Christmas is. Wes stands me up to hang with his dad and Iesha. I don't hear a word from Jasmine. But at least there's peace in our house. Even Jayson knows better than to act up on the holidays. We do our Christmas Eve thing. Uncle Kid comes over to hang afterward. Mom and Dad mix their drinks and play music, swooning over each other like they're teenagers all alone. Then the next morning we unwrap our presents, but there's no surprises there. Jayson gets the newest version of NBA2K, then quickly disappears into his room for a marathon session. Kid rattles around rubbing his head after having a few too many on Christmas Eve. Mom and Dad open small simple presents from each other and declare them the most thoughtful things ever. I get mostly clothes, which is how it's been for years now, like my parents are trying to turn me into some young professional. It's not like there's anything I really want though. At least nothing anyone can give me as a present.

Later, when my parents and Kid have dropped off for naps, I text Wes. Turns out his dad came through this year and got him his kicks. We set up a time to meet later. I know he'll be sporting those proudly.

Then I get down to business. I throw on my cleanest pair of jeans and a slick new shirt my parents got me. Coat and boots and then I hit the street, heading for Central. The sky is one massive cloud. Everything's closed. Nothing but me is moving. It's like the buildings are just a row of faces staring at me. For a second, I imagine someone looking out of their apartment window and seeing me, wondering what in the world Derrick Bowen is doing kicking it down the street on Christmas afternoon. I regret all over again that I didn't take the time to get my license last summer. The wind kicks up and icy flurries sting my face. More snow is coming—snow and ice on top of snow and ice. I put my head down and move faster. There's a car now and then, but mostly the only sounds are my boots on the concrete, my breaths, and the wind.

Soon enough, I hit my destination. Even from the outside, their place is distinguished. The wood around the windows has a new coat of paint, nothing peeling like on all the other buildings, and the steps are spotless. Again, it seems like they think they're better than everyone else—but maybe they are. Suddenly I wonder if maybe Jasmine's never really let her guard down with me because she thinks I'm not good enough for her. I bet her parents have fed her that. Standing here, my finger an inch from their doorbell, I suspect it about myself. She's going places. No doubt. She's college scholarship material. And I am too, but people like her parents look at athletic scholarships like it's cheating somehow.

I ring the bell. It takes an eternity for the door to open. When it does, it only swings back a foot. Just enough for Mr. Winters to frown out at me. He's got a thick sweater on, a heavy gold watch on his wrist. His face has that same smooth skin tone of Jasmine's. His frown isn't

Slump   85

even angry, just this look like he's perplexed at what could possibly be interrupting Christmas dinner. Behind him I can see some candles and other Christmas decorations lit up. It looks warm on his side of the door, like a scene from a Christmas movie—near the end when everything's come out just right.

"Derrick?" he says. That bass voice of his has always intimidated me. It's slow and syrupy, not any of that ragged anger that someone like Coach Bolden has, but it drips with judgment.

"I thought I could—" I trail off. God, what a terrible idea. I feel as out of place here as I used to when Kid would take me to ball at the park when I was twelve, going up against men twice my size. "Is Jasmine home, Mr. Winters?" I finally ask. It comes out all tentative, like I'm admitting to some crime. And it's a stupid question. Of course she's home. I'm the only person in the city not home right now.

"Jasmine is engaged with family right now," he says.

"I know, but—" I trail off again. What was I hoping for, some Christmas miracle?

"Derrick," he says, then he checks over his shoulder quickly. He steps outside and swings the door shut behind him. His hand's still on the knob like he wants to make this quick. He shivers once in the wind, and it strips him of some of that power he seemed to have—him on the warm inside, me shivering out in the cold—but it also backs me up, puts me down two steps from him so I have to look up. He smiles at me. "You seem like a nice kid, Derrick. You've always been polite to me and Mrs. Winters, and Jasmine has always said nice things about you. So I don't know what happened between you two. But you have to understand that she doesn't want to see you right now."

Kevin Waltman

It's all a shock to me. I figured the first thing Jasmine did was burst home in tears and tell her parents about how horrible I am. The fact that she didn't gives me hope. But then I think about her suffering in silence. I imagine her moping around the house dodging her parents' questions.

Mr. Winters makes a motion like he's going to put his hand on my shoulder, but then he thinks better of it and shoves his hands in his pockets. "Young couples fight, Derrick," he says. "Sometimes they make up. Sometimes they don't. But I can tell you that coming here right now isn't going to fix anything. I know my daughter, and if she changes her mind it will be her doing. Go home and spend Christmas with your family."

There's not much to say after that. Nothing to do but head right back up the blocks I just came down. I didn't really expect much more than what I got. I was just hoping that maybe I'd see Jasmine, ask her if she liked my present. It had been sitting, wrapped, in her living room for a week—that scarf she'd gone nuts over a month ago down on Mass Ave. Maybe she just threw it out without even opening it.

Later, we're checking the Christmas Day game, watching the San Antonio Spurs school people. Jayson's made it out of his room, his X-Box shut off just long enough for him to eye some real hoops. Kid's back in good spirits. He chatters more than the play-by-play guy, pointing out all the little things he thinks the players do wrong. To hear him, you'd think he knew more about the game than Duncan himself.

My dad's racked out for yet another nap in his chair, little snores

Slump

escaping now and then. And Mom's cooling it back in their room, taking a rest after the melee of Christmas morning.

"Oooh!" Jayson explodes, reacting to a Tony Parker floater. Dad stirs a little on the couch, but settles right back down to sleep. "He's still filthy good," Jayson whispers, "even if he is getting to be an old man."

"You get older, you get wiser," Kid says, full of himself.

I don't say a word, still smarting from my rejection at Jasmine's door.

It goes on like that until the fourth. Kid tries to bait me more and more, saying things he knows I disagree with—like that the game still revolves around the big men or that no team today could hang with the Lakers of the 80s. The most I give him is a *whatever* now and then. I just want to be left alone to watch some ball.

My dad finally wakes up from his tremendous nap and then goes in their room to check on my mom. They come back out and announce they're going to find a place open for coffee. For the first time in a while, they look happy. When they open the front door and get a face full of cold, they cinch up against each other like teenagers.

"Your uncle's in charge," Dad calls over his shoulder. "Try not to let things fall apart completely while we're gone." Mom laughs and pulls tighter against Dad, and then they're gone. The door seals behind them, but there's still an aftermath of cold that seeped in. It sets me on edge.

"You heard the man," Kid says. "I'm running the show now." He looks around the house, frowning like something displeases him. Then he snaps his fingers at Jayson. "Go fix me a plate of leftovers, and then clean your room."

Jayson stares at him for a second, indignant. Then he gets it. "You crazy," he says.

They both laugh. But when Kid sees that I won't join in, he shakes his head. "What? You can't even break a smile? What the hell's biting you? Still that girl?"

I don't respond. I don't want to give him the satisfaction of being right. Instead, I try to act interested in the pick-and-roll being replayed for the millionth time on the TV.

Kid keeps after me. "It's that girl! I knew it. Man, I told you—ex girl to the next girl."

Jayson laughs again, probably thinking that phrase is a Kid original. "That's good. I like that."

"Just cut your shit out, Kid," I snap. "Quit acting like you know every damn thing in the world."

That frosts the room over for a while. We go back to watching the game. At the next timeout, Jayson slips off the couch and heads to his room to hit up more NBA2K. Can't really blame him.

After a while, Kid clears his throat. He's not angry, but he's not fooling now. "Well, I do know one thing, Derrick. You go around thinking how bad you got it, and life has a funny way of showing you what bad really is."

Slump 89

11.

A few days after Christmas, we have a little tourney up at Cathedral. Our first game, we put it to Decatur pretty good. It seems like maybe all we needed was some time off to get our legs back. Devin buries some Js and his wheel seems fine. And I make damn sure I get Moose rolling down low after our little dust-up. I even get a couple to fall from range, then get some nice run-outs to show off my hops. Fuller picks his game up too, rebounding like a beast. And Stanford gets his here and there.

It ends up a 67-42 pasting. Toward the end, while I'm catching a rest with the other starters, I keep scanning the crowd hoping to see Jasmine. No sign.

We get several hours to kill before we need to be back at the gym for the night game, so we all go out to eat. Coach takes us to an Italian restaurant with a huge buffet. "Fuel up," he says, then turns us loose to chow down. Moose makes a line for the buffet, showing off some quickness we didn't think he had. He loads down a plate with spaghetti and a mountain of lasagna, then stacks up two different desserts.

Kevin Waltman

Murphy stands back and marvels at the big man. Then he says, "Moose, it's a buffet. You don't have to get everything at once. You can come back for more."

Moose responds with total sincerity. "Oh, I'm still getting seconds." Then he heads to our table, already starting to eat as he walks.

It seems like half of Marion East is there killing time between games. I get that feeling of being watched. When I look around, I see Daniella Cole staring at me. She's with a group of her friends in the far corner of the restaurant, but she's locked in on me like there's nobody else in the place. She's got this smooth coffee-colored complexion, and she has her hair pulled into braids that gather into thick curls on the side. She has a nice, easy smile too. But everyone knows she's all hit and run. Her stare makes me uncomfortable. When she wraps her lips around her straw and takes a slow sip, I turn away.

The band came too. On my way back to the table, I almost literally bump into Wes. I have to dodge him because he's walking with his head down, texting. Iesha, no doubt.

"'Sup?" I say.

"'Sup, dawg," Wes says, but he doesn't even look away from his phone. He might as well be talking to a stranger.

"Those shoes are some sorry ass kicks," I say. That gets his attention. He looks up with an expression of disgust, like how *dare* anyone crack on his style. Then he sees it's me, and his snarl gives way to a smile.

"Hey, D. I didn't even see it was you."

"I know," I say. "You got your head buried in that phone so much you're about to crash into the buffet."

Slump 91

Wes gives this shrug, playing embarrassed. "You know how it is, D," he says. "Gotta check in with the female."

Somehow this hits me wrong. I feel like now he's trying to put on a show for me, maybe for everyone in that restaurant—be the big man with a pestering woman. "Shit, Wes. You know you're the one chasing after her every waking second. Iesha's probably somewhere else right now running shit to her girlfriends about how you won't stop hassling her."

It was meant as a joke, but it cuts Wes. His mouth pinches down into a tight O, and he squints his eyes at me. Now, I've got eight full inches on him, but I'd swear Wes would be ready to throw down with one more word. "Well, maybe you don't know how it is," he snaps. "Mr. Basketball and still can't get any."

I hear the sound of a fork clanking against a plate nearby. I hear murmurs of conversation all around us and the bustle of workers bringing out more food for the buffet. But it feels like the whole restaurant has stopped and is listening to us. "Shit, Wes, you get chopped up a few times and all of a sudden you think you're some bad ass."

"At least I'm not strutting around like God's gift even though I'm only scoring nine points a game!"

Now people really *are* listening to us. I don't want to make more of a scene than we already have, but I'm just done with Wes. He thinks he can run smack at me like that? "Just go sit at your table," I say, motioning over to the section the band's camped out in. "You do you and stop worrying about me."

"Done," he says.

And that's that.

Kevin Waltman

Against Cathedral, Moose controls the tip to me, and I don't even hesitate. Before we even get set, I attack the rim and gangster one in. Cathedral turns it over and I attack again. I drive right, looking at Devin in the corner, then fake it to him and knock a little runner off glass. I'm not done though. I jump into their point and get him off balance, then get a fingertip on his pass. It sails wide of its mark. Fuller scoops it up. By the time he gathers, I'm already running free, like a wide receiver behind a blown coverage. Fuller finds me and lobs a long pass my way. I gather it in, take a power dribble into the lane, and throw one down—reverse for good measure.

Time out, Cathedral, and our crowd's in a frenzy. Our bench is up and into it, Reynolds the first one off to high-five me.

"What got into you?" Devin asks in the huddle.

"Nothing," I say. "Just about time I got it together." I mean, this is how the season was supposed to be. Me controlling things.

"Hey, great start," Bolden shouts, "but it's just a start. Remember to stay patient as the game goes on. It's not always going to be this easy."

I'm not hearing it. No more passing it around the perimeter for five minutes hoping someone gets open. No more settling for long range Js. I'm in full-on attack mode. As the game continues, I just drive and drive, no matter how many people jump into my path. I go around them to the rim, rise over them for leaners, shuttle the rock past them for dimes to Stanford and Moose.

With a few minutes to go in the first half, the aggression catches up with me. I lower my shoulder and get a whistle. It's a cheap charge

Slump 93

call. Our crowd howls in protest. I can't help myself. I throw my hands in the air and shake my head—apparently too demonstrative for the ref because there's a second whistle real quick. Technical. I turn to Murphy and Bolden, my palms turned upward in a plea. I didn't even *say* anything. Rather than take my side though, Bolden just points to the bench. Rules are rules, even for me.

I angrily snatch a towel from Darius and sit. Reynolds makes room for me and pats me on the back. "That was a bullshit call, man. A bullshit T too."

"Whatever."

"Naw, D, you were ballin' out. The refs are just trying to keep Cathedral in it."

"I don't want to hear it, Reynolds!" I snap. I stare down at the floor between my shoes for a full minute, feel the throbbing in my temples. I'm so angry I could strangle somebody. Starting with Bolden. When I finally look up at the game, I see our lead evaporating. With me off, Cathedral gets it rolling. Bolden slides Devin over to point, which isn't his strong suit. And then Reynolds comes in and tries to play hero, missing on two straight threes.

The lead drops to five, then three, then one. Then Reynolds tries to slip one into Moose, but it's a low pass—off Moose's shins and out of bounds. Behind us, our crowd is stone silent. Cathedral's fans start to clap in rhythm while their boys hold for the last shot of the half. Bolden watches intently, perched on the edge of his seat with his head jutting out, like some bird of prey about to attack. But Murphy stands and walks my way. He crouches down and then drops to a knee beside me. "You've got to keep your cool out there, Derrick," he says.

"I know, Coach."

"No, you've got to *understand*. You lose it like that and you hurt the whole team."

"I *know*, Murphy."

Murphy gets off his knee and stands next to me. He bends at the hip, lowering his head so it's just inches from mine. "I know I'm just the assistant, Derrick, the one who's supposed to be all supportive when Bolden cracks the whip. But you take that tone with me again and you'll see just what a son-of-a-bitch I can be."

"Look, I get it, man," I pop. I point to the court, where Cathedral's working for a good look. "Shit, we wouldn't even have a lead to lose if it weren't for me."

Murphy doesn't say anything. He stands and walks away. Behind him, Cathedral knocks one down at the buzzer and their crowd roars.

"We can't just let teams back in that easy!" Devin snaps. "Come on, boys."

"I'll get back out there and get us straightened out," I say.

Moose snaps at me: "Just make sure that includes a post feed now and then. This isn't the Derrick Bowen Show."

"I feel you," I say.

"You say that, but you sure don't act like it."

"Come on, guys," Fuller says. "We're all on the same team here. We never got after each other like this where I used to play."

About four of us shout in unison: "Shut up, Fuller!" I add, "Nobody gives a shit about where you used to play."

Finally, Murphy and Bolden come through the door. They'd

Slump   95

been conferencing outside the locker room for a good five minutes, and Murphy's still in Bolden's ear as they walk in. Bolden nods a few times and then walks briskly to the front of the locker room. He snatches a marker up and starts writing on the white board.

5 – GREEN
4 – STANFORD
3 – JONES
2 – FULLER
1 – VARNEY

It takes every ounce of willpower I have not to scream. I turn my head toward Murphy and get met with his icy stare. Then he mouths, real nice and slow so I can make it out—*I told you not to test me.*

Kevin Waltman

12.

Mrs. Hulsey throws her hands up in despair. She can't believe none of us did the reading over break. In the weak light of the January morning, you can almost see it creep across her face—a deep desire that American History weren't a two-semester deal at our school. She doesn't know if she can take another semester with this class.

"It's the most important book ever written on Vietnam," she sighs. "How could you not care?"

We don't even have the energy to give her lip. It's the first day back from break, and we'd all rather be sleeping. I'm still stinging over that Cathedral loss. They just rolled us in the second half, but Bolden never budged. Wouldn't even look my way. The practices since then have been tense. He's got me back with the ones, but he's been super critical. If I even think about attacking the rim before looking for a post-feed, he jumps my case. And Murphy hasn't said a word to me. He nods hello when he comes in, but it's about as icy as if he were walking past a panhandler.

"I was going to show you a movie, but I can't do that now,"

Slump 97

Mrs. Hulsey says. She leans over and puts both hands on her desk, like she's about to fall over under the stress of teaching us. She sighs again. "Okay, just take out your books. Let's read the first chapter together right now and we'll discuss it."

Some of us start to dig into our backpacks, but Martin Germain raises his hand.

"What, Martin?"

"What book you talking about?" he asks.

Everyone laughs then, except for Mrs. Hulsey. I swear tears well up in her eyes. She might not last here, but she doesn't know how good she's got it. Marion East is no Harvard, but if she thinks this is rough, she ought to try out some other city schools. Some places are complete chaos, like trying to learn in a war zone.

Before she can respond to Martin, there's a knock on the door. It's someone with a note again, but as they hand it to Mrs. Hulsey, they motion for her to lean in. Then they whisper something in her ear. Something bad happens on Mrs. Hulsey's face, like she saw a ghost or something.

She takes the note and looks at me. "Derrick," she says. The class starts to *ooh* again. I gear myself up for yet another showdown with Bolden and Murphy.

"Stop it!" Mrs. Hulsey snaps. "The rest of you mind your own business and read!" It's for-real anger, and everyone shuts right up.

I take the note, but this one sends me to the principal's office. Strange. I know I've screwed some things up—with Jasmine, with Wes, with my coaches—but I haven't done anything to get me in trouble at school. I hurry down the hall to see what's up. When I come into the main office, Ms. Chambliss, the secretary, looks like she's been waiting for me. She motions toward the principal's door. "Just go on in, Derrick. Mr. Markey's waiting for you."

I push open the heavy door to Markey's office and see him brooding. He's got busts of MLK and Malcolm X anchoring his huge desk, pictures of black political leaders hung all over the walls. His desk has this kind of military organization, like if you moved even one piece of paper he'd cut your hand off. Markey sits behind it just staring at me. Nobody messes with Markey. Never. He's 6'5" and a good 250, his face as big and dark as a bear's.

"Derrick," he says, his voice booming low and loud, "sit."

I do as I'm told.

He doesn't waste any time. "Your father's in the hospital, Derrick," he says.

PART II

13.

Uncle Kid looks bad. There's always a ragged look to Kid, like he's just waking up in his clothes, but now he looks worse than I've ever seen him. He doesn't say a word for the first mile in the car. His right hand keeps drumming against his leg and his jaw is hanging open like he's just been punched in the mouth.

I don't know what to say. There are about a million questions zooming through my head, but they clamor on top of one another, and I can't pick any single one out. The hospital starts to loom in front of us as we go along 16th. I feel a panic in my chest. Finally, Kid's eyes focus on me. "Aw, D," he says. It's as if he just now noticed me. Then he repeats it, "Aw, D," and his voice cracks as he tries to hold back tears. He starts to slump down toward the steering wheel, but then he stiffens his back again and looks at me. "He's gonna be okay," he says. But I can tell Kid's not sure. It's the kind of thing grown-ups have to say at a time like this, and Kid's not practiced enough to be convincing.

Inside the hospital, nurses and doctors breeze by us, some studying clipboards, others sipping cups of coffee. The hospital creeps me out. It's not that it's got that sickening hospital smell, but that they've made attempts to try to make it cheery. There's art on some of the walls, flowers on nurse's stations, TVs broadcasting midday soap operas. It all just seems unreal right now. We round the corner, and then reality hits me. Mom is sitting in a small waiting area, a sick expression on her face. Beside her, Jayson is just staring at the television. Not watching, really, just zoning out.

When Mom sees me, she stands. She pulls Jayson up by his hand and walks toward me and Kid. "Derrick, it's going to be fine," she says. She's much better at this than Kid, her voice as smooth and sure as if she were explaining something on the news to me. She glances quickly at Kid and tells him thanks, then ushers me and Jayson both back to the waiting area. Kid stays where we were standing, lingering in the middle of the hallway like he's not sure if he's allowed to join us. He turns to the nurse's station like he wants to ask a question, but when the nurse holds up her hand and tells him to wait a second, he just shoves his hands in his pockets and shuffles down the hall.

"How much did they tell you at school?" Mom asks.

"Just that Dad was here. That he was in a wreck."

Mom nods. She takes a deep breath, like she's bracing herself to actually say the words she has to say. But then she just tells us straight: "He ran off the road and hit a telephone pole." I recoil. Jayson's lip starts to quiver, and Mom reaches out and holds his hand to calm him. "It's going to be okay. His leg's in bad shape, but he's stable. They just need to find out exactly what happened."

At last, a specific question emerges from all the noise in my head. "How bad is his leg?"

Mom blinks a couple times, taken off guard. But she goes right back into Mom-mode—speaking in reassuring tones but telling us the truth we need to hear. "I don't know. It's not something where he'll never walk again. But it's not like he just bumped his knee either."

And like that we all fall silent, as if speaking a single word would be an insult to Dad. Every time the door behind the nurse's station opens, Mom comes off her chair just an inch, then settles back down. All I want is to see my dad. Except when I picture him in my mind—in a hospital bed, maybe tubes running into him, monitors beeping out signals—I don't know if I can actually handle it. In truth, I'm afraid to see what he looks like now.

We sit in a smaller room. No art on the walls here, no television. Just a chair for the doctor and chairs for family. There's also a little screen where I guess sometimes they put up X-rays or MRIs for people to see. We sit in a semi-circle around the doctor. Uncle Kid stands by the door. There aren't enough seats for him. He almost got shut out by the doctor until Mom finally identified Kid as family. Now he stands there fidgeting, like he's not sure of himself. Maybe he's worried he'll get pushed away from the family now that my Dad can't speak up for him. I don't have time to feel sorry for him though.

"Your husband is stable," the doctor says, speaking only to my mom. He introduced himself to us, but I've already forgotten his name. And he hasn't looked at me or Jayson since that introduction. "Physically, he can recover. We'll do surgery for the leg, and then he'll have several weeks of rehab. But the tests showed a seizure. That's what made him lose control. We need to monitor him so it doesn't happen again. We'll give him a prescription, but he can't drive until he's cleared. He'll be walking again before he can drive. But he should have full recovery if all goes well."

"Thank God," Mom says. She reaches over and squeezes Jayson's hand. "Can we go see him?"

The doctor raises his eyebrows. He's got a cold, washed-out look, like he's been on call for a whole week solid. He's older, with wrinkles setting in around his eyes, and his brown hair is broken up by splotches of gray. "You can, but you have to understand that he needs rest. His body went through some trauma." Then he looks at me and Jayson. "Do you two know what I mean when I say 'seizure'?"

I don't want to admit my ignorance. All I can picture are epileptic seizures, people convulsing on the ground, but that doesn't sound like what happened to Dad. Jayson shakes his head no. The doctor goes on. "There are all different kinds. What your dad had doesn't make him lose consciousness, but it means he's not in control of what's happening. So we want to be sure it doesn't escalate into something worse. We've run blood tests and what we call an EEG—that's a test that measures brain activity."

We sit there and absorb it. Strangely, there's something comforting in how clinical and cold the doctor is. It's like he's talking about some scientific experiment in class instead of my dad.

"What do *you* think, though?" This is Kid, his voice quavering like he might just fall apart in front of everyone. Mom shoots him a look, angry that he'd dare speak up right now, but then she turns her attention right back to the doctor. She wants to know too.

The doctor shakes his head. "I can't really say anything until we get the results of the tests," he says.

Slump 105

"But what do you *think*?" Kid repeats. "Is this going to happen again?"

The doctor won't bite. "I don't know. This can go any number of ways. He could be back to normal in a month, or—" he breaks off here. He's turned to Kid and it's like he forgot Jayson and I were in the room. He corrects himself. "I don't know. We'll run tests. We'll do some surgery for the leg and then he'll have to rehab it. That's all I can say with certainty at the moment."

He stands then, a signal that we're all done. He takes one last look around to see if we have any more questions. But when we freeze up, he simply shakes my mother's hand and tells her that a nurse will come get her when we can go see my father.

It's forever in that waiting area. Kid keeps offering to run get us something to drink or eat, and my mom keeps refusing. It's hard to know exactly why. Maybe she feels like eating while Dad's alone back in his room would be some kind of insult. Maybe she's really not hungry. Maybe she just doesn't want Kid's help.

I alternate between watching the TV above us and walking over to the window. It's just a view of the parking lot and 16th street. We're on the third floor. Below us, people wheel in and out. I wonder how many go with heavy hearts, shouldering news as bad—or worse, maybe—than what we've got. The sky goes from a bright blue—you'd think it was a nice hot day out there if it weren't for the bare trees and the unmelted snow plowed into piles—to another gray, dreary January afternoon.

When we finally do go back to see my dad, I wish we hadn't. He's got an I.V., and there's a tube running into his nose. All that, I can handle. It's his face. It's bruised and looks gaunt, like the skin is sagging away from the bone. And even though I can see his chest rising and falling beneath his sheet, he looks as cold and lifeless as a corpse. When Mom rushes to him and puts her head on his chest— "Oh, Tom. Oh, Tom. Oh, Tom," she keeps saying—I have to turn away. When I do, Kid's right behind me. He catches my shoulder as I turn. For a second he gives me this half hug, but then he pushes me back around. "Don't be scared," he whispers. "You gonna have to man up."

My mom pulls herself together, apologizing to me and Jayson for making a scene. Then we pull up chairs and sit around Dad's body. Again, Uncle Kid's the odd man out and has to stand over by the door.

There's just the sounds of the monitor for a while and a small rustle of the sheet each time my dad breathes. Finally, my mom talks to us. She tells us that, before we were born, her grandfather had died of a heart attack. He was over-stressed and over-worked and refused to rein in his diet. I can't believe she's telling us this now. But then she stands. She grabs Dad's hand as she talks to us. "But that's not happening to your father. He had an accident, and he can get better. And he'll be around for a long time to watch you two grow up and go to your weddings and play with all the grandchildren you're going to give him. But he's down right now, and he needs us. We're going to be there for him too. I want each of you"—she nods at Kid to let him know she means him too—"to talk to him. I know he can hear us. Just tell him he's going to be okay and whatever else you want to say to him. In private. You can say anything."

Mom goes first and then it's me, Jayson, and Uncle Kid out in the hall. Nobody knows what to say. We can barely look at each other.

Slump

It's like we all know some terrible secret the other is keeping, and we don't want to have to talk about it.

Mom doesn't take long though. The door to Dad's room comes open with a soft whoosh, and there she stands. Her eyes are wet, but she wipes them briskly, like she's angry at herself for showing vulnerability. She lifts her chin back up and takes a deep breath. "Who's next?" she asks. None of us respond. She closes her eyes, just for a second. It's like every decision requires more energy than she has. She's trying to dig down deep for one more effort. She opens her eyes and looks at Jayson. "You go," she says. Then she walks past me and Kid and back toward the waiting area. She seems to slump a little lower with each step. She even puts her hand on the counter of the nurse's station as if she needs support. Then she reaches down for the arm of the nearest chair and collapses into it. Maybe she doesn't think I can see her from down the hall, or maybe she doesn't care. Either way, she buries her face in her hands and gives two heaving sobs.

Later on, when it's my turn, I pull my chair up close to Dad. His face looks ashy. It's like it's not even him. Like maybe I've come into the wrong room, or they've switched him out with someone else. I start to reach out to touch him, but I stop short. If he's cold and clammy, I don't want to feel it. I rest my hand on the rail of his bed instead.

"Dad," I say. "If you can hear me…" But then I go quiet. All these things I want to tell him, but nothing comes. He just needs me to say something, anything, let him know I'm here. And I choke. "Dad," I say again, but then nothing else. What frightens me is that I could say the wrong thing. Like maybe he really *can* hear me through the painkillers but what I have to say would just be more of a weight on him. I hate myself for it. Here's my dad in trouble, and all I can think about is how awkward *I* feel, how worried *I* am. *Me.*

A minute or two passes. The room is dark except for the light right by the door. Once it seems like enough time has passed that people will think I've actually talked to him, I get up. I move the chair back to its original spot, since everyone else has already taken their turn. Then I head for the door, fast. Maybe if I wait another second they'll shut me in here for the night too.

When I hit the hallway the light feels harsh on my eyes. People are still milling about. All of a sudden, it seems like the hospital is some hub of action after being in that still room.

"Derrick," a voice says. I turn. It's Coach Bolden. Coach Murphy's standing beside him. The clock behind their heads says it's 6 p.m. The whole day has passed. For a moment, I think they're there to get on me about missing practice. I didn't even think to call anyone to say I'd miss, but if they can't cut me some slack for *this*—but before I can even finish that thought Coach Bolden's hand reaches out and grabs my shoulder. He pulls me in and gives me a hug, thumping me on the back a few times with his other hand. "You hang in there," he says.

He lets me loose, and I step back. His gesture almost makes me cry, but I don't want to let him see that. Murphy looks away from me, and I get a glimpse of how it's going to be—everyone avoiding eye contact because they don't know what to say. He tries to say the right thing, but he's looking at the floor. "You know, D, you need anything, anything at all..."

He's struggling to finish his sentence, so I let him off the hook. "I know, Coach. Thanks."

Slump 109

Bolden doesn't have any problems making eye contact. He stares right at me with that intense gaze, leaning forward a little bit like he does in timeouts. "Now listen, Derrick. Your father's a young man and he's gonna come out of this. You keep your head together for him. As far as hoops,"—he waves his hand in the air—"don't even think about it. You need time off—take it. There are things way more important than basketball, okay?" Something in my expression must not satisfy him because he raises his voice a little—not in anger, but just to make sure I'm paying attention. "Hey, I mean that. Like Coach Murphy said, anything you need."

Then they walk with me over to where my family's standing. They all stand up, except for Kid who just looks away from Bolden. My mom thanks the coaches for coming by.

"Have you all eaten?" Bolden finally asks.

"No," my mother says. "I don't think I can."

"You gotta eat. I'll call my wife, and she'll run something over so you don't have to think about it."

My mom starts to protest, thanking him but explaining that we don't want to put her out.

"Mrs. Bowen," he says. "It's the least we can do. Really."

Finally, she nods. "Thank you, Coach," she says. "Derrick couldn't play for a better man."

"Oh, I'm sure he could," Bolden says, "but players who have good mothers make my job a lot easier. So I should be thanking you every day."

Then, at last, it's time to go. It seems like there should be some formal show since we've been here all day, like the doctors should all come out and acknowledge us. But they've all moved on to other patients, breaking bad news to other families.

Slump 111

14.

It's as if my classes don't even happen. A bell rings, and I move to a room and sit. Then another bell rings, and I move to a new room. In between, there are people talking, there are even things put on the board that I write down, but none of it registers. I glide through each day like I'm in a dream, like if I were to touch anything it all might evaporate. Reality is somewhere else. A hospital room with Dad, Mom sitting patiently by his side. Or a living room with Jayson staring at the TV for hours on end, Uncle Kid standing over him like he should instruct him somehow—make him crack a book and turn off the tube—before silently retreating to the kitchen to fix us something basic—beans and rice, maybe some sausage stirred in if we're lucky.

Right now it's Geometry II, an hour that seems to stretch out for an eternity. Without Jasmine to help me this semester, I feel like I'm slipping further behind every day. I crack my book to act like I'm paying attention, but all I see on that page is a blur.

We've learned some things. First, the doctor told us that Dad's earlier episodes—those times he lost his balance and train of thought, like when he'd get overly worked up at Jayson—were probably smaller seizures. They said we should have had him into the emergency room after the first one. I'll give Mom credit for not launching into an *I knew it*, even though she'd all but begged Dad to see somebody. Then the doctor started talking about what he called a "brain episode," which made it seem like something that happened to someone on TV instead of to my dad. But the point was that it wasn't major. They'd put him on meds for at least a month and then bring him back to run tests again.

What it meant, really, was that we could start envisioning a "normal" dad again. Maybe not right away. But there was a future version of him that would be past all this.

Still, I think of him in that room, his leg propped up, that hospital smell sunk all the way into his skin. It makes me shudder. I try to focus on what the doctor said could help my dad make a full recovery—physical rehab at the hospital and home, a better diet, more exercise—but my mind keeps coming back to him knocked out from painkillers. It's a hard image to shake—like he's ready for his coffin.

I sure wasn't shaking that thought in our game last night at Lawrence Central. Same old story. We were right there all game, but couldn't buy a bucket when it counted. Dropped to 5-5. The whole night I felt like if I could just make a play, just knock down a J to loosen the defense, we could get it rolling. But it never happened. And my heart wasn't really in it. I knew Uncle Kid had brought Jayson to the game, but I couldn't bear to scan the crowd for them. I was afraid that if I saw them I'd lose it right there on the floor.

"Derrick?" the teacher says. It's Mr. Brandon, who always has this wry half-smile on his face. He's got a lighter complexion, almost sand-

Slump   113

colored, and he never lets you forget that he knows more than you do. He won't raise his voice, but when he turns his attention your way it can be withering. "Do you care to respond?"

"What?" I ask.

There's silence in the classroom. Brandon's smirk disappears. He just looks down at the piece of chalk in his hand. "I'd asked you if you knew the answer to number four." He angles his thumb to the board, where there are ten questions listed. They've been up there the whole period, but it's like I'm seeing them for the first time. "It's okay," Brandon says, and he takes a shot at giving me an actual smile, but it just comes off as a pitying look. Then he asks another student and the class hums along like I'm not even there.

It was like this last night too. For as poorly as I played—as many turnovers as any other number on the stat sheet—nobody got on me. Coach didn't snap me up in the huddle. Murphy didn't try some pep talk. Moose didn't bitch about a lack of looks. I know it was out of some sort of compassion, but it felt like they suspected my problems were contagious, like saying something to me would put their own fathers at risk.

In some ways, that's as bad as anything. If people would just act normal—if Mr. Brandon would just go ahead and embarrass me like he would any other student—then maybe I could forget about the whole ordeal, just for a second.

Classes, practice, hospital. It's Dad's last night before he gets discharged, and I'm almost as eager for it as he is. I don't know if I can take many more evenings here.

Kevin Waltman

"How was school?" Dad asks. He's trying to keep things as normal as he can.

"Good," I say. A lie, really. He fumbles for the controller for his bed, and I look away. I hate to see him so weak. In the hallway, doctors rush past. They flip pages on charts and talk in serious tones. In here, there's just the murmur of the television. Dad has it on some old cop movie, but the sound's so low you can't follow what's happening. He just has it on to distract both of us.

He finally finds the button he was looking for and raises up. "They're sending me home tomorrow," he says.

"I know," I say, then realize my dad probably needs more enthusiasm than that. "I mean, that's fantastic."

"Any rehab I'm doing here, I can do at home," he says. Then he takes a breath. The man's worn down. "Just leg lifts until I can put my weight on it again. They might bring me back here for rehab some each week."

I don't say anything then. It's this way every night. I freeze up. I find myself praying for Jayson to come in so he can fill the room with his chatter. Then I can say I have to get home to do homework—not a lie, but a lousy excuse. We turn our attentions back to the movie. In his room, there's always a smell of medicine covering up something sour. But I try not to think about it.

"Derrick," my dad says, "I'm so sorry." He starts to tremble and tear up.

"It's okay, Dad," I say. "You don't have to be sorry." This happens almost every night, and it makes me feel awful. "You didn't do anything."

"No, no. I'm just…I'm just so sorry."

And then we don't say anything. And then he nods toward the remote and asks me if I want to find a game on television. Then, finally, Jayson—back from the hospital cafeteria—comes in and I make my exit.

"I don't know how we'll make it work."

"You'll make it. You always do."

Mom smiles patiently, but shakes her head. "Saying that isn't going to pay the mortgage. It sure isn't going to pay for Thomas's rehab."

Uncle Kid throws his hands up in the air, offended for being contradicted. But then he just nods, tells her he knows what Mom says is true. They're both staring out the waiting room window. They don't know I can hear them. They don't even know I'm back from visiting Dad, so they talk freely, not choosing their words for my benefit.

"They already told me they won't do worker's comp for things like this," Mom says. "'Unrelated medical condition,' they say. Like the wear and tear on him didn't have a damn thing to do with working at those places."

"You got insurance though," Kid says.

"Yeah. It'll help. But without his income? I don't know, Kid. I don't know."

Kid shakes his head, not at my mom but at the whole situation. He looks out that window as he does, like he's disapproving of the whole city. Then he reaches over and takes her by the elbow. She resists at first, but he stiffens his arm so she can't pull away. Mom slowly leans into him, buries her head on Kid's shoulder. He runs his hand up and down her back, smoothing her blouse. "We'll think of something," he says. "We've got to. For Jay and D."

Then, as if mentioning my name makes them aware of my existence again, they both look my way. Mom straightens up immediately, but it's too late to hide the tears that are on her face. "I'm sorry, Derrick," she says. "I don't want you to see me like this."

"It's okay, mama," I say. The *mama*—a word I haven't used for her in years—comes out spontaneously, and I can see it melt her a little. She walks my way and hugs me, and I let her, leaning my head down to hers.

"Don't you worry about these things," she says. "It's all going to be okay."

But now I know better. When I sneak a peek at Uncle Kid, he's back to staring out the window, shaking his head. So now, along with all those images of my dad broken-down, I imagine us having to move, cramming into some slum apartment.

Hamilton Academy, I think. Should have jumped there last year. Maybe it's all my fault, but the thought somehow just makes me resent them more. Now it's like I *have* to beat Vasco and Hamilton, like some kind of redemption hangs on it.

Slump

15.

Forget Hamilton and Vasco. Right now we've got enough trouble with Indianapolis Northwest. We should blast these clowns, but we're down at half, 21-19. At home too. As we ran back to the locker room, I thought I even heard a few boos from our crowd.

Everything's gone wrong. Devin tweaked that ankle again and had to come out. Fuller got in foul trouble. Moose snapped and got another T, then about lost it on Bolden when Coach took him out. And I can't get a thing to drop. Hell, our best players have been Stanford and Jones, who have six apiece—which probably explains why we're down to Northwest.

The locker room bristles with bad energy. If someone so much as moves the wrong way, a riot will break out, every man for himself. Talk about a slump—it's like I've infected the whole roster.

Bolden comes in and walks to the chalkboard. He erases everything and starts over, drawing a half-court on there. He starts to put Xs up to walk us through an offensive set, but then stops halfway through.

"Does it matter?" he asks. We all stare at him, a little bewildered by that question. Bolden just flings the chalk down and it cracks into countless pieces on the cement floor. "It doesn't, does it? I can draw up plays until my arm falls off, but it doesn't matter unless you guys decide you want to get after it."

There's more silence in the locker room. I don't know what Coach expected, but when nobody says a word he just shakes his head. He stares at me for just a second but then looks away, settling on Moose instead. He laces into the big man, telling him he's the leader of the team, the senior starter. It's supposed to be up to him to get us going. "I'm too damn old to be lighting the fire for you every night," Bolden winds up. "But fine. I guess I have to. Here's the story for the rest of the night. I'm not drawing anything else up. All I'm going to do is count how many times I see a player taking it easy. I mean, you give anything less than all you've got and I'm marking it down as a checkmark. And then tonight, when you're all out doing whatever it is you do, I'm gonna tally up all those checkmarks. And that's the number of times you'll run the stairs next practice."

With that he bolts out of the locker room, just motioning angrily at Murphy as if to say *You try talking to these fools instead.*

In Coach's wake, Moose stands. "You heard him," he shouts. "Ya'll better get your heads out your asses."

"Yeah!" Fuller shouts, and he gets echoed by most voices in the room, but it's all hollow. You can tell when people are for real into it and when they're just trying to kid themselves. The chatter in our locker room is all make believe.

Murphy takes a stab at it, talking us through our sets the way

Bolden would. When he's done he gathers us in the center of the locker room to put our hands in. We do, just like always. And we shout *Team*, just like always. But the sound is thin and quick. No throat to it.

Still, we gotta hit the boards again for the second half. Northwest isn't just gonna lay down and die for us. But before I can make it down the tunnel to the court, I feel a hand grabbing my wrist. I try to pull free, but the grip is strong. When I turn, it's Bolden, who'd hung back by the locker room door. All that heat from a few minutes ago is drained from his face. He talks to me as calmly as he would if he were a stranger on the street asking for directions.

"Derrick, now don't you take all that stuff personally," he says. "You're dealing with something else that these other guys don't have to. Remember what I said stands. You need time away, you can take it."

"I'm good, Coach," I say. God, I just want to be back on the floor with my boys, not talking about this again.

Bolden peers at me sharply, like he's trying to read something on my face. "Okay. Long as you know what I said stands. But now,"—and here he leans in even closer—"if you're here, then be here. Let's get out and give it hell, okay?"

"I feel you, Coach," I say. But in truth, I feel nothing.

Fuller and Moose have the stuff in the second half. It's not like they come out bottoming everything they put up, but they get after it. Every rebound, every loose ball, they just snatch it up. Soon enough it infects a few other guys. Stanford knocks in a couple from the shallow wing. Jones rises up for a deuce in the lane. Hell, even Reynolds jumps off the bench and buries a J. The only guy not with the program? Yeah, the guy standing in my kicks. I mean, it's not a total loss. I rack up a couple assists to Moose. I get a couple deflections and a block on D. And late, when Northwest is in panic mode, I drain four straight at the stripe to ice it. But in between all that are more missed pull-ups and even a couple ugly turnovers.

With the clock ticking to zeroes, I dribble it out top. Northwest, down 8, has given it up. The crowd counts down with the clock, happy to head into the night fat with a win. But it doesn't feel that way to me. The horn sounds. We shake hands with the Northwest players, then bust it back to the locker room to whoop it up, but I just can't get into it. I mean, when I ball out, it all backfires and we lose. Now, I just go through the motions and we win. It's like the more I do, the less value I have to the team. It makes me sick. And I'm not one to get hung up on my numbers—I'm in it for the wins—but I'd like to at least play well, to at least feel like I'm making the engine turn.

Bolden makes his rounds in the locker room, mixing congratulations with little tweaks of advice. He always does this, even when we've been at our best, just so we know there's always room to improve. Then he hits my locker and says, "Way to work out there, Derrick."

"Yeah," I say. "That's one way to put it."

He shrugs. "So some shots didn't fall. They'll drop soon enough. Be happy with the win."

"Yeah," I say again.

He leaves it at that. He knows my head's not in it. I mean, a blind man could see that. But he doesn't press.

After a long, soaking shower and after listening to Moose talk shit about how much play he's gonna get tonight—I walk out into that

Slump 121

gym and there's nobody there to greet me but Uncle Kid. No Wes. No Jasmine. And no Jayson.

"Jay's waiting outside," Kid says. "You know he can't stand still for long."

I nod, but I think to myself that Kid's no parent. No way my mom or dad would be letting Jayson kick it outside with nobody watching him. We stand across from each other for a second, neither of us talking. Kid and I are right near midcourt. Behind him I can see his jersey hanging on the wall, cast in deep shadows now that the main lights are off. I wonder what it must be like for Kid to come to these games, to walk this hardwood in his street shoes. Once he was the favorite son here. And then, senior year, things blew up on him. There were run-ins with Bolden, suspensions, and I know by the end of it he went from a Big Ten prospect to a player scuffling at Junior College.

"Better head back," Kid says.

"Yeah."

We shuffle toward the doors, our heads bent down. I dread going home, seeing my dad laid up. With any luck, he'll already be in bed, worn out from his rehab and zonked from his meds. I hate thinking that, like I'm laying some curse on my own dad, but it's the truth. I just can't deal with things right now.

"Good game," Kid tells me. It's an afterthought, like someone wishing you a belated happy birthday.

"I guess," I say.

We hit the cold night air and Jayson, who peels off from a group of freshmen girls he's been trying to flirt with, is less polite than Kid. "Damn, D," he says, "you guys sure know how to take the fun out of basketball. I checked the Pacers score and they had more in the first quarter than you guys had all game, I think."

"All right, Jay," I say. "I don't need it from you." I laugh though. He means well. Just trying to lighten the mood, which is something we could all use these days. I give him a little mock shove, and then the three of us hit the pavement back to Patton.

Mom is on the couch, not doing anything. Not even watching TV. Just sitting there, exhausted. When we come in, she looks over at us once and then down at her feet like she's willing them to move.

"Just sit, Kaylene," Kid says. "I got it."

She slumps back on the couch again in silence. She asks me about the game, but that's about as much energy as she has. Jay and I know enough to keep quiet. We kick on the tube in search of a game, but mute it so Mom can relax. Out of nowhere, she sighs. "Your father's getting better," she says. "It's a slow process. He can't put weight on the leg yet, but his muscles are strengthening again. He's got more motion." There's neither hope nor dismay in the way she says it. Just an update. A statement of facts. Then she rises and heads back to bed. She traces a finger across Jayson's shoulder as she passes by, like she's trying to keep contact with us in some small way.

Meanwhile, Kid heads to the kitchen and starts whipping together a late dinner for me and Jay. The smell of an onion in oil hits us. We migrate from the living room to the kitchen. We watch Kid work. He throws in some garlic and tomato sauce, dashes a few spices across the top. It's like he's been doing this all his life. He almost scalds himself when he drains the pasta—"Son of a bitch!" he says, still soft so as not to wake anyone, while he runs his fingers under cold water—but

Slump

he pulls it all off pretty seamlessly. Then without a word the three of us dig in.

"Thanks, Kid," I say when we're done.

"Eh," he says. He waves his hand like it was nothing.

Then that's it. Kid clears the dishes, setting them in the dishwasher so delicately you'd think he was handling the world's finest china. Jayson and I go back to the game and then Kid joins us, but we still don't turn the sound on. It's like if any of us says anything then we're going to have to really *talk*, just hash it all out. And so we retreat into the basics—grub, sports. Thing is, I can't imagine being anywhere else. I know there are parties going on. I know my teammates are out in the city enjoying a win. But where would I go? I go to a party and I'm liable to bump into Wes or Jasmine, and I don't feel up to that. More than anything though, I just feel responsible to be here, even if I don't know how to help. It's as if having a good time seems like a sin right now.

"I'm gonna hit it," I say after a while, and I slink back to my room.

The silence in the house kills me. I wish Jayson would crank up his music just to annoy people, anything. Hell, I'd take the noise of last year this time—Kid and his friend Brownlee talking nonsense about me transferring, my mom tearing into them. Anything but this deathly quiet. Thing is, I can't even text my people—no Wes, no Jasmine—and I can't bear to try and read something. Even *that*—cracking a book—reminds me of Jasmine, like maybe when I read before it was all some strategy to impress her.

Instead, I kill some time online. And the bad news is there too. ESPN's updated their class rankings for mid-season, and wouldn't you know it. I've dropped all the way down to the #6 point guard for sophomores. Even worse, I've been passed by some in-state kid down South, Dexter Kernantz. I've never even heard of the kid before now, but I click around and he's dropping almost 8 dimes a game, a big reason why Evansville Harrison is off to a 10-2 start.

Dexter Kernantz ahead of me? "Whatever," I say. Then I look around like, *Who am I even talking to?*

I decide to hit the rack, feeling about as alone as a body can.

16.

"One more, Tom," my mom says. "You can do this."

My dad grimaces in his chair. He goes back in for weekly check-ups, but in the meantime the doctors told him that he could strengthen his left leg if he worked on moving it with his right leg stabilized. Other patients probably get some expensive equipment for their rehab, but here? Our equipment is Jayson. He's crouched on the floor, pinning Dad's right leg to his recliner while Dad tries to do lifts with his right.

"One more, Tom," Mom repeats.

"I can't do it," he says, then flops back into the chair. "Hell, I can't even get that leg five inches up."

"Come on, Tom," Mom says, "one more try."

"You can do it, Dad," Jayson says. He rises up on his knees, like some little lapdog begging for food. His eyes are wide and earnest. "You're doing better than yesterday."

My dad laughs, but it's a dark, disgusted sound, the kind of thing I've come to expect from other grown men, but not from my dad. "If that's 'better' then I'll have full motion by the time you graduate from college."

Jayson takes the hit and just settles back on the floor to hold Dad's leg. Mom shakes her head. "None of that, Tom. Besides, thinking about Jayson graduating from college isn't going to make anyone worry less." She meant it as a joke, but nobody even cracks a smile.

Dad tries again, and that right leg comes up—maybe halfway—before he slouches back in the chair again, defeated. "Goddamnit," he says. Then he catches his tone. "Sorry, Jayson," he says gently. "I shouldn't use that kind of language."

"No sweat, Dad," Jayson says. Of course, if my parents could hear some of the stuff that comes out of Jay's mouth when they're not listening, they'd near lose their minds.

It's a depressing scene. I wish like crazy that we were spending Sunday at church instead. Anything but this. Dad's too embarrassed to go though. He can walk on crutches, but he doesn't want everyone looking at him and pitying him. Especially those old church women who, he says, feel closer to Jesus every time they gaze upon someone's misfortune. Plus, he hates his meds, always complaining about how dizzy they make him. In general, he's just pissed.

"Who am I kidding?" he says then. "I'm lucky. God, I'm so lucky." And then he gets almost weepy until he checks himself.

It's like this with all of us. We feel like the whole world's turned against us, but then we remember that Dad could be a lot worse. A lot. I never saw the car after the wreck, but I was foolish enough to Google images of cars wrapped around telephone poles. That's something some people don't survive.

Still, here we are. My dad is stuck in that chair. My mom walks around this house with her face drawn so tight you'd think it would

Slump 127

crack. She doesn't say it, but I know that tension is more than my dad's health—it's the bills coming due, the fridge getting bare.

The doorbell rings. I all but bounce to it. I mean, I don't give a rip if it's someone trying to convert me to their religion. I'm jumping at any distraction that presents itself.

I open that door and have to lower my gaze before I see who it is: Wes. He can't meet my eyes, staring down at his shoes—the Timberlands I got him last year. Then, when he looks up, he immediately looks away.

"What up, man?" I say, cold as if he's just some stranger I'm passing in the hall.

"D," he says, then he shakes his head. He knows there's nothing to say that fits this moment. "Aw, man, I'm sorry," he says.

Wes shakes the ice around in his cup, then digs a piece out and crunches on it.

"I don't know, D," he says. "It's like she just got cold all of a sudden. Like I did something wrong and it's my job to figure out what it is."

Tell me about it, I want to say. I know what it's like to be worrying about every little thing with a female.

We're kicking it at a sub shop on College, just killing time really. How we got onto Wes' static with Iesha, I don't know. If it were anyone else, I'd be all tensed up about it. Like, *How dare you moan about your troubles when I got all mine?* But not with Wes. All it took was him hanging his head and saying he was sorry, and we were hugging it out right there at the front door. I told him I was sorry too, about a hundred times, and then we knew just to get out of the house, away from everything. And truth is, I'm happy to hear Wes talk about his mess. Anything but what's going on at home—or even the way we're trudging through the season.

"You think she's messing around on me?" Wes asks. He bites at one of his fingernails, then, realizing how bad that looks, goes back to crunching ice.

"Shiiiit," I say, trying to act all cool about it. Truth is, I have no idea. There's always been this feeling like Iesha's just a little out of Wes' league, but I'm sure not telling him that. Besides, the reason she seems a little past him is because sometimes he acts that way himself. He's like a guy who's walking to the stripe for two, down one late, and he's got the skills to bury the shots, but he doesn't have the confidence. And, man, if you don't think you can get it done, then you can't. "She's lucky to have you, man."

Wes smiles, but it's brief, like he can't really accept that answer. He looks away again. "Thanks, man," he mumbles.

We chill for a few minutes, just watching people come and go. There's a guy bumming change out on the sidewalk. Everyone around here knows him. He's got some line about needing bus money to St. Louis, but any fool knows he's scrounging change to hit up the liquor store. Still, some people drop a little something his way. He makes this real exaggerated bow of thanks every time, then starts his act all over for the next person. Finally, the manager goes out and chases him off, but he'll be back. Until then he'll just be a problem for some other manager at some other store. I love this city, but sometimes it just looks like the same scene over and over—people hustling and nothing changing.

"Let's hit it, D," Wes says. We hoof it to his car—well, his mom's car, but he calls it his—and cruise the few blocks back to our street.

When he parks, I don't want to get out. I'd give anything just to kill the whole day with Wes. Not to see my dad struggling.

"You want to head on up to Ty's Tower?" I ask.

Wes perks up for a second, but then shakes his head. "I'm gonna hook up with Iesha later. *Supposed to*, at least. She might bail at the last minute again."

"Ah, it's cool," I say.

"Want to catch the Colts somewhere tonight?" he asks.

Now I'm the one perking up. "Most definitely," I say. "Bring that honey of yours."

That finally coaxes a real smile from Wes, that wide goofy grin that makes him look like the same kid I used to kick it with when we were runts. That puts me in a better frame of mind, too. I feel like now I can go in and tackle whatever scene is playing out behind our door. As I walk up those steps, I even tell myself that I'm going to really sit down and talk to Dad, like I should have so many times before. This time I'm not freezing up on him.

Then, when I open the door, I see the last thing I'd ever expect. It's not Dad rehabbing, not Jayson causing people grief, not Mom sweating over a stack of bills, her hand trembling up by her temple. It's Uncle Kid. At the kitchen table. Unpacking bags of groceries. Mountains of food. Even walnuts and oatmeal for Dad's new diet.

"Hey, D," he says, like this is as natural as bumping into him down at the Fall Creek court. He tilts his head toward the fridge. "Stocked up on those frozen burritos you like. Better get your feed on."

I tell him I already had a sub with Wes, and Kid just shrugs. Like, *No sweat. You want more grub, it's there.*

I retreat to my room, but Jayson peeks his head out of his door first. Behind him, I can see his video game frozen on pause.

"You see Uncle Kid?" he asks.

I nod. "What up?"

"I don't know, D. He came in a few minutes ago. Took him four trips to the car to get all that food in here."

We don't even have to talk it out. Just give each other a look. Only way Uncle Kid's got money to burn is if he's running some game again. All we need around here.

17.

We should've hung 80 on a squad like Manual last night. Should have run them in circles. Instead, more of the same. An ugly win to Coach's liking, but nobody else's. I mean, when I hit the stripe in the third, I could swear I heard yawns while I was going through my routine.

38-29. Final.

Devin knocked in a single three before limping off late. I rang up a whole nine points. Only Moose cracked double digits. Typically, those kind of numbers at the end of a game would mean we got smacked around pretty good, but it's a win. Take it and move on, I guess. So I try to put the way we won aside and focus on the team warming up across from me—Scecina.

While I'm stretching my hamstrings near mid-court, Murphy comes over. "Let's get after it tonight," he says. "Stay locked in. No looking back, no looking ahead." He rubs my shoulder a couple times then moves on to Devin, giving him a little pre-game chatter too. Problem is, he said exactly the wrong thing to me. I was doing my best to get over that Manual game, but when he said *no looking ahead*, it only made me think about it. Hamilton Academy's next on the slate. Vasco Lorbner. Deon Charles. Undefeated and storming toward a third straight State Championship.

I look down the court at Scecina. They've got a decent big named Harold Stubbs. A couple shooters with size to boot—Marble and Carfino. We'll have to get it cranked up to win this thing. But Hamilton next weekend? The way we're playing, we'll need a damn miracle.

"Let's go now, D," Moose says. "Get your head in it." He's come up next to me and all but shoves the rock into my gut. I dribble down the court beside Moose. The other guys make some space for us. The big man posts and I stay on the perimeter, both of us moving at game speed. I shot fake and take a dribble to get free. Moose goes drop step, then turn-around, then next time whips one back out to me for a three—bottom, of course, but in the back of my head I wonder why all year it's been net in warm-ups and bad rolls during games. *Gotta get rid of that thinking*, I tell myself, and keep feeding Moose. For just a second, I relax and watch him work. The man has gone through a change, for sure. Last year, he was a load, but he was carrying about fifteen extra pounds on that frame. Now he's got himself cut up pretty good. He's still far too large to uproot if he catches low, but he's not looking to Bolden and pulling on his jersey anymore. That's some work Moose put in. I want our season to work out, for us to get rolling again, but I figure Moose actually deserves it.

One good thing is I can check Wes again before tip. Make eye contact with him and get a little fist pump of encouragement. The only other person I have in the stands is Jay. Wes gave him a ride to the game, but Mom wasn't coming if Dad couldn't. This time even Uncle

Kid ditched, claiming obligations. I try not to think about what that means for him on a Monday night.

Soon enough, everyone's at mid-court for the tip. I take one last look at the gym—the splashes of school colors, the fans hurrying from last-minute stops for concessions, the cheerleaders bouncing on the sidelines—and then the ball goes up and the world shrinks down to what's between the lines. Scecina controls and comes at us. They've got a nice little clip to their pace right away. They work inside to Stubbs. He tries to deal on Moose but then rifles it crosscourt to Carfino. A shot-fake and drive, then another crosscourt to Marble on the baseline. He lets fly—checked pretty good by Fuller—and sinks a trey.

Their whole squad claps once, all together like they're in military lock step, then sprints back down on D. There, they do the Duke thing, smacking the hardwood with their hands. Nothing pisses me off more than that stuff. I mean, if you wanna get after it, just get after it. You don't need to smack the floor to D people up. I give their point guard a little sneer to let him know, then rip past him left. I get into the lane and draw some company, making for an easy dump down to Moose for two.

"Atta look, boy," he hollers, and then it's our turn to go D up.

Part of me is tempted to smack the floor right back at them, just to taunt, but I know that wouldn't fly with Bolden, so I just meet my man at mid-court. I dig into him pretty good, even bump him off course once he gives it up. He gives a pleading look at the ref but gets nothing out of it. "Gonna take more than a few slaps on the floor tonight," I tell him.

He gives this little snorting sound, like he's about to show me, but when he catches on the wing, I dig in again. He's back on his heels immediately and I stay up tight. When he tries to sweep the rock through, I poke it away. Devin scoops and we're gone.

I get a step on my man by mid-court and Devin leads one out to me. I gather it in stride and sprint toward the rim. Their three-man scrambles back. I know I could force it over him, but I just leave it to Fuller. Easy lay-in and we've got a quick lead. *Finally.*

Our crowd gets into it. When Scecina looks a little lost on their end, the crowd just gets louder. Every time a Scecina kid passes on a look, our people get more boisterous. Finally they get an entry to Stubbs again. Moose has him bodied, but he starts backing down. One dribble, two dribbles, just inching back. He's checking for Carfino and Marble, but we've got them locked down. I know what's coming next. He picks up his dribble and lodges a shoulder into Moose's chest for some separation. Soon as he does, I come crashing down. When he rises, I'm there with him. His shot gets spiked back so hard, he almost ends up with **WILSON** imprinted on his forehead.

Devin rips it again. We run. This time Scecina gets set, but I see no reason to wait around. I catch it out top with a head of steam and just fly down the lane. Stubbs comes over late, so I can't get a free run, but I kiss one in for a quick 6-3 lead. Gym is jumping and those Scecina kids look shook. When they call time, I backpedal to our bench, eyeing them the whole way. Carfino and Marble are snapping at each other, pointing back to the court in anger.

"Hey, hey, hey!" Bolden yells. He grabs me by the jersey and pulls me back to the bench. Not so hard he makes a scene, but enough to get my attention. "Don't be thumping your chest over a single

Slump

bucket. You think they're gonna roll over? They've had teams rip off six straight before."

I sink back onto the bench. I try not to show my disgust, but, man, it's like it kills Bolden to see us have fun on the floor. *Can't the man see?* If we get up-tempo, nobody can check us. It's only when we settle into half-court that we have trouble. What's even more frustrating is that just last year he *wanted* us to run. We went small and came within five seconds of ushering Hamilton Academy out of Regionals. Now he wants to shift into low gear? *Killing* me. Just *killing* me.

"You okay, D?" This time it's Murphy with a hand on my jersey, right before we head back out onto the floor.

"I'm good," I say.

When I try to turn away, he keeps hold of my jersey. I want to just rip myself free, but I don't want to make a scene. All we need is everyone thinking there's static on the sideline. "Really, D," he says. "I mean it."

"I'm good," I say, but it comes out like a hiss. Murphy shrugs and heads back to the bench, disappointed in the response. But what does he expect? Does he want me to spill it all out there on the hardwood in front of every damn body? I'm not okay. Not with a lot of things. Last time I went round with Murphy it landed me on the bench, but he and Bolden are slow to come down on me now.

Before I can dwell on that too much, we're back in the thick of it. Scecina gets themselves set, and they iso Carfino up with Fuller. Shot fake and drive, and just like that it's a one-point game again. Their crowd makes a ruckus now, and our people settle into their seats.

I clap for the inbound from Stanford. When I bring it across mid-court, they do it again—they all slap the floor in unison. It makes me boil, but this time there's a little more determination in it. They've all got more focus in their eyes. When we start clipping through our offense, they pick up the intensity. They talk on screens, jump passing lanes, bump cutters. Basically, they get into us for real.

About fifteen seconds of this and Stanford gets twitchy. He fires a baseline J that's about three feet beyond his range. Even as it's in mid-air, Coach is off the bench, yelling that it's too quick, that we need to work harder for better shots. By the time Scecina rebounds, I can see Coach motioning to Chris Jones to check in at the next dead ball.

No more runouts. No more jumped passes. No more easy anything. And with two minutes to go, Scecina's got it up one. They've got it out on the side. While they send in some subs, Moose calls us in.

We gather at the top of the key, everyone huffing and fatigued. Stanford bends down and puts his hands on his knees, lowering his head. He looks up, some pain from fatigue in his eyes, and it shows off how young he still looks. He can add as much muscle as he wants, but when he gets that kind of expression, he looks like an unnaturally tall fifth-grader.

"Hey, head up, man," Moose snaps.

Stanford raises his head a few more inches, but he's too beat to stand up straight.

Fuller hollers at us all: "Come on, guys! We can get this one. Let's dig in and get a stop!"

Moose curls up the corner of his mouth and cocks his head. We're all getting a little tired of Fuller's rah-rah noise, but Moose probably just doesn't want an underclassman popping off in his huddle.

Slump

Then he shakes his head and smiles. I realize I haven't seen that smile during a game in a long time. It's like with all those pounds Moose burned off in the summer, he shed his good spirits, too. "You know what?" he says. Then he points at Fuller, jabbing him so hard with his finger that Fuller rocks back on his heels. "What Fuller said. Let's go!"

That makes everyone laugh. Even Stanford raises up a little more. I have to smile too, even though I really don't want Fuller thinking he's some leader all of a sudden. Down on the other end, I see Coach Bolden narrow his eyes at us like some old hawk sensing a threat: *How dare those kids have a good time!*

Too late to think about anything else though, because Scecina throws it in and the game's back on. They're in no hurry with the lead, so they work and work. What they want is to get Stubbs in the post and then spread Carfino and Marble around him. Fuller and Devin do a good job on the perimeter, keeping pressure on them to make an entry more difficult. Finally, after about thirty seconds, they pull it back out. Their point guard circles way up top and looks over at their bench. Their coach motions with his hands—brings them into a circle and then pulls them apart. Spread out. They do just that, fanning everyone out into the corners, with just Stubbs in the middle.

Their crowd reacts. They rise to their feet and start clapping in rhythm, right on time with the ticking clock. These kids aren't even going for another look. They're just running clock.

I hate it. *Hate* it. I mean, there should be a shot clock at every single level. At freaking Boy's Club games. But it's the smart move. I glance down to Bolden and he just sinks into a mock defensive crouch, telling us to just keep guarding. No fouls yet.

They know how to play this. We get into them tight at all, and they send a cutter to the middle. We jump that, and they pop it right back out to the perimeter. And the floor's so spread that if we overplay at all, they've got an easy back door for a lay-in. A minute left now, and their crowd seems to get louder with each tick. Bolden motions for us to stay after it. Still no fouls.

Thirty seconds left. When I glance down at Bolden he's checking the clock. We have to bite soon. Can't wait too much longer to put them at the line. That's when it happens. Stanford's man cuts middle and Stanford lunges at the pass. He misses by a mile. His momentum carries him out toward mid-court. His man's all alone at the top of the key, and he turns. God, you can see it on his face. Wide open, Stubbs down low, Carfino and Marble on the wings—*Attack!* Soon as he takes a dribble, I'm crashing down off my man like a maniac. The kid drives to the lane, and Moose has to help. Stubbs comes free, but now the Scecina kid's off balance. That attack mode on his face has been switched to fear—he knows he shouldn't have gone for it. He jumps and looks toward Stubbs, sees me jumping the lane at the last moment, and then turns in mid-air to float a pass out toward Marble.

Devin swipes it easy. I dart back middle, and Devin hits me in stride. My man's backpedaling like mad. Our crowd's roar just edges out the Scecina crowd's moan in volume. I take a dribble to mid-court. I see Stanford all alone. The man was too gassed to even help back on the defensive end, but now he's running free, fast as a greyhound. No sense in wasting time, so I lob it ahead and Stanford's got such an easy run even he can't choke it away. A simple two-hand flush, and *bang*, we're up one.

Scecina calls time. Our whole bench is up to meet us, Reynolds leading the way and pumping his fists like he's the one who drained the bucket, but my eyes are on Scecina. Every one of them wears this look of disgust. I could swear Marble's about to spit on the court. Yeah, they got some ticks left, but their faces say it. *They're beat.*

"Just one stop now. Just one more!" Reynolds is shouting in the huddle, but Coach raises his hand to tell him to ease off.

"I think we all know that, Reynolds," he says. Then he goes about drawing up what he thinks Scecina will do on their last shot.

In the end, it doesn't matter. Even when we break huddle, their crowd's dead. And so are they. A few guys clap their hands trying to get the team up, but that look of disgust is still on their faces. Carfino takes the ball from the ref, looks toward the perimeter once or twice, then lobs a terrible pass toward Stubbs in the post—it sails over his head and out-of-bounds. Our ball. End of story.

18.

Even I can't sulk after that one. Who cares what the pace of the game was? You sneak out with a win after trailing late, and everyone's feeling good. For once, I can taste it—a little of last year's magic coming back. Hamilton might be in for more of a fight than they think.

Moose spread the word on the bus ride home about a blowout at a JaQuentin Peggs' place. Our whole roster is there whooping it up pretty good. Peggs isn't exactly the type of guy you want to be tight with. In fact, he's got one foot in the banging life. Maybe both by now. He shows up to Marion East so rarely now people think he's lost. But who cares? The house stereo's bumping. Every fine-looking girl at Marion East is here, looking tight on a Saturday night. Well, I guess that's every fine girl but one. No Jasmine. And it's not like I'd know what to say if she were here.

Wes and Iesha are kicking it over by the kitchen, so I hang with them for a while. I hate to say it, but Wes is right about Iesha. I mean, she's standing there, but the girl's a thousand miles away.

"You see Marble get after his teammate on the way back to the locker room?" Wes asks.

"Nah, what happened?"

"He was onto that kid who gacked away the ball with the lead, just riding him the whole way. And then the kid had enough. Just stepped up and pushed Marble. They were about to throw down before their coaches broke it up."

I laugh, that full-of-yourself laugh that's the reward for anyone who's won a game like that. A bounce the other way, and that could have been us. But we won and nothing's gonna turn that W to an L now. When I glance at Iesha though, she's got that distant stare, like she sees something beyond the kitchen, beyond the walls, maybe way down onto the South side for as much as she seems to care about what's going on here.

"What up with you, Iesha?" I ask, trying to draw her back in. "What's the word in your world?"

She turns back to me. It takes her a second to piece together what I've said. "Oh, nothing," she says. She gives Wes a quick smile, but it's fake.

Wes can feel it. He looks at me, but I just shrug it off. I shake my head real quick, trying to tell him not to sweat it. He's looking pretty tensed though.

"You guys wanting something to drink?" he asks. "JaQuentin's got plenty of stuff in the next room."

Now I *know* my man's getting desperate. Look, it's not some huge deal. We're sixteen. It isn't like he's slinging rock, but this is Wes we're talking about.

"I don't need anything," I say. I squint my eyes at him, but he just turns to Iesha.

"Sure," she says. "Whatever."

Wes high-tails it, leaving me standing next to his girl. And it becomes clear real fast that we don't have a thing to say to each other.

"Catch you round," she says, and she heads off to talk to some girlfriends.

I hit up the living room, where everyone's dancing. Moose is doing his thing—stone sober, I might add, since he's trying to stay in playing shape—dancing with just about every girl in the room. He gets all up on some girls, letting them grind on him to some Wale. But then somebody drops some old school Outkast—a cut Coach Murphy probably listened to back in the day—but it's one *everyone knows*, and the whole mood of the room changes. In about five seconds, it turns into the kind of scene that makes my mom lose sleep at night and makes my dad think that our generation is doomed. Basically, every honey in the house starts grinding like their lives depend on it.

I lean back against the wall and soak it in. I don't care what my parents say. Just people being young. Not a thing wrong with that. And then I see her—Daniella Cole looking right at me. There's no confusing her look, but just to be sure she motions to me with her index finger.

I should know better. Then again, not like I'm ever gonna get that attention from Jasmine. In a split second I'm on the floor with her, and she's got her ass pressed against me so fast, it's all I can do to play it cool.

"There's the man!" Moose shouts. He leans across her and gives me a high five, like I've just buried a big J. Everyone—Stanford, Devin, even Reynolds—is smiling and living it up. For the first time in too long, I feel a little release from all the serious noise in my life. I mean, this is what sixteen is supposed to be—out with the boys after a win, a honey coming on strong. All good.

And people can say what they want about Daniella. The girl is put together. It might be January, but in the heat of the house party, she's stripped down to short-shorts and a tight t, and she's about to bust loose from that. When the song ends, she turns to face me. She has a little sweat beaded up on her forehead, but I don't mind that a bit. She smiles at me and bats her eyes.

"Hey, Derrick," she coos, smooth as honey.

"'Sup, Daniella?" I say. I try to act cool, but now, as everyone's chilling to a slower song, I can feel all those eyes on me. I feel nervous, so I lean back against the wall. Daniella just moves right on in. She pretends like she's got to make room for some people squeezing by, giving her an excuse to press her chest right up against me. She laughs then, all flirty. It doesn't take a genius to figure out I can have this girl if I want her.

I look around one more time, see Moose giving me a wry little smile, like, *Go on, man. Nobody's gonna judge you.*

I don't know what to say to make it happen, but it turns out Daniella does. "Hey, let's go upstairs where the music's not so loud," she says. "We can talk." But when she says *talk*, she traces her fingernail down my chest to my stomach. This girl doesn't *play*.

I follow her across the living room, watching her hips switch as she walks and trying not to look too eager. The only thing that slows us down is Moose. He puts a big paw out in front of me just before we get to the stairwell.

He leans down, all nonchalant. "Be safe, dog," he says. He presses something into my hand. Without looking I know it's a condom. I have one anyway—a single I'd carried in my wallet the whole time I was with Jasmine, just praying it would come in handy one night—but I appreciate the big man looking out for me.

When we get upstairs, Daniella leads me down the hall like she knows what she's doing. She knocks lightly on a door and then pushes it open, revealing a dim room with a large, unmade bed inside. There's a pile of dirty laundry in the corner. It makes me feel like we're doing something wrong. Like any minute someone's mom is going to come in to pick up that laundry, snap on the light and scream at us.

Daniella doesn't seem nervous at all. She leans up and kisses me on the neck, traces her tongue in a crazy pattern. She grabs a fistful of my shirt and pulls me to her, backing up to the bed. Then she flops down on it and peels off her shirt. I stare for a second—part of me thinking that I shouldn't be doing this, that somehow girls like Daniella are meant for someone else—but then she leans forward and grabs me by the belt. Every other thought in my head, other than what she's doing with her hands, fades away. There's just a loud thrumming between my ears that keeps getting louder when she pushes me down on the bed and climbs on top of me.

When I came out of that room, I expected that half the school would be gathered there like witnesses. I wasn't sure if I'd act all swole up like some badass or hang my head like a perp being walked to a cop car. But it turned out there wasn't a crowd at all.

I knew I was supposed to feel like a real man. Supposed to swagger and talk smack. But instead I couldn't even look her in the eye. She

Slump

didn't seem to care. She pulled down on my arm so she could lean up to my ear, then gave me a little bite and told me thanks, probably trying to inflate my ego. Then she was gone down the hallway. Slick as that.

Even now, standing in front of my house, it doesn't quite seem real. Down the block, Moose's car rumbles around the corner. On the ride home, he just kept laughing. "You a dog, D," he kept saying. "Getting down with dirty Daniella." He'd reach over and slap me on the leg. It made me laugh, but now that he's gone I'm just standing here alone on the block. There are still some lights on along Patton. I see a silhouette moving in Wes's kitchen—probably his mom waiting up for him. To hear other people tell it, the whole world's supposed to change when you finally hit it, but this looks like the same old street to me.

My feet crunch through the crust of ice on top of the snow. The sound echoes in the cold night. I turn the key in our door, walk in, and see Mom and Uncle Kid huddled at the kitchen table. Everyone else is probably long since in bed, but they both seem tensed. She's holding a piece of paper in front of her. It flaps in the air like a wounded bird when she waves it at Kid. He's got a wad of cash in his hand, extended halfway between them.

"You need it," he says.

"Not if I don't know where it comes from," Mom says. "I can handle this." She looks down at that piece of paper, but as she does she shakes her head like she doesn't believe her own words.

Then they see me standing there and they shut up. Mom lets the paper float harmlessly down to the table. Kid stuffs the cash in his back pocket.

"Derrick," Mom says all surprised, like I wasn't supposed to come home at all. "Do you need something to eat?"

"I'm good," I say. I drop my bag on the living room floor, let it thud down like some huge burden I've been carrying. Then I figure I better head for my room before my mom senses what I've been up to or notices that I'm ten minutes past curfew.

"You okay, Derrick?" she asks, and I can hear that tone in her voice—like she knows something's up—but my back's already turned. I call over my shoulder that everything's cool. She lets it go at that. I know it's because she doesn't want me asking questions about what she and Kid were hashing out, not because she actually buys my answer.

It doesn't take Kid but a few minutes to make it back to my room though. He leans against my doorjamb all nonchalant, like he's just killing time on a corner or something. "Nice win tonight," he says.

"It's a W," I say. I unlace my kicks and drop them on the floor, hoping Kid gets the hint that I'm too beat to talk.

"What you get up to after?" he asks.

"Nothing," I say.

"Come on, D," he says. He leans into my room, then, gives me a big knowing grin. "Hell, I can see it on you. You got a piece, didn't you?"

I flop back. Cross my arms behind my head. Act like it's the stupidest thing he's ever said. But inside I'm wondering how in the world he knew.

"Fess up, D," he says. "Ain't no shame." He walks into the room, stands over me. He leans down and fakes like he's going to punch me in the gut, getting a big flinch out of me. I curl up into a ball, hands over my stomach in a defensive pose. "Yeah," he says. "It's good for you.

Slump

Put a little strut back in your stride for once." Then, his point made, he turns to leave. He lingers at the doorway again, his hand on the light switch. "Just don't let it mess up your head," he says. Then he kills the lights, and I'm alone at last.

19.

It's only Jayson and Kid in the stands, even for the Hamilton game. My dad's not off the crutches for a little while longer. I've accepted that he's not heading out before then.

The good news is, with Vasco and company on the slate, I haven't had time to sweat Daniella. There's been no noise about it anyway. I hit the Marion East halls on Monday morning half-expecting Daniella would be shadowing me, all up on me like I belonged to her. Didn't happen. Still, every time she texts me I sense these crazy expectations from the other end, like now I owe her something. And maybe I do. I mean, would it be the worst thing in the world? It's not like she's boring. Or dumb. She might not get the same grades as Jasmine, but Daniella's quick as anyone. Get her started on what's wrong with Indianapolis, and she can drop some history on you in a hurry.

But all that fades away. Everything that isn't ball—Dad, Daniella, even Wes going full heartbreak mode because Iesha's cooling him out—it's all gone.

"First off, we know we can get these guys," Coach says. We're gathered in the visiting locker room, just a big gray cell instead of that palace their players are enjoying. All eyes are on Coach. He holds up his index finger. "One shot last year. We were one shot away. And everyone thinks it was that last bucket Lorbner made, but forget about that. A one-possession game means you could have won it with a free throw you missed in the first half. An easy back-door you gave them in the third quarter. Any one possession could have changed it." A quick peek at Moose and Devin and I see that their jaws are set, scowls ripped across their faces. My boys are locked in.

Coach keeps on. "It's not easy. To beat these guys, we've got to defend. That means doubling Lorbner in the post. They have shooters, but we can live with that." Then he snaps his attention to me. "Except Charles. Derrick, you stick that kid from the tip. Don't leave him. Not for anything."

Coach stands. We all rise with him. He steps into the center of the locker room and puts his hand out. We all come in and stack our fists.

"Let's get after it," Coach says.

Then Murphy smacks that pile of fists. "Team!" we all shout.

It's hard not to think about last year this time, when Hamilton invited me up here to get me to transfer. Then, the gym was empty and Coach Treat kept telling me about how incredible it was on game nights. Now I see.

It feels like we're in a college arena. They've got a state-of-the-art scoreboard rolling Hamilton highlights. They've got their students packed down front, all head-to-toe in school colors. They've got music pumping crisp and clear over the sound system. I wouldn't be surprised if, in addition to the local sports crew, ESPN showed up to capture the action.

We go through the layup lines, everyone trying to get a good lather going. Every pass pops, and we all chatter with each other. *Bucket*, every time a shot drops, or *You'll get it to fall* if one rattles out. I stroll out to mid-court, trying to gather my thoughts. I take a long look at the Hamilton end. There's Charles, weaving between his teammates, dashing back and forth with his crossover before burying a step-back. He doesn't even glance at our end. I check their coaches—Treat and his top assistant Campbell, who's hated me ever since I scored some free shoes off of him last year, only to gift them to Wes and then stay put at Marion East. As soon as they see me, they look away, trying to pretend like I'm just any other point from any other team. Without thinking, I let a smile curl across my face, but then I sense someone staring me down.

"Derrick," he says. It's Vasco, who's also walked all the way to mid-court. "It is always good to see you," he says. He extends his hand across the mid-court stripe. A few flashbulbs pop as I accept it. He's the *now*—top recruit in the land, lined up for Michigan State—but it's like they know he's shaking hands with the next guy in line. "We haven't had enough challenges," he says. "I hope you make us sweat a little."

Any other player—*anyone*—and that kind of smack talk would make me hate him. But with Vasco, it's just so matter-of-fact, like he's not even saying it to act all cocky. Just stating facts. The man doesn't even have a sweat up yet. In fact, he looks so relaxed that if he weren't in uniform, you'd think he just rolled out of bed.

"We gonna bring it," I say. Only thing I can think of.

"Good," he says, flat as can be. Then he turns, catches the rock from one of his teammates, takes a dribble to about twenty-five feet and calmly drops a J.

Slump   151

Makes me shake my head. Hell, I like the guy. But it'll also make it sweeter to knock him off. When I turn back to our end, Fuller's up in my face.

"Man, where I transferred from, we had this guard," he says. "Any time he needed to shut down a good opponent, he'd just follow him everywhere. Even at dead balls. Like, even if the guy walked all the way over to his bench, our guy never left his side. Just to get in his head. Try it with Charles, D." His face is as earnest as ever, a little sweat on his top lip. He makes me think of some guidance counselor trying like crazy to tell you how it is. But it's just that—his eagerness, his old-man-Denzel-Washington-haircut—that makes it impossible to deal with his routine.

"Fuller, you ever think sometimes I don't need any advice?" I pop him on the shoulder once, just to let him know I'm joking, but he sulks away, dejected. Well, he's just gonna have to get his head right himself. I need to take care of me right now.

I get back into the warm-up line, but after one time through we break out of it and just start shooting around to get loose. A missed shot by one of our back-ups kicks my way. I scoop it up. I start under the rim. Just a two-footer, one-handed without jumping. It's a little routine to get my stroke down, the same one Uncle Kid used to have me go through at the park if my shot got out of sorts. The ball slips through and kicks right back to me. Next, five feet, same form. Then ten feet, with my left hand on the rock to keep it straight. I keep working out, a few feet at a time. Straight on. Bucket, bucket, bucket. The clock's ticking down to game time. When it hits 10 seconds, I step back out to the three-point stripe. Let that clock tick while I pound the rock with my left. Then, at 2, I cross back between my legs and let fly. *Wet.*

Game on.

When they announce the starting fives, Hamilton advertises all their flash again. They kill the lights and pump in more music. Then spots come swirling down from the rafters, like at some NBA game. You can barely hear their public address guy over the beats, but when he announces Deon Charles, the crowd gets hyped. He races to mid-court, bumps fists with me and mouths something, but I can't hear what. Then he's off to their side, waiting for the other starters to join him. The crowd stays amped up, but when they announce Vasco's name, the place really erupts. So loud you'd think the gym would crack apart.

I look at our guys. All of a sudden that steely focus from the locker room is gone. Instead, they're all bug-eyed, geeked from the ruckus around them. Even Moose looks a little rattled.

"Hey!" I scream. "Noise isn't gonna beat us, no matter how much they make." I figure now's the time to lead, like I should have been all along. "It's just their five and our five. Ain't nobody coming down from those stands to ball out! Now let's go."

That seems to shake the boys out of their fog, but I know that just to be sure I better get after it early. At last, the music quits. Everyone comes out to center court, settling in on top of that big white Giant they've got painted there. Vasco controls the tip easily enough, but when Charles zips a quick pass ahead to their swing-man, it sails. Right away, they've got a turnover and we've got a chance to jump out ahead.

As I bring it up, I hear Coach hollering. "Be smart now. Make every possession count!"

Fair enough, but just this once I know what we need. I cross mid-

Slump 153

court and pop it to Devin on the right side to start our offense. Only, instead of cutting left, I fake that way and double back toward Devin. I swing behind him so he can run a little handoff with me. As soon as that leather hits my fingers, I'm *gone*. Push into the lane hard and Charles can't do anything but ride my hip. Come to a jump stop and look straight at Vasco, who fakes like he's going to help but stays glued to Moose. *Easy*. I lean in and kiss home a ten-footer, that little pull-up I've been missing all year.

2-0, good guys.

The look on Bolden's face is mixed. His eyes are narrowed in frustration, but he's biting his lip. Even he doesn't want to kill any early mo.

I've been through this drill with Hamilton before—no way they're sitting back and worrying over one little bucket. They race it at us hard. It's all I can do to cut Charles off before he gets a look. He doubles back to the top of the key to set the offense, but they don't waste any time. Not ever. A kick to the wing and a quick post-entry to Vasco. Devin crashes down to help. Vasco busts out a move I haven't seen before—a quick ball-fake back to Devin's man to shake the double and then a quick-as-lightning turnaround before Devin can come back again. Tied, fast as that.

"Ball!" I shout to Fuller, who's slow getting it in. No sense in waiting on them to get set before we attack. So, again, that rock hits my hand and I run it at them. This time Deon's ready, but I set him up—give a little rhythm dribble to the right before spinning back left. Into the lane again, and this time Vasco runs at me. Just an easy dish to Moose for two.

Before I can even tell Moose *Good shot*, Hamilton's back on top of us. Charles comes screaming up the court. When Fuller helps on the drive, the rock gets kicked out to his man—a nice long look at a three that he bangs home.

"Stay put on that," I tell Fuller. "I don't need help on the drive."

He nods, but he's got that dejected look on his face again, like I've just stolen his iPod or something. This time down, I figure the man needs a touch. Ball zips to Devin on the right wing. Cross-screen for Fuller. Then I flare out to set Charles up for Stanford's screen. I take a step baseline, then cut middle, shoulder-to-shoulder off Stanford.

Devin hits me with a crisp pass just as I hit the right elbow. I immediately duck into the lane. The defense dives. This time, instead of dropping to Moose, I ball-fake back over my shoulder to Fuller. He reads me—back-cuts just as his man lunges, and I hit him in stride for an easy ten-footer. Rattles home and we're back up.

"Way to be, boys!" I shout. "Now let's get a stop!"

By the time that's out of my mouth, Charles has it in the front-court again. They set their offense and get it humming. Ball to the wing. Ball to shallow baseline. Back to the wing. Cross-court to Charles. Look into Lorbner, then cross-court again. The crowd's buzzing the whole time, but the pace is so quick that they barely have a chance to really get loud. You can hear the squeak of cuts, the shouts of encouragement from the benches. I love it. Finally, a game with some jump to it.

Charles tries losing me on a screen, but I get through and keep a hand in his face so he can't squeeze off a shot. Instead, he rifles a pass into the post, where Stanford's sealed deep. Rather than give up the bunny, Stanford reaches before the shot can go up. Obvious foul.

Slump

Hamilton aligns to take it out. We all keep eyes on Lorbner so he doesn't get an easy one off the inbounds. But then there's another whistle.

Bolden's halfway onto the floor, hands on his hips.

"Timeout, visitors," the ref says.

What the hell? We're humming, up a point early, and now Bolden's waving us in. "Come on now. Come on. Good start!" This is Murphy's chatter as we come to the sidelines, but when we sit Murphy eases back, and Bolden squats in front of us.

He eyes each of us with that wild stare. Then, over-enunciating to us like we're little misbehaving children, he says, "Slooooooow dowwwn!"

I want to scream at him that we've finally got some zip, and if he wouldn't kill it, we might just knock these guys off. But I don't.

"What, Derrick?" Bolden snaps.

"I didn't say anything, Coach."

"Your body language says plenty," he snaps. I guess I must have leaned back the wrong way or shaken my head slightly or looked away at the wrong time. Who knows? It's like any little thing can set Coach off.

Now I look back at him. He wants to give me a stare-down, I'll stare. Around us, the gym hums with people chattering away the timeout. The Hamilton band kicks into their fight song. Finally, Coach drops his gaze. His eyes just waver at first. Then I see it flash across his face—he still doesn't have the heart to really get after me, the kid with the banged-up dad. *Damn.* I'd rather him rip me than give me a pity pass. But he turns to the whole team and explains how if we try to run with Hamilton, they'll leave us behind. "We've got to play them possession by possession," he hollers. Then he sends us back out as the horn sounds.

Problem is, even if he can convince us to play it slow, nobody's giving that order to Hamilton. They get Vasco in the post of the first reversal and he banks one in. On the other end, I try to do what Coach says—just work methodically for the best possible look.

But right away I see something different. Every other school we've played has been content to sag back in on us, take away my drives and Moose's posts. Hamilton doesn't roll that way. They're out in passing lanes, up tight on the ball even if it's Stanford twenty feet from the rim. I understand why—with the talent they've got and with Lorbner roaming the paint, why sag back in and play soft?

It's like an invitation to drive. Every time I catch it, I can see creases. It's like all season we've been playing against seven defenders, and now things have finally evened up. Still, with Coach's orders, I wait. A cross-court to Devin. No look. A screen to pop Fuller out to the wing. Nothing. An entry to Moose, but even he can't get a decent look on Vasco. When he kicks it back to me top of the key, I can't control myself anymore. Trying to slow this game down is like trying to hold back a freight train with a dog leash. I jab step right to get Charles leaning, then dart left into the paint. Vasco jumps at me, and I drop one on Moose for a lay-in.

I sneak a peek at Bolden. He nods his approval on the bucket, but he motions with his hands—palms down in a patting motion toward the floor: *Slow it down.*

Keep dreaming, Coach.

At halftime, Coach paces back and forth while we sit and catch our breath. Murphy goes locker to locker, slapping people on the knee. "Way to get after it," he keeps saying. "One more half of that."

Slump

We damn near melted the scoreboard. It's 41-40 Hamilton at the break, meaning we dropped more on the best team in the state in one half than we've been scoring on scrubs for a whole game. This is what we were built for. This is why I busted my ass all summer and why Moose burned that fat into muscle. *Run.* I've turned Charles around so many times I'm surprised he doesn't have whiplash. When I get past him I'm just dealing—Devin spotting, Fuller and Stanford cutting, Moose getting to the rim. Hell, even Reynolds got in to drop a J. *Run,* I think. *We can run all damn night.*

"We can't keep running with these guys," Bolden says. He avoids looking at me as he says it. He doesn't look at any players, really. He just stands in the center of the locker room, head bent down. "I know you don't want to hear that, but we're playing right into their hands." He looks up then. Not at us, but at the ceiling, like now he's calling down divine intervention. "I swear to God," he says, "you guys are going to kill me." And on that *kill* he looks at us, eyes bulging with anger. He doesn't scream, but any fool can see he's about to burst. "They're the number one team in the state. Champs two years running. Undefeated. And we're on their floor. Are you guys out of your *minds?* You think you can come in here and *run them?*"

Wearily, his shoulders slumped like a mourning man, he goes back to the board. He draws up our half-court sets one more time and pleads with us. "Slow it down and they'll get frustrated," he says. "But you're not going to scare them with your speed."

He's right. Well, with any other point guard in the state, he'd be right. But we get first touch after the break. For a couple possessions I try to do what he says. That just gets us a travel on

Stanford and a forced miss by Fuller. Bang bang on the other end and Hamilton's up 5.

I dribble it up, and it's like Coach can see me itching. "Take it easy now, Derrick," he says as I cruise past him.

Instead I take it straight to the rim. I don't even bother throwing a move on Charles, just pound it past him and attack. Lorbner slides over, but I just rise for another pull-up. Silk. Game on again.

The rock just gets ripped back and forth. On one end, Lorbner gets to work on Moose. A drive and a dish, a post-up for two, a rainbow from range, even a behind-the-back pass to a cutter for a deuce. But I've got the answer every time. It's like seeing Lorbner light it up brings out the best in me. I finish at the rim, get a step-back J to rattle home, find Fuller cutting, then drive and kick to Devin for a three so deep you can hear the crowd *ooooh* as it's in the air. Bucket, bucket, bucket.

By the end of the third, the game's got all the markings of a shootout that won't stop. Hamilton's up 63-61, but it feels like whoever has the ball last is going to win it.

At the break, Bolden pleads one more time. "We've got to get the pace under control," he says. "We keep running with these guys we'll get burned." Even as he says it, you can tell he knows we've tuned him out. Nobody wants to slow it down now. Bolden gives us his stare, going player to player with his eyes, imploring us—then we break that huddle and I don't even have to be the one to say it. "Keep after these sons-of-bitches," Moose shouts at us.

We do. First touch I get, I dart into the lane and hit Stanford with a dime to tie it. I steal a glance at Bolden and see him wince. Man, it's almost like he doesn't even *want* us to score if we won't do it his way.

Slump

There is one thing I've done according to plan though—stick the hell out of Charles. I know from experience you leave that kid and he'll drop bombs on you. Every time down, as soon as he gives it up, I'm chest-to-chest. I might not play mind games like Fuller told me, but it doesn't matter how far Charles floats away from the basket, I'm following. He's had his looks here and there, but as the fourth wears on I see him start to get anxious. They're up two, but he catches it a good twenty-five feet from the bucket and—even with me up tight—launches. It barely scrapes iron and then skims out of bounds. Our ball with a chance to tie.

"We don't need that shot," Lorbner tells him.

Charles squinches up his face. "I don't need you yapping at me," he fires back.

Lorbner straightens up, right there at mid-court. "Deon, I said we don't need it. You'll get yours when you get yours."

Charles slinks on then, bullied by his star. Maybe it's seeing that exchange, or maybe it's that we finally got a stop—either way, there's a little nervous buzz in the Hamilton crowd. It's been so long since they've witnessed a loss, they probably won't know how to handle it when we hang one on them.

I can sense it. These guys are like a wounded animal. Time for the kill. I bring it into the frontcourt and kick to Devin on the wing. I screen the other way, then cut through the lane off of Moose. All game long, Charles has stayed on top of that screen and chased me all the way to the opposite baseline, but just this once he trails. All the opening I need. I open up in the lane. "Ball!" I shout. Fuller feeds me from the top of the key, a nice pass to my strong side, and I gather and rise in one motion. Charles hacks at me, but he's too late to do anything but get the foul.

Bucket. Whistle. Chance for an and-one to put us up.

Our crowd erupts. The boys on the bench get so amped that Murphy has to sprint down to restrain them. "That's what I'm *talking* about," I shout, screaming it up to the rafters for everyone to hear. Moose comes flying at me for a chest bump that almost knocks me into the third row.

Once we settle, I take my place at the stripe. As the ref hands me the ball, I glance at the Hamilton players on the lane. Their heads are hung. We've got 'em. Except for one guy—Lorbner. He just stares at me, calmly and curiously as if I've just shown up at his doorstep selling magazines. Like he's just biding his time until he can tell me *No*.

I go through my routine. Deep breath. Two dribbles, then spin the ball in my hand. Line it up and let fly. *Just* off, a tad to the right. Lorbner rips, but it's no sweat. We still have it tied, and they're feeling tight.

Charles dribbles out top for a while, still looking impatient. He dips his shoulder and tries to drive, but I cut him off. He has to pick it up, and our crowd—all squeezed into the far corner—heckle him the best they can. He squeezes off a pass to the wing, then waves at his teammate for a screen. And when he doesn't get what he wants right away, he gets snippy: "Move, man," he snaps at his boy.

Got 'em rattled, I think.

Except for Vasco. He catches on the short baseline and, calm as a kid chucking it up in the driveway, sinks a seventeen-footer over Moose. The Hamilton crowd gets back on their feet, but when I sneak a look over at my shoulder at Charles, he's still sniping at his teammate instead of paying attention to me. Two quick claps of my hands draws the in-bound from Stanford, and I'm off before Charles knows what's hit him. I'm past him and into the lane. Vasco comes late. I've learned my lesson with him, so I drop one to Moose who's filling the lane. He rises, but there's one problem—he doesn't have the rock. One of their wings clipped just a piece of it, and now he scrambles after it in the paint.

There's no chance to get back. My feet are still on the baseline when they turn to run out. I sprint like hell, but all that means is I get to Charles just a beat after he releases an open three, the kind he's been waiting for all night long. I don't even watch it drop. The Hamilton crowd's explosion tells me all I need to know.

No time to sulk. I know we've got to get those points right back, so I race into the frontcourt again, wanting to shut those people up as soon as possible. This time when I drive, the whole defense sinks in so I snap the rock back between my legs for a step-back. It's a quick move, and it frees me at the three-point line. Charles doesn't dare run at me, or he knows I'll blow by him so I just set the feet and rise.

It feels good leaving my hands, but the rotation just doesn't have that snap. Maybe it's from tired legs, but the shot scrapes front iron and Hamilton's off again. We sprint back, and I can feel the burn in my muscles from the pace. Their crowd rises in pitch, sensing the knock-out blow—the kind I thought I was going to give them. We get back in time so there's no easy look, but we're starting to hit the wall. All game long we've been talking on the defensive end, calling out cutters, warning each other of screens. Now we're silent. Soon enough I turn to get a faceful of Vasco. A solid back-screen to free Charles, and there's nothing I can do but watch him rise from range again.

Bucket.

Just like that, we're down eight.

Their crowd gets deliriously loud, and Charles eggs them on. He nods his head real big and slow as he backpedals on defense, his mouth pursed in an *oooh* like he's the baddest thing on earth.

Fuller inbounds it to me, and I slow it down. When I cross mid-court, I look at Bolden, expecting he'll want time. He just looks right back at me. "Go on," he shouts. "You got it all figured out." Then he turns to the bench and leans back on his seat. He stretches his legs out in front of him and laces his hands behind his head, like he's kicked back in the shade on a summer's day. Damn, that old man can be one mean son-of-a-bitch.

86-70. Final. No use in saying more.

Coach just walked into the locker room, said, "You played hard. I'll give you that." Then he shrugged his shoulders and said, "Shower up and hit the bus."

The only sound on the bus ride home was my phone buzzing with texts. There were the usual: *Tough luck* and *Hang in there* from Wes and Kid. Then another one came in. *U still the best baller in the state.* This one was from Daniella. While I didn't exactly want to hear from her, that little message made my pulse race. When I didn't respond right away, the phone buzzed again: *Come over?*

Part of me—maybe most of me—wanted to hop right off the bus and sprint to her place, but something made me not trust her. I texted her back to tell her I should get home, that I'd hit her up next week.

Slump

Phone buzzed again. *U sure?* And this time a pic accompanied it—Daniella stretched out on her bed, stripped down to her skin, only the sheets pulled over her in the most crucial spots. I don't know why she does it. It's like everyone's talked shit about her for so long she's just going to live down to what they think of her. And I know she doesn't actually want that. I know she wants to be more to me than some hook-up. If she didn't come off as so desperate maybe I'd take her seriously, maybe give our thing a real chance. Still, that pic gets the job done on me.

So here I am, knocking on Daniella Cole's door on a Saturday night. Not a light on in the whole apartment complex. Wasn't a month ago I was knocking on Jasmine's door on Christmas day, saying a little holiday prayer that she'd let me in. That's when it hits me. What if Daniella's dad opens the door? There aren't a lot of explanations for my presence other than the most obvious one. But I guess Daniella Cole didn't get to be Daniella Cole because her dad was keeping a real close watch. The door opens a few inches and a hand reaches out from the darkness to grab my wrist and pull me in.

She leans up on her toes and her breath is hot in my ear. "My mom won't be home for another couple hours," she says. Then she turns and pads over the carpet toward her bedroom. There's a little moonlight shining into the window and I can see that this place is nothing like Jasmine's. A flat screen anchors the living room, looking like it cost more than any other piece of furniture in the joint. There's a splash of old checkout line mags on the floor, but not a book in sight. *This isn't who you're supposed to be with*, I tell myself. But the moonlight shows off something else—Daniella switching those hips as she walks. Lord, there's no saying no.

Kevin Waltman

By the time I make it to her bedroom, she's already climbing up on top of the covers. She looks back at me over her shoulder. "I bet you're frustrated after that game," she says.

20.

At breakfast, Mom can't even look at me. She knows. And she also knows that whoever I've been with isn't Jasmine. I know for a fact that she never had in mind for me to be with someone like Daniella. Daniella and I actually talked some last night before I had to get out the door, and it was almost sweet. We just hashed out school, cracked on Mrs. Hulsey. Daniella pulled up a video I hadn't seen before of some pint-sized kid in Detroit—maybe he was ten—just cutting grown men off at the knees in a rap contest. It was like if I could just turn myself off from thinking about Daniella a certain way, things could actually be cool with her. But I can't turn that off.

"Rough night," Mom says. She's putting the finishing touches on an omelet.

"What?" I say, recoiling. I can tell without her saying anything that she knows every last thing—but the one silver lining in that is that we don't talk about it. Hell, I'd rather lose to Hamilton every night for the rest of my life than talk to my mom about sex even once.

"The game," she says. "Rough game." She slaps the plate

down in front of me and then hollers for Jayson to get himself out here for breakfast.

Jayson and I eat in silence. Mom sips her coffee. She stares out the window at a January morning that's gray as gravel. The door opens and my dad stumbles in on his crutches, Uncle Kid trailing behind. Another snowstorm is brewing behind them, the early flurries gusting in through the open door. Kid sets a bag down by the door and tries to help my dad, but his hand just gets swatted away—Dad's pride taking over. Only problem is that effort about sends my dad to the floor. We all gasp, but Kid catches him just before he crashes down.

"Thanks," Dad says, but the word comes out almost like an insult. He's so sick of needing help that he's starting to resent the people giving it to him. He makes it across the room, drops his crutches and sinks into his chair, then roots around angrily for the remote. I was worried about him never walking again, but I wasn't prepared for this—my dad growing angry and sulking in his chair, like some old man who's soured on the world.

Kid shakes it off and retrieves the bag he set down by the door. He brings it into the kitchen and starts unloading groceries again—fresh fruit, milk, eggs, three packages of bacon. We all just watch him as he puts them away, natural as if he were in his own apartment.

"Kid," Mom says. Just one word, but it's loaded. Any time she says your name with that cool tone you better run for cover. Kid doesn't even answer, just keeps stocking the fridge. "Sidney!" she snaps.

He doesn't turn around, just looks over his shoulder like he's eyeing a cutter on the court. "Yeah?"

"Where are you getting the money for all this?" Mom asks,

Slump

voicing the question we've all been wondering for weeks. After Kid tried to play Hamilton for a job last year, there's added skepticism. I don't think he'd do it, but he wouldn't be the first uncle to try and make some bucks off colleges eyeing his nephew—and if that ever happens, Mom will go nuclear on him.

"I got cash," he says.

I watch my mom. She closes her eyes for a second. Takes a breath. I've seen this. She's trying to give Kid one more chance to really answer before she unloads on him. She walks over to where Kid's standing. Jayson glances at me, looking as nervous as if he's the one getting grilled by Mom.

"We appreciate the help," she says, "and Lord knows we need it for those doctor bills, even though Tom can start working again once he's off those crutches. But I need to know where the money's coming from." She's doing her best to keep her temper, but her hands are firmly on her hips, and she's leaning forward just a little as she speaks. Last chance for Kid.

"Jesus Christ!" he snaps. He slams a bag of oranges down on the counter and storms for the door. "This damn family! You try to help and all you get is a bunch of conflict. You people are impossible." He tries to zip up his coat, but he's in such a hurry that it gets stuck. He struggles with it for a second before making an angry, guttural sound, then barging through the door and whipping it closed so hard the house shakes.

My mom's still standing in the kitchen. Her hands are on her hips, but now she's leaning back, as if knocked off balance by Kid's tirade. Jayson catches my eye again and raises his eyebrows like he's impressed by Kid's tactics—blow up at Mom and beat her to the punch.

Jayson's probably filing that strategy away for future use, but I ought to tell him it probably won't work as well for him as it did for Kid.

I figure that's about enough for me. I get up and head to my room, but Dad—who didn't even look up from the tube the whole time Mom and Kid were at it—clears his throat. "Derrick, come here," he says.

I stop at the corner of the hallway, but he curls his finger to beckon me, like I'm a toddler about to get scolded. I do as I'm told, and when I get close he reaches out with his left hand and snares my wrist. He pulls on my arm so I have to lean down toward him. "Look, son," he says, "I'm not proud of having to get helped around all the time. But—" He trails off.

"I understand, Dad," I say.

His eyes dart back and forth like he's looking for the right thing to say. He takes up the remote and snaps off the television with an angry, stabbing motion. He stares at me. His eyes start to water behind his glasses. Scared that I'm going to see him cry, I start to pull away but he squeezes tight as a vise. "It'll get better," he says. Then he starts searching for words again.

"Okay," I say. Right now, I'd say anything to be free of his grip. Somewhere inside, I sense he's got an important point, that if I'd try as hard to listen as he is trying to tell me, I'd get it. Or maybe instead of listening I'm supposed to talk now, fill up the silence that he's running against. Dad sees that I just want to get away, so he gives me another squeeze on the wrist and then lets go.

"Just do me two favors," he says.

"Anything."

"Tell Jayson to get over here to help me work on my exercises and hand me that phone." He points to the cordless over on the couch. "I need to call my brother to smooth things out."

Jayson, listening in, doesn't need to be told a thing. He pops up from his chair and comes over to Dad, then squats down to hold Dad's good leg still. I hand the phone to Dad, but when he dials, the front door opens again, and there stands Kid holding his phone. He didn't even make it off the porch.

He looks at Dad, who breaks into a broad grin. "I was just calling you to apologize, Sidney," Dad says. "But what the hell were you still doing out there?"

Kid stares down at the floor and shifts his weight from foot to foot. "Ah. I got about halfway to my car before I realized that I'd left my keys on the counter." We all turn to look at the kitchen, where Mom walks to the counter and picks up Kid's keys. She holds them up like some piece of incriminating evidence and just shakes her head real slow, like she can't believe her lot in life is to be surrounded by the four fools in her living room.

"I'm sorry, Kaylene," Kid offers to my mom, but he doesn't have the stones to look at her.

She huffs. "Have you eaten breakfast?" she asks.

"No." He still won't look up.

"Well, you brought all this food. Least I can do is make you some eggs."

With that, a tenuous peace is restored. I stay in the living room and read for class. Kid sits at the table while Mom whips up some food. Dad and Jayson work on Dad's exercises. Nobody says a word. But there we are, all together, sticking it out the way families do.

21.

I've seen this script before. Hit up practice on a Monday night and the gym's dark, like the foot of snow we got has shut everything down. Make it to the locker room and nobody's saying a thing. Just Coach Murphy telling everyone to stay in their street clothes for a team meeting.

I can deal with this. I mean, last year this time Bolden finally took the shackles off of us and let us run. It meant me playing the four-spot, but it also meant I started getting some easy run-outs for jams. And it turned our season around. Just like that, we went from treading water to stomping teams.

Moose catches my eye and gives me a quick wink. He knows what's up. And Devin gives me a nod—though it turns into a wince when he goes to sit at his locker and has to put pressure on that bad ankle. By this point, any fool knows Devin's just gonna have to grit it out and play through the pain. That wheel's not getting better without some serious rest.

A quick scan of the younger guys reveals they're not breathing quite as easy as Moose, so I figure it's another chance for me to be a leader. I head over to Reynolds first to give him a quick fist bump. He sits all bundled up in his winter coat and hat, like he's trying to protect himself from the coming blizzard of Bolden's wrath. It makes him look like a little kid scared of his dad, so I just put my hand on his shoulder. "All good," I say. "Don't sweat this."

"Even after last game?" he asks, conjuring up our collapse against Hamilton.

"Hell, yeah," I say. "Besides, not like you booted the game away." Then Murphy makes his way over. He doesn't say a word, just hovers over my shoulder like some cop waiting for someone to make the wrong move. So I ease back to my seat and we wait.

And we wait. And we wait some more.

I bet Bolden lets us stew for a solid twenty minutes. By the time that locker room door swings open, even I'm starting to sweat this meeting a little bit. Even then, Bolden doesn't say a word. He just strides in, all business, an old VCR cradled in his arm. He hooks the thing up to the dumpy old dusty TV that stands on a rolling cart in the corner. It's so embarrassing, I almost feel sorry for him. It's like we're stuck in the 90s, watching things on tape, when every other locker room in the civilized world has gone digital. But Bolden doesn't seem to care.

"Watch!" he shouts. "Watch these offenses."

It's not exactly a riveting film session. At first, he just shows us some Memphis Tigers footage from last year, and only their offensive possessions. They get it out and go, a long outlet leading to a fast-break pull-up. As soon as that ball goes through the net, the tape jumps to their next possession. But if anyone so much as leans their head back in fatigue, Coach is on them. "Don't you dare act like this doesn't matter," he snaps, and everyone's back to attention again.

Kevin Waltman

So we go through every possession of an entire game, watching Memphis rack up 82 points in the process, a ton of them on fast-breaks. You ask me, Coach is the one that ought to be taking notes. Then, when the tape ends and the lights come up, we all start to stir, but Coach Murphy claps his hands, just once and loud as a gunshot. "Not done!" he shouts. "Just hold tight."

It feels like a teacher keeping you past the bell, like what they've got to say about some Langston Hughes poem is so life-or-death that where you have to get to doesn't matter. Bolden takes his sweet time too. He ejects the first tape and then methodically walks over and hands it to Murphy, who hands him another tape that he's had sitting on a chair. Brutal.

The lights go down and the video starts up again. This time, the teams that hit the hardwood projected over our chalkboard are Wisconsin and Illinois. I'm hoping he'll have us watch Illinois' possessions. They're no Memphis, but they'll get it out and go when they get a chance. But no. It's Wisconsin. Long, boring possessions like with each trip down the floor they're trying to single-handedly set the game of basketball back fifty years. If it weren't for fear of Coach's fury, every head in this room would droop down in sleep. And Wisconsin does their thing. They roll up a game that barely hits the 50s. I know now what I'll do if a doctor ever gives me one day to live—I'll watch a Wisconsin game, because it makes 40 minutes feel like eternity.

Mercifully, the lights come back up, and there's no more tape. Bolden strides to the blackboard and starts writing, while Murphy unhooks the VCR. When Bolden steps away, he's written *Memphis 82* on one side and *Wisconsin 58* on the other.

"Question," he says. "Which team had the better offensive game?"

Slump 173

We sit there dumbfounded. It's like someone asking you who the president is. You've got to be from outer space not to know. Then again, Bolden's always got something up his sleeve so the veterans play it cool. Not Reynolds. His hands shoots up like a missile.

Bolden nods at him. Reynolds says, all eagerness, "Memphis did."

Bolden just shakes his head slowly, with that pitying expression parents give you when you tell them something so dumb they can't believe it. "Sorry, Reynolds," he says. "But be honest. How many of you thought the same thing?"

One by one the hands go up, until the only people in the room with their hands by their sides are Bolden and Murphy. "Now why would you think that?" Coach asks.

Reynolds keeps jumping at the bait. He practically leaps off his seat and blurts, "They scored more points! You got it right there: 82 to 58."

Bolden nods, then motions with his hand for Reynolds to settle. *Poor freshman*, I think. Sure, I would have had the same answers, but I had the sense to keep my mouth shut.

Bolden walks back to the board and says, "Let me show you a little more information." Under the *82* he draws a horizontal line and then an *80*. Then over on the Wisconsin side he does the same thing, except it's *58/52*. He turns to us and folds his arms. "Those second numbers represent how many possessions each team had. Now, you can do the math, right? How many points—*per possession*—did each team score?"

Fuller, showing off that he's got a calculator cranking in his head, rattles it off almost immediately. "Memphis scored *1.025* per possession and Wisconsin scored—" he pauses for a second to be sure, then —"*1.16.*"

Coach nods, impressed, then scrawls those numbers on the board, *1.025* next to Memphis and *1.16* next to Wisconsin. "Get it?" he asks.

People start to nod, but Reynolds shakes his head. "Memphis still scored more points," he says.

This time Bolden has to take a deep breath so he doesn't erupt. He reels it back in. At the end of the day the man would rather instruct than scream. He smiles and lifts his eyebrows, then exhales again. "Reynolds, the scary part is I bet there are a half-dozen other guys in this room who still think the same thing. It's like this. The goal isn't to score a bunch of points, but to make each possession end in points. Get it? In other words, if Wisconsin—playing the way they play—had the ball as many times as Memphis did, then they'd have scored—?" He stops and snaps his fingers, points to Fuller.

Fuller squinches his eyes up to think, but finds the answer fast. "Ninety-two points. 92.8 to be exact."

"You see?" Bolden continues, scanning the entire room now. "The lesson here is that, dunks be damned, Wisconsin's a better offensive team than Memphis." Then he cracks another smile, not able to help himself. "And I guess the other lesson is that if you need help with your math homework, ask Fuller."

Guys laugh then, happy to have any kind of joke to lighten things up. But Bolden's not about to let the levity last. "One more thing!" he shouts. Then he takes the chalk and scrawls against the board so hard, I'm surprised he doesn't shatter it. Under Memphis he writes a huge *L*. And under Wisconsin he writes a big, jagged *W*. "Memphis lost and Wisconsin won!"

"Last I checked, that's the point, boys," Murphy chimes in.

Bolden snaps up a folding chair, spins it around and plants it right

Slump 175

in the middle of the locker room. He settles down into it like every move makes his joints ache. "Boys," he says. Then nothing else for a second. He looks around the room, peering at each of us one by one. Most guys look away when he gets to them. "It's not about Xs and Os at this point. It's about what you guys have in here." He points to his chest, jabbing it so hard it probably leaves a bruise. "Do you know why?"

Nobody says a word. Even Murphy stands in the corner still as a statue, like if he so much as twitches, he'll send Bolden tumbling over the edge.

Bolden takes a few angry, raspy breaths, then continues. "Well, I'll tell you. It's because you want things to be easy. You're good, but not *that* good. You guys need to be grind-it-out good. Floor-burn good. But you don't want that. No. You'll defend for a few minutes at a time, but not for a whole game. You'll stay patient for a few possessions, but not all thirty-two minutes. It can't be that way." Now he stands. He walks out to where we sit, passing close by each player as he talks. He's so close guys lean back as he passes by, like they're trying to get out of the way of a truck rumbling past. "You've got to *grind!* Do you hear me? Possession by possession by possession. Grind!" Then he squats down right in front of me. He reaches out and bangs on the floor with his fist, imploring us. "But here's the best thing. When you do that, you'll start beating people. And it'll hurt 'em. More than just any old loss. You've been there, right? Losing to a team because they out-toughed you? Riding home on that bus sick to your stomach with wondering how in the hell you lost to them?"

Bolden stands, walks back to his chair and sits. He stares out at us with that sharp watch again, waiting for an answer. But he's so intense, it makes everyone scared to speak up.

"I've been there." This is Fuller, almost spitting out the words. He's even got the weary voice of some old man telling stories in the barbershop corner. Now it's like he's dredging up some baggage from his last school, offering it up for a counseling session. "It feels—" he breaks off for a second, wondering if he should say precisely what he wants, then plunges ahead— "it feels like shit."

Bolden lets his face relax into a twisted smile. "Yeah, Fuller, that's exactly how it feels. Now wouldn't you rather have other teams feeling that way instead of us?"

"Fuck yeah," Moose says, taking the license on language and running with it.

"That's right!" Coach Murphy yells, partly to try to get people pumped and partly to say something before Bolden can get mad at Moose for his choice of words.

"All right!" Bolden shouts. "There it is. We got to be more like Wisconsin. Just get Ws, and don't worry about style points."

Still, something doesn't sit well with the team. I can sense it and so can Bolden. He scowls, upset that we don't look more impressed. "What?!" he shouts. "You tried it your way against Hamilton. What more proof do you need?"

I look down at my hands. Shuffle my feet back and forth on the floor. Fidget in my seat. It seems to be going around, but finally Stanford has the brass to raise his hand.

"What?" Coach asks.

Stanford has a hard time spitting it out, but finally he just shrugs his shoulders and lets it rip. "Wisconsin, Coach? Really?"

"What's wrong with Wisconsin?"

Slump 177

Stanford looks around, hoping someone will let him off the hook. He's tried growing some mid-season facial hair, but it's just little wisps—another attempt to look tough backfiring. When nobody bails him out, he plunges ahead. "Coach, they're so white. I mean, my freshman year we went down to play Martinsville, and even they didn't have that many white guys."

Everyone laughs again, but we try to stifle it. Sure, that's what everyone in the room was thinking, but we know better than to get too carried away.

Coach puts his hands on his hips and lets the laughter die down. This time he doesn't even give that patient smile he gave Reynolds. He practically barks at us, his body shaking with the volume. "Fine! But if I've got a roomful of players who'd rather lose as long as people don't think they're 'playing white,' then I'll walk out that goddamn door right now!"

Nobody's laughing now. There's an itch in me, some buried nerve that always jumps under Bolden's restraints, that wants to take him up on his challenge. Let him walk and get someone in here who's entered the 21st century. But I don't.

When a full minute of silence—and I mean *funeral silence*—passes, Bolden relaxes his stance. "Be back for practice tomorrow night, but if you're not ready to play my way you might as well hand in your jersey on your way out."

22.

I'm halfway home, re-reading a depressing text from Wes—*Iesha's done with me. Done.*—when another comes in from Daniella. It's the eighth one today, even though I've only replied to one of them. She just keeps on. And this time she says something that really chills me—she refers to me as her "boyfriend." I know this is something I'm going to have to deal with, but I don't know how. That's when I hear footsteps behind me. I whirl around to see Reynolds trailing me, his hood pulled so tight around his face that I recognize his coat before I recognize any features. He drops his hood back and there's that amber baby face, his eyes glassy in the cold. Around him snow swirls up in a little cyclone.

"Hey, D," he says. He kind of leans forward in greeting instead of sticking his hand out or anything, like any movement more than that and he'll turn to ice right on the spot.

"What do you want?" I ask. I'm in the same cold night as he is. I know he's not headed in the opposite direction of his house unless he wants something.

He looks around, then waits until a car passes, like he's about to make some illicit deal and doesn't want anyone to see. Then he walks a little closer and half-whispers: "Do you think Bolden's losing it?"

"What?"

"Coach Bolden. I was talking with Stanford after the meeting tonight, and he thinks Bolden's going off. Like not all there anymore."

I roll my eyes. I'm only a sophomore, but trying to make it through a season dragging along Reynolds makes me feel like a ten-year vet. "Man, Bolden's the same as he ever was. And he's gonna be wearing down Marion East players long after you and I have graduated." It's crazy. I've been bucking under Bolden's saddle for almost two years now, but as soon as somebody else talks even the slightest shit about him, I don't have time to hear it. "One thing I know about Coach," I say, "is that all he wants to do is win." That's when I think about him and Murphy waiting outside of Dad's hospital room, about how long Bolden took it easy on me this year. Hell, even this last game against Hamilton—it's not like it was Moose and Stanford pushing the pace. It was all me. And he didn't single me out even then. "The other thing I know is that Bolden's always got his players' backs," I add.

Reynolds shrugs his shoulders. He doesn't seem convinced, but he doesn't have it in him to argue. He's about to turn back, but then stops. "You know, that's not even what I wanted to say," he starts. "I was talking to my mom last night. We got to talking about the team and then about you." He stops, embarrassed.

I don't have time for this. Too much going on to stand here and listen to Reynolds mutter around. "Go on," I tell him.

He looks away for a second. "Well, man, she lit into me good when she found out I'd never even told you how—" This time when he looks away he says the rest of his words into the street, so I can't hear.

"What?" I ask, getting truly annoyed now.

Reynolds huffs, then gathers himself up to say what he has to say. "I never came down here to offer help to you and your mom when your dad had his accident. I didn't even say how sorry I was."

Now I'm the one who's embarrassed. For a second, I get angry at him. How dare he bring up my dad like that? How dare he pity me? But even on a frigid night like this, that feeling melts away. Maybe it's seeing how my parents made peace with Kid. Maybe it's coming to grips with the fact that there's no winning a fight with Coach Bolden. Or maybe I'm just tired of being at odds with everyone.

"It's okay," I say. That's all, but it seems like that's the only thing that needs to be said. Then we stand there for a few seconds, our breaths making little clouds in the night. Finally, a car zips past, rumbling like it's lost its muffler, and the roar snaps us out of it. "Just come on over. I bet my mom's got enough food if you want. And then we can run you home so you don't have to hoof it in the cold."

While we eat, my phone gets hit up three more times. Daniella, Wes, Daniella again. While Mom's re-filling a pitcher of water, I sneak a quick text back to Wes, tell him I'll hit him up later and we'll hash it out. But Daniella? Man, I don't know what to do about that girl. Don't get me wrong—she can flip a switch in me—but she's creeping pretty hard.

Reynolds packs the feed away for a wiry freshman. Mom barely has time to sit down before she's got to pop back up and get him more mashed potatoes. At least he gives her a sincere *Thank you, Mrs. Bowen* each time.

"You're welcome," she says for about the thirtieth time. "You just eat until you can't squeeze any more in." Then she smiles, kind of to herself. "My mom used to have a saying—'Even when there's not enough, there's always enough to share.' And, believe me, getting to *enough* was a lot harder for her. So you just go on." Then she finally takes a chance to eat herself, still kind of shaking her head as if she's lost in that memory of her mother. Jayson and I pause, waiting to see if maybe there's more story to be had. My grandparents on Mom's side are both gone. I only have the faintest memories of Grandma, so Jay and I soak up whatever stories we can get. I know they moved up here from down South when my mom was a baby, and I know that times were so tight that their perseverance has taken on a kind of mythical status with my mom. It means that, for Jayson and me, there's no obstacle too big, and there's no room—not even a little—for us to complain about things being hard.

This time that's all we get though. It's not like when Mom's around her siblings and the stories come flying out—the way Granddad used to pull triple shifts when other men were drinking up a weekend. Or the way Grandma got so mad at my uncle once that she kicked in his bedroom door, and it stayed off the hinges until his next birthday. No story this time. Maybe that memory of Grandma kicks in just a little bit, because Mom does look up from her meal. "One thing though," she says. "With three able-bodied boys sitting at this table, I don't see any reason why I should clean up even a single plate when we're done."

"Yes, ma'am," Reynolds says. Smart kid. But then he's got to add on: "I wash the dishes for my mama every night."

"Oh, really?" Mom asks. Then she takes this long curious look at me and Jay. "You two hear that? I think this new friend of yours could be a good influence, Derrick."

I look at Reynolds and just shake my head. Man, that kid can't help people for trying—busts up Devin's ankle, turns the ball over every time he touches it, and now he sets me and Jayson up to clean dishes forever. Reynolds grimaces, that apologetic look he gets on the court when he screws up, but I just smile, let him know no harm done.

A few minutes later we're toiling away. We've got a good system working. Jay clears and scrapes, Reynolds scrubs, and I dry and put things up. It gives Jayson a chance to grill someone else about the team too.

"You guys ever gonna get things rolling?" he asks Reynolds.

"Yeah. Most definitely," he answers, thinking—mistakenly—that a basic answer like that will satisfy my little brother.

"But how? You got nobody at the three that can stretch the defense. Devin's only half strength. You got no depth at the big spots. What's gonna change?"

Reynolds pauses, the hot water streaming over his hands. He tries again. "We'll get it. We get a little closer every time out."

Jayson thwunks down a couple more pans for Reynolds to scrub. "Not against Hamilton you didn't. Shoot. Those guys were just toying with you. You don't have enough shooters for the half-court, and you don't have enough speed to run."

Reynolds shuts off the water and steps back. He looks at me for a little help. Chalk it up as one more fool who didn't know what they were getting into when they talked hoops with my little brother. "Easy, Jay," I say. "Can't you let a man visit us without quizzing him to death?"

"Fine. Fine." But he's clearly not satisfied. He gives a half-assed scrape of the last pot and then slaps it down beside Reynolds before walking away.

As Jayson makes his exit, Dad comes limping in. I go from laughing at Reynolds and Jay to feeling my throat tighten up. I realize I'd been fearing this the whole time. The only person outside our family who's visited Dad is Wes, and now here's Reynolds—practically some stranger—gawking at my dad as he almost falls into the living room.

He catches himself, then sees that we have company. He'd been sleeping, so his hair's matted down on his head a little bit, making him look like one of those shiftless men who can barely keep themselves together. Still, he straightens up and puffs out his chest a little bit. "Thomas Bolden," he announces, and sticks out his hand toward Reynolds, who, after hesitating, walks into the living room to get a handshake.

"I'm Reynolds," he says, meekly.

"That's it?" Dad asks. "You just go by one name? Like Prince or something?"

Reynolds sputters out a nervous laugh. My cheeks burn. It's like my dad's trying to over-compensate for his frailty by cracking some lame joke that's about ten years out-of-date. It just doesn't suit him. It's like as his body's weakened his personality has too. Now that heat I felt in my cheek spreads down through my neck and chest. Soon I feel that same swirl of emotions—shame at my father and shame at myself for feeling that way about him. It will only get worse if Dad sinks down in that chair and starts rehabbing, lifting that bum leg up with such effort you'd think there were a fifty-pound weight on it.

Reynolds and Dad are still facing each other, both waiting on the other to say something to break the awkward silence. We're all saved by the doorbell. I all but sprint to answer it. Instead of Kid standing there with yet another bagful of groceries, I get a different kind of shock— Jasmine Winters, bundled against the cold, wearing that scarf I gave her for Christmas.

"I can already see my dad's heart breaking when I talk about it," Jasmine says. We're sitting in a coffee shop on Mass Avenue. Outside in the night, people hop from the street to the curb, weaving between piles of plowed snow. I know enough to realize they're not all as rich as they look, but they're decked in pretty expensive coats and boots. Even the college kids who look like they picked their clothes up out of a dumpster have haircuts that cost more than my whole wardrobe. I try to ignore all that. If this is where Jasmine wants to hang, I'm in. Shoot, girl could ask me to chill in a war zone, and I'd be game.

"I thought that's what he wanted," I say. "I mean, I've been to your place. They didn't pack those bookshelves with all that stuff just so their daughter could go to, like, Ball State."

Jasmine smiles. Seeing it just tears me apart. We're not here to start things back up. Even I know that. Besides, I've still got the Daniella issue to deal with. "I think they were hoping I'd go to some little Midwestern liberal arts school. Not out on the East Coast." She's talking schools in Boston. Talking New York or Philadelphia. I know that if she gets the scholarships she's hoping for, she'd be crazy not to go, but just the thought of it—hundreds of miles between me and her—depresses me. I'd rather her be close, even if I can't touch her.

"What about you?"

"Me?"

"Come on, Derrick. I know I'm not the only one who has mail piling up from schools. Granted, my mail's because I'm first in my class and already rocked the ACT in my junior year, but I guess some people think basketball's just as important."

I lean back. "Damn, girl. You coming at it a little hard, aren't you?"

She laughs. Getting a rise out of me never fails to brighten her up. "Okay," she says. "For real. You got any favorites?"

Truth is, I haven't even thought about it all that much during the season. I mean, it's always there, always a topic waiting every time the mail comes, but I just kind of stifle it all during the season. "Maybe Coach Bolden's wearing off on me," I say, "but I swear to God I've given more thought to Howe on Friday night than I have about where I want to play three years from now. All I know is my parents want it by the book. We're not gonna be hitting schools up for cash and cars like some players do—even though I know we could use it."

"Oh, come on, Derrick. Give me something."

I shake my head. I watch an older couple hugging each other like they're still giddy teenagers. They walk up to the counter and place an order. The woman leans over and whispers something in the man's ear and he just smiles, reacting to something deep and strong and secret between them. "Tell me your list again," I say to Jasmine. "Let me see which ones have decent hoops."

"Derrick," she says. "You should give it real thought. It's a big deal. And it'll come up faster than you think. I've still got a year left here, but that doesn't mean I'm going to wait to think about it."

"I know," I say, hitting that dejected tone of a kid just scolded by a teacher. "But the recruiting doesn't get real until next year." There's so much else I want to be talking to her about. I want to know why I've barely even seen her shadow at school. I want to know if she's gone out with anyone else. But mostly I want to beg forgiveness, just sink down on my knees right here in the coffee shop—let people stare, let people record it and post it for the world to see, I don't care. It's like my dad's wreck and the aftermath, the constant frustration of this season, all of it would be okay if I could just get Jasmine back again.

"I want things to work out for you," she says. She's not looking at me now, instead staring down into her cup. It reminds me of those times last year when I stumbled upon her in the bookstore, how just the sudden sight of her sent me racing. "Just because we broke up doesn't mean I've ever wanted anything bad for you."

There's a long silence after that. Then, I can't help it. The words just come bubbling up even though I know it's the last thing I want to talk about, like I'm some thief in the interrogation room who can't help but tell on himself. "You know about me and Daniella, I guess," I say.

Mid-sip, Jasmine freezes. It's just for half a second, but she stops and narrows her eyes, like she's tasted something not quite right in her drink, but then she moves forward, setting the drink down in front of her and exhaling. "I heard," she says, like we're talking about some little random thing in the news. "Marion East is a big school, but it's still a high school. When people hook up, it doesn't stay a secret." I'm tempted to go through the whole drama with her, let her know just what's gone down and how Daniella's clinging now. But Jasmine shuts

Slump 187

it all down. "You might need to talk to somebody about her," she says, "but, Derrick, I'm not the one."

"I know," I say. "I'm sorry."

"Well, I forgive you," she says. "Looks like I probably always will." She finishes her drink and then stands. *Time to go.*

Outside, as we're heading for her car, she slips. Just a little patch of ice on the sidewalk, but she about goes down. I catch her by her arm and steady her. For a second, we're pulled in close to each other and I can feel her warmth, even through our coats. But it can't last. She separates from me and pulls out her keys, punches the button to unlock the car. On the way home, we just listen to music until we get a couple blocks from my house. Then she starts asking about my dad. She wants to know it all, but I just offer up general stuff. "He's okay," I keep saying. "He's getting better."

Finally, when we're stopped at an intersection, she reaches over and grabs my arm. "Derrick, have you talked to him about it?"

I shake my head no.

A pained expression washes across Jasmine's face, one far more troubling than that little flash I saw when I mentioned Daniella. "Derrick," she says. "You've got to talk to him. You've got to. You've just got to."

Jasmine's never told me anything but the truth.

23.

It hits me as soon as I walk in the door, that unmistakable smell of meat hitting heat. The Howe game tips in a couple hours, so I'm not going to overdo it, but my mouth starts watering. I march toward the kitchen.

I round the corner and there, apron and all, is Uncle Kid. I can see the bowl off to the side where he had the steaks marinating. He says hello to me but doesn't look up from the stovetop where he's got three burners going with three pans full of steaks. There are several more stacked on a plate beside the stove, the marinade dripping off of them.

My mom is in the corner with her hands on her hips, like she's been banished to a time-out in her own kitchen. Jayson comes out from his room, the aroma luring him from his Xbox. Then, behind him, comes my dad. He's off the crutches. Free to go back to work. But he can't drive yet with his meds, and he's still limping pretty bad. It keeps him pretty prickly all the time. When he turns the corner and sees Kid, he just shakes his head.

"Sidney," he says. "What are you doing?"

"I'm making everyone dinner! Five steaks, big brother.

Seriously good cuts." He tilts his head toward my mom. "I thought maybe Kaylene could pull together a salad to go with it?" He jerks his thumb toward Dad. "Gotta make sure to healthy it up with some greens for you."

Weariness fills my dad's face. He's been down this road so many times with his brother. It's like the more enthusiastic Kid gets, the more he shows outward signs of good times, the surer my dad is that something's about to go really wrong. "No, Sidney," Dad says, "I mean what are you doing? I'll buy that you scraped enough together to help us with milk and bread. But steaks? Where are you getting the money for that?"

Uncle Kid doesn't answer. He just flips the steaks, one by one. Then he goes to the fridge and pulls out a stick of butter, starts cutting off a few pats to put on the steaks. He mutters something to himself that we can't quite make out, but there's an audible *could just say thanks* at the end.

"Sidney!" my dad shouts. His voice reverberates in the kitchen. The window panes tremble with the force. When we all look to him there's a tremor evident in his hand—from anger this time, not any seizure. "You've helped us, and we've thanked you. But if you don't tell me where you're getting the money from, then you can just take those steaks back where you got 'em."

Uncle Kid shakes his head to himself. Out of the corner of my eye, I see Jayson edge toward Mom. She loops an arm around his shoulder as if to protect him. There's never been a gym—not even for a tie game with the clock dying—as tense as this kitchen is right now.

"Does it really matter?" Kid asks.

"Yes," Dad says. His voice is calmer now, but he's not about to let Kid off the hook.

Kid shrugs. "I got a job," he says. "Okay?"

Dad smiles, then takes a deep breath. "Where are you working, Sidney?"

"Why's it matter?"

"Because it does. Where are you working?" I recognize that tone in Dad's repeated question—he thinks Kid's lying and wants to pin him down to see if the story holds.

"Faces," Kid says. Mom and Dad look at each other, both searching for some kind of meaning in that response. Then they look back at Kid. He doesn't even wait for them to ask the question. He talks while he tends to the steaks. "Faces. It's a bar. Way down on Keystone. I got a job tending bar. My friend Brownlee hooked me up because his uncle owns the place. So that's all. I'm not doing anything that will shame you, brother. Okay?"

It's a solid answer. But something in Dad's expression still shows some dissatisfaction. He cocks his head and peers at Kid. "Don't you need a license to tend bar?" he asks.

Kid nods his head up and down in an exaggerated fashion, almost like a player who's trying to get the crowd going. "Yep. Yep. You do," he says. Then he turns to my parents. "But have either of you ever been in Faces? Jesus, either of you ever been to that intersection at night?" My parents' silence tells Kid that they haven't. "Well. There are places that follow the rules, places where people order drinks that take a damn scientist to make. Let's just say that Faces ain't that kind of establishment."

Slump 191

Dad, still doubtful, stays after him, claiming that there's still no way he can afford this on a bartender's salary.

"Look," Kid says, growing exasperated. "People talk when they drink. And the things some of those guys say they don't want repeated. So they tip well. Got it?"

There's silence in the kitchen again, filled up by the sound of Kid pulling the steaks from the pans, then slapping down fresh ones, sizzling at high volume. My parents look at each other again. Finally my mom shrugs at my dad. *What else can you say?* it seems to suggest. She pats Jayson on the shoulder and points him toward the table. He sits down. We all follow suit, leaving Kid to tend the steaks. Then she starts pulling together a salad, like Kid asked a while ago. But midway through chopping a carrot, she stops and turns to him. "Sidney, I'm sorry. We should have trusted you. But if that was the answer, why didn't you just say that a month ago? Having a job is a *good* thing."

Kid nods again. He lifts one of the steaks with his tongs, but puts it back down, not ready to flip it just yet. "Ahhhh," he says. "I didn't want to go ruining my reputation."

At Howe, we stick to Coach's script. He wants a grind? We'll just go ahead and grind. But it's more of a grind than even he might expect. Devin re-tweaks his wheel mid-second, and Reynolds just comes in and falls apart. I'm beginning to think there's no helping the kid. I can't get a look to save my life, and whenever Moose gets a touch, he's got three guys hanging on him.

Halftime: 20-18, Howe. End third: 28-27, Howe. So we slog back out there for the fourth, ready to keep on slugging it out. Only this is no prize fight. It has the feeling of some back alley brawl instead. If I had to bet, I'd say that every player who's seen time has more bruises than buckets on the night. There's no sign of anyone breaking loose.

We get a deuce from Fuller. I get a little runner in the lane. Moose gets a put-back. That's it. But Howe's got their own issues, and it's enough to put us up 33-32 late. Howe ball.

Their coaches call in a play from the sidelines, but whatever they called it doesn't do any good. They run their three man baseline, but Fuller sticks him and there's no shot. He kicks it back out to my man, and I dig into him. He's no shooter, but I'm not taking any chances now. Finally, they pop Reynolds' man flying to the wing, but when he catches, he hesitates instead of firing. Then, remembering the clock's running down, he chucks an off-balance three that clangs off the crotch, bounding way out to the perimeter. Howe controls it and all of a sudden they're in panic mode. Out of the corner of my eye, I see their coach signaling time-out, but in the madness—guys cutting this way and that, the crowd screaming for them to shoot—they don't see it. My man launches from twenty-five and I get a piece, so it falls like a rock at the baseline. Howe saves it to their three man who fires a wild three— off again, ricocheting all the way to the other side. Their two man gets one more look, but now he chokes it back, kicking it to one of their bigs in the corner instead. He's got no choice, so he fires up an air-ball that, at last, Moose wrestles away. When they hack him and the whistle blows, I look up and it's over. Well, not totally. But with two ticks left, they'd need a full-court heave.

Moose rattles in the first. He misses the second, but in their hurry to grab the rebound they mishandle it. The rock trickles out of bounds with one tick left. Our ball. The Howe faithful start streaming out into the Indianapolis cold. I sigh in relief. It's a win. But damn if it feels like it. I mean, can you really say you beat someone if that's all the fight they could put up?

In the locker room Coach tells us it's progress. *Baby steps*, he tells us. Whatever. On the bus ride home, there's less chatter than after most losses. I'm pretty sure every man on our roster is pretty sick of taking baby steps.

24.

Wes texts me: *What am I gonna do?* I think of what to say, but he hits me right back: *She won't even text me.* My boy's coming unraveled over Iesha. I start to text him, but before I hit send he hits me again: *What I gonna do, D?*

I finally get enough breathing room to get some messages through. I tell him we'll hash it out tomorrow night, that he's got to just cool it. I don't say it, but if he's texting Iesha as frantically as he is me, then she's gonna do all she can to shake herself free. I know, because when I look up from my phone as the bus pulls back into Marion East, I see a car I know in the parking lot—it's Daniella, waiting on me.

"Good win tonight, boys," Bolden says. "Way to gut it out. But we got Pike coming in here tomorrow night. Gonna take even more guts to win that one."

It'll take more than 34 points too, I want to say, but I'll just worry about Pike tomorrow night. As soon as I file off the bus, my main problem gets out of her car and calls my name, acting like it's totally cool that she's there crowding.

I take a deep breath and walk over.

"Hey, Daniella," I say. "What you up to?"

She acts all offended. "I can't see my man after his game?"

That phrase—*my man*—makes me wince. I'm not anyone's man, certainly not Daniella's, but at the same time I feel sorry for her if she thinks so.

"Look," I say, but I just trail off. The other players stream off the bus. A few look my way. At least none of them gives me any grief about Daniella. They're all just ready to get free for a Friday night. And then I think, *Why not? Why get so hung up on what people think of Daniella?* I mean, here she is—wanting me—looking real good on the weekend. Even as I tell myself these things though, my heart's not in it.

"We need to talk, don't we?" Daniella says. I nod, but I can't make eye contact with her. She opens her passenger door with a quick jerk—the sound of metal-on-metal screeching into the night—and tells me to get in. "I know somewhere we can go," she says.

My front door is closed, and my hand trembles a little as I go to unlock it. Through the window, a flickering light tells me someone's up watching television. I say a silent little prayer that whoever it is will click it off and go to bed. I don't want to see anyone.

I intended to break it off. The whole car ride I kept formulating what to say—just the right phrases to let her know it was done without sounding too cruel. Daniella didn't say anything as we drove. She just kept flipping through songs on her iPod and smiling at me. She cruised downtown, finally pulling into a dim parking lot right under I-65. There were a few other cars, but no lights, no signs of life.

"So, Derrick," she said, "what you want to tell me?" But as she said that, she leaned over, breathing on my neck. And her hand slid to my thigh.

We did a lot of things in that dark parking lot, but breaking up wasn't one of them. And now I feel sick. I can still smell her perfume on my clothes. Every time I do, I feel like I'm going to pass out—partly because I can't believe I let it happen and partly because I want to text her to do it all over again. Afterward, we sat there in the dark. We weren't far from where 65 and 70 merge, all that traffic criss-crossing our city on the way to distant places. Daniella said she thought it was the saddest place on earth. "The middle of the city, in the middle of this state, in the middle of the country," she said. "Those highways are just waiting to take people places, but it makes me feel like I'll never get out of here."

"You want out?" I asked.

She nodded. "More than anything." But then she caught herself, not wanting to be some drag, and she kissed me again and smiled and drove me home.

That light inside our house keeps flickering, so I go ahead and unlock the door. I mutter a quick *Hey* to whoever's in the living room and try to slide down the hall to my room. But my dad calls my name. He tells me to come in and sit down. I have no choice but to obey. When I sink back into the couch, he clicks off the television, sits upright in his chair and snaps on a lamp. The light floods the room and burns my eyes a little bit.

"Heard you won," he says, casual as anything.

"If you can call that a win," I sigh. The way we're playing disgusts me, and I can't hide it.

Slump   197

My dad snorts at my reaction. "Wait a minute," he says. "I thought you were all about winning. What happened to the player I knew?"

I pop off a little more loudly than I want. "This team! We could be so good, but it's like I've got to carry everyone. We should have beat Howe by thirty."

My dad nods and pinches up his mouth. His eyes go down and to the right, a look he gets when he's mulling what to say. Then, almost as an afterthought, he reaches down and gives a quick rub of his bad leg. "I don't know much about basketball," he starts, "but when you say you're carrying everyone, does that mean you're scoring all the points?"

"Nah. Moose was our leading scorer, but—"

He cuts me off. "So you must get all the rebounds? Or maybe you have to guard the other team single-handedly?"

"That's not what I mean, Dad. I mean—"

He puts his hand up again. "Maybe you mean you're running the practices and coming up with the game plans and teaching all the young players so they can get better. Maybe you've taken Reynolds and Fuller under your wing to help them along."

This time I don't respond. *Shit.* My dad hasn't been to a game in months, and he's going to lecture me about the team? I know he's hurting, but it just makes me seethe. He must sense it because he doesn't keep on. He leans back in his chair and folds his hands in his lap, tilts his head back and closes his eyes like he's going to sleep.

Just as I'm about to get up, he speaks again, not even opening his eyes. "I've been absent on you, son. I've been here, but I've been absent." Now he opens his eyes again. He leans forward and looks at me intensely. "But I've got to tell you something you don't want to hear.

Derrick, you're not carrying anyone." He pauses to let the words sink in. "Neither am I," he adds. "No, everyone's been carrying me. Have you noticed your mom busting her ass to keep this house together? You notice your uncle getting a job so he can help pay for our food? You notice Jayson helping me with my exercises? Or your friend Wes and that kid Reynolds coming over to take your mind off things? Or maybe Coach Bolden taking it easy on you?" I must flinch at that last bit, because he smiles. "Your mom told me everything. How Bolden and Murphy came to the hospital that night. How—"

And now he trails off. He starts to choke up, thinking about all that's gone down, and I get that old burning shame. I can't take it to see him get emotional. I almost resent him for it. We sit in silence for another minute. It's so quiet I can hear him breathing. I can barely take it.

I get up and slink toward my room, fling myself down onto my bed. *Damn it all.* I mean, I won a basketball game and got laid on a Friday night—the stuff pretty much every sophomore in Indiana dreams of—and things still feel all fouled up.

I climb back off the bed. I know there's something I've got to do. When I round the corner to the living room, I almost bump straight into Dad, who's limping off to bed himself. He steadies himself against the wall. "You okay, son?" he asks.

"Yeah," I say. I look down. When a car goes past, the headlights seep in through the windows and wash us, just for a second, in their brightness. I look back up and meet Dad's eyes.

Neither one of us knows what to say, but at last I feel bubbling up in me all the millions of things I've meant to say to him. How scared I was for him. How ashamed I was of myself for not being able to

Slump 199

say that. The thing is, I know I won't be able to say it—not just quite right—even now. Still, I point back to the living room. "You too tired to stay up and talk for a while, Dad?"

He smiles at me. "I got all night, Derrick," he says.

We tread back out to the living room and sit in silence until our eyes adjust to the darkness. Even now, I don't know where to begin.

"Now tell me about the girl," Dad says.

"What?"

He actually laughs, a short, sharp belly laugh that I think might wake up Mom and Jayson. "Derrick, you're sixteen. You don't hide this stuff well. You think we don't know what's going on?"

I sink back into the couch, resigned to the fact that there's no getting around the truth. I tell my dad what's up with Daniella, leaving out some details but providing enough for him to know the deal. My folks aren't fools. They didn't expect I was going to stay some pure virgin until my wedding day, but even as I talk to my dad I picture my mom's expression when he relays all this to her. Which, no doubt, he will.

When I finish, Dad cocks his head at me. "How do you feel about this girl, son?"

"Feel? I mean…"

That's all the answer Dad needs. He leans up in his chair just a little bit more, the springs creaking underneath him. "You can't do that to her, Derrick. You can't take advantage of a girl."

That gets my back up a bit. "It's not like she doesn't want it," I tell Dad. "I don't see how I'm taking advantage."

He raises his eyebrows and pulls his head back a little. "You don't see how? Okay." And with that he leans back again. I know that's not the

Kevin Waltman

end. He waits a few seconds and then points toward the hallway. "All that mail you have piling up in your room, all those brochures from all those schools? It's just the beginning, Derrick. Soon enough they'll be calling you, texting you—in your ear all day every day. And they'll be offering up things to you, just about anything you can dream of. It'll be there for the taking. But it won't be right to take it. If you can't see that sometimes it's not right to take things just because they're being offered, then you're headed down a different path than your mother and I expected for you. You need to look that girl in the eye and tell her the truth."

He doesn't raise his voice. He doesn't even tweak it at the end like some cold parting shot. He just says it all matter-of-fact. And, man, that kills me. It's no breeze being the son of Thomas and Kaylene Bowen. There are some dads who would listen to what I had to say and tell me just to use Daniella up until I got tired of it. Or tell me to take what I can get from schools, because you only get one go-round, and there's no sense in making things harder on yourself. I think about all those NBA stars decorating the walls in my room. No way all of them denied themselves. No way they all took the hard road. But I guess that's not the point. I look back at my dad—see him still waiting on my response, and then I realize—here he is, still helping me, even when I've not been there for him. Being the son of Thomas and Kaylene Bowen is no breeze, but it does mean I know right from wrong. And when I remember that, I'm more of a man. Or at least it makes me closer to being a man than I am doing all those things with Daniella.

"I know you're right," I say. Dad nods. There's no judgment in his face, just understanding that what I'm acknowledging doesn't come easy. "And, Dad?" I go on. "I'm sorry."

Slump 201

"For what?"

"For not being there for you," I say. I start to choke on the words again, so I just plunge on before I bail again. "For not talking to you in the hospital. For not helping you with your exercises. For not doing— God, for not doing *anything*."

He shakes his head, then smiles. "Derrick, don't you see? You're talking to me now." And there it is—these things I've held against myself, Dad never did. He never would. "You're a good person, Derrick," he says. "And I know you'll always do the right thing. But you have to understand—I also know you're a sixteen-year-old guy. Which means that before doing the right thing, you might wear out every other possible option." He laughs at his own joke, then his face straightens again. "Your grandpa—on your mom's side—he used to have this saying. He'd say, 'All a man can do is his dirty best.'"

He stands up and motions to me. I get up and walk to him. He gives me a hug. I'm not ashamed at all to accept it. "Let's do our dirty best from now on," he whispers to me. And I can feel, standing there, that even if I'm already three inches taller than him, he's the one with all the strength.

Kevin Waltman

PART III

25.

There was Wes blasting my phone again and me texting him down from the ledge and promising him over and over again that we'd hang after the Pike game tonight.

There was Devin in street clothes, foot back in a walking cast, his face as long as if he'd just been told his cousin passed.

There was Bolden and Murphy huddling in the corner, casting looks over their shoulders at Reynolds, trying to figure out their best strategy without Devin.

And now there's the blast of our fight song, the buzz of our crowd. They might not be thrilled with our style of play, but there's new promise in the air. It's the first of February and today the snow melted. Anyone who's been through an Indiana winter knows we're not out of it yet, that a week from now we might be shoveling out from a fresh foot. But seeing the streets wet with run-off, seeing the ground peek out from beneath its cover for once—it gives you hope.

There's the refs stretching their hammies, telling all the players to have a good, clean one. And there's Major Newsome, all-city, all swagger, already jawing pre-tip. I played with Newsome on the AAU circuit, but he and I didn't exactly make friends. He didn't care for the fact that I wouldn't pass it to him every time, and I just flat didn't care about him. Newsome yaps at Moose a little, but can't get a rise out of our big man. He bumps Reynolds, trying to intimidate him. Then he heads my way.

"Gonna be fun running you off your own court," he says.

I don't even look his way.

"Yeah, just like AAU. Too damn full of yourself to even talk," he says. "Or maybe you ain't got shit to say."

My jaw clenches, but aside from that I don't react.

The refs are telling us to get set. The lead official is about ready to toss it up, but Newsome's not done. "Gonna put the hurt on tonight. Shit. Trying to check me with some slapdick freshman? And the mighty D-Bow in the middle of a sophomore slump? Shit. Not even the best point we've faced all year. That kid Kernantz in Evansville would turn you around all over the floor." This time I look at him. He eats it up, thinking he's in my head. "Yeah, you hear me."

I smile at him. I wink. Because what Major Newsome doesn't know is that there was also a sit-down between me and Bolden. He caught me just after he wrapped his pre-game talk. As the other players filed out for warm-ups, he looked me in the eye. "Don't try to get in a race tonight," he said.

"I feel you, Coach," I said. I looked right at him. "I know you're right about the way we need to play, especially without Devin."

"Good."

"But can I say one thing?" I asked.

"Say it, Derrick."

I took a deep breath, but I kept eye contact. "You know Pike's going to get theirs. I just want to know that if I get a chance—maybe just one-on-one before everyone gets down—can I attack the rim?"

I expected him to say *No*. I'd promised myself I wouldn't blink when he did. Instead he put his hand on my shoulder. "I lost some sleep last night thinking about this very thing," he said. "You know, it's possible—just maybe—that I get carried away with wanting you to grind it out." He gave me a pop on the shoulder. "You get a run at it, go for it, Derrick. But I'll do you one better. We spent a lot of hours last year working on your shot. When you hit a rough patch this year, we abandoned it. Hell, I kind of made you. But tonight you get a look—a *good* one, you hear me?—you stick it to 'em."

Yeah, Newsome doesn't know any of that. But he's about to learn a few things.

Moose gets the tip to Fuller, so we get first crack. Fuller throws it ahead to Reynolds, but there's nothing there, so he circles it back out top to me. Even on first touch, they're sinking back so far I've got a look from about twenty-one feet. I'm tempted, but I know not to rush. So we run the offense. Hit Stanford at the high post. He kicks to Fuller baseline. He enters to Moose, who gets doubled. Then a kick-out to Reynolds, who gives a shot fake. It doesn't get Newsome to leap, but he does draw him in tight enough that Reynolds can get by. He's going nowhere, but when my man jumps to help on the drive, I float to the open wing. "Ball ball ball!" I shout. Reynolds is slow to see it, so my man has a chance to recover. Doesn't matter. I dip my shoulder and blow by, then dish to Stanford for a quick deuce and—*bang*—we're up

2-0 and our crowd's hopping. I make sure to arc toward Newsome as I hustle back. I don't say a word, just nod real long and slow at him.

"Shit," he seethes. "Ain't nothin'."

Problem is, he's right. I go out to check their point guard, but he gives it up to Newsome early. He doesn't even have to throw much of a move on Reynolds. It's just a quick bounce right to get Reynolds to turn his hips, then a silky pull-up from twenty-two. Their lead.

"All night!" he woofs on the way back down. "You got nothin' for that!" A ref tells him to cool it. But if Reynolds can't put up more of a fight than that, then Newsome will back up every bit of the smack he runs.

On our end, we stay patient. Look for Moose. Nothing. Reverse to Fuller. Nothing. Give to Reynolds and he drives into a mess, so I go rescue him and re-set it. Even as I circle it back out top, I can hear Newsome woofing at Reynolds—"Yeah, you best give that up," he says. But while he's yapping, Moose is busy sealing his man. I hit him right in time, and he muscles one up before the double arrives. We're up 4-3, and our crowd goes nuts. Back-to-back buckets out of half-court sets! Hell, they probably feel like they're watching the Pacers.

But we hit the other end, and it's the same story. They just flatten out and let Newsome work. This time Reynolds stays up tight on that drive, so Newsome has to go to his bag of tricks. Thing is, that bag's deep. He crosses behind his back to shake Reynolds and lets fly just behind the stripe. Bottom. 6-4 and Newsome just howls, pursing his lips up toward the rafters like he can barely take how good he is.

I would very much like to shut that kid up. But it's not going to happen in the first quarter, so I bring it up and get us set. After a few passes, Coach calls time. As we shuffle to the bench, our crowd cheers

Slump 207

in encouragement, except that everyone in the house knows that if we don't find some answer for Newsome, it's gonna get ugly fast. They saw the Hamilton game. We can't keep up an offensive clip like this, but a guy like Newsome can.

When we sit, Coach looks at us so intensely it's like the eyes are about to pop out of his head. First, he starts with Reynolds. "You like having that punk yap at you?" Reynolds shakes his head. "Well, what are you gonna do about it?" When there's no answer, Coach looks around the huddle like someone else ought to jump in.

When nobody does, I backhand Reynolds on his arm. "You good," I say. "Nobody's asking you to stop him cold. Just stay in front and keep a hand in his face. He's not gonna go all Kevin Durant on you." It's not the greatest pep talk ever, but Reynolds nods in earnest, sets his jaw a little like he's ready to dig in harder.

Then Bolden makes a sweeping motion with his hand, ushering Coach Murphy into the center of the huddle. A strange move. Murphy smiles and puffs his chest out a little. He doesn't get center stage very often. "You all know anything about me as a player?" he asks. Of course nobody does, so he plunges on. "Well that's because I only scored about four a game for my career. But, ooh, I could guard. You know who Zach Randolph is?" he asks. Now we nod. He's only the best big to come out of Indiana in a generation. "My senior year I got matched up with him. Let me tell you something. I outscored him! Eight to six, baby." He sees the shock spreading through the huddle. "I swear on my grandma's grave! And I'll tell you how. Boys, we beat the hell out of him. Just beat him up. And I promise you this: Freakin' Major Newsome is about a million times softer than Zach Randolph. So listen.

That kid doesn't touch the ball, doesn't dribble the ball, doesn't make a cut, hell, that kid doesn't so much as breathe without somebody putting a body on him. You hear me?"

We nod. Then the buzzer sounds, calling us back to the court, but we don't get away without a parting shot from Bolden. He points to Reynolds, then to Fuller, then to Stanford. "You got five fouls each. Don't be afraid to use every damn one of them."

The first time down, when Newsome cuts baseline Fuller catches him square in the chest with his shoulder. Newsome lands in the front row. While there's a little Hollywood in his act, it's enough for the refs to warn Fuller that he'll get a flagrant next time around. Newsome's teammates help him up. Even before he's on his feet, he's bitching to the refs that they can't let stuff fly.

"Shut your mouth and play," Moose tells him.

That gets Newsome's back up, but he knows better than to tangle with the big man. Even as he puffs out his chest, he's glancing for the refs to step in. They do, restoring order, but Newsome's just in for more. He gets the rock on the wing and squares Reynolds up. He gets him to leave his feet on a pump-fake and then drives into the lane. Mistake. Moose doesn't even let Newsome come to a jump-stop before he puts him on the hardwood. Again, it's just short of a flagrant, but this time there's no acting—when Moose bodies him up, Newsome drops like a rock. And this time he's not yapping as he gets up.

Next time he catches, he gets past Reynolds again, but instead of driving into the paint, he pulls up from seventeen and misses. Just like that, it's clear—Newsome can ball out, but he wants no part of Fuller and Moose. And, yeah, our crowd lets him have it on the way back

Slump 209

down the court. Newsome acts like he loves it—nodding to the crowd and motioning for them to get louder—but about that time Stanford catches with a back screen—totally clean—and puts him on the floor for the third time in a minute. On that one, our crowd hits a volume they haven't reached all winter.

By mid-third quarter, it's still tight. We're nursing a 33-32 lead, Pike ball. And I'll give Newsome credit. Nothing's come easy since those first minutes, but he's stayed after it, methodically piling up the fouls on us and calmly sinking the freebies at the stripe.

Reynolds is riding pine with four, so Fuller is tangling with Newsome now with Jones back at the three. Fuller's doing all he can, but it's a tall order. Pike keeps setting screen after screen. Fuller slips through one, then another, then another, but finally he gets hung up and grabs at Newsome, who flails his arms as if he's been shot. Theatrics aside, it's an easy whistle, and that's the fourth on Fuller too.

Our crowd works on the ref as he signals the call to the scorer's table. Everyone's getting frustrated that we've been whistled twice as often as Pike, but this is the flipside of Coach Murphy's advice. That's when Coach motions me over. I hustle, since it's Pike's in-bound as soon as the ref is ready, but Coach's message is short.

"Switch with Fuller," he says. "Check Newsome. No more cheap fouls."

I nod, then sprint back to inform Fuller. He nods, but he knows that now he's got to check the point, which is way out of his skill set. I smack him on the back. "You got this," I say. "Just stay low on my guy. He doesn't want to shoot. Just wants to drive. Got it?"

Fuller says he does, and then we're into the action again. Pike keeps looking to feed Newsome, but he has a tougher time getting free against me. He can't shake me on cuts, so he tries posting, but I've been through that action with guys a lot bigger than Newsome. I keep dancing around him—fronting to scare off the entry, then beating him to the other side of the lane so he can't seal me on reversal. Finally he gets a clear out up top. They hand it to him and he dribbles leisurely, sizing me up. I know that behind me everyone's flattening out, so it's just me on an island with Newsome. He grins, like he thinks he's gonna turn me inside out.

A rhythm dribble to the left. A crossover between his legs. A hard dribble right. And nothing. I'm glued to him, and he can't even budge me with a shot fake. "Dead! Dead!" I shout, and everyone else clamps down on their men. All of a sudden I see fear flash in Newsome's eyes. Panicked as a deer in headlights. All he can do his throw up a leaner to beat the five-count, and it barely catches rim.

Stanford controls. He outlets to Jones, who zips it to Fuller in the middle. I fill the right wing and we're off and running. Pike isn't quite back, but Fuller doesn't want to do something stupid, so he pulls up at the top of the key and waits to set the offense. Through habit, I start to head back out toward Fuller to get the ball, but as I do, Pike just flat leaves me. With us switching assignments, they've got themselves crossed up. I'm all alone on the right wing. I clap, but Fuller doesn't need told. He zips it to me. As it's coming my way, I know—this is dagger time.

The thing's true as soon as it leaves my hand. You can feel the crowd collectively inhale as they watch it arc toward the rim. They explode when it finds bottom. Four point lead. As I head back on

Slump 211

defense, I can hear a voice—Bolden's—knifing through the roar: "That's it, Derrick! That's how it's done!"

Pike doesn't call time, but they should. Our crowd's in full-on bully mode, heckling them on every pass. In this kind of tight spot, I know they want Newsome to take the shot so I stay glued. He catches me trailing him and curls to the rim, but he sees Moose, Fuller, and Stanford waiting on him, and he just doesn't have the juice for an attack. Instead, he pulls up and I get a piece from behind.

As I race toward the hash for the outlet, I can see Newsome out of the corner of my eye, whining to the ref. He's got his hands spread wide and he's jawing pretty good, but all that matters to me is that he's left their point guard as the only one back.

Moose catches me right in stride. I see everyone on our bench—Bolden and Murphy included—windmilling their arms telling me to push. *Fellas*, I think, *I don't need told.*

I'm on top of their point guard in a heartbeat. I can see our crowd rising as I push it toward the lane. That guard knows he's got no prayer, so he just bails to avoid the foul, leaving me a free run. And I thunder that thing as hard as I've ever thrown one down in my life. It's like I'm trying to get rid of a whole winter's worth of frustrations with one tomahawk. When I hear that crowd explode in response, I feel freer than I have in months.

This time Pike does call time. But it's too late. I've seen beaten teams before. And Pike's beat. For good measure, Newsome offers a parting shot at the ref on his way to the huddle. A sharp, shrill whistle pierces the crowd noise. The ref Ts up Newsome. He gives the signal with a little flourish too, like he's been waiting all game to do it.

I thought our crowd couldn't get any louder than they did after my jam, but I was wrong.

"That's what I'm *talking* about!" Moose hollers as we burst into the locker room, fresh from finishing off Pike 53-41.

Even Jones and Reynolds are chest bumping and running smack. Devin limps around gingerly but makes sure to high-five everyone he sees. I sink back at my locker and take it all in. I could puff my chest out and talk trash about how I stuck Newsome down the stretch, or how I shook their whole squad with that rim-rattler. But I don't. I just want to watch my boys living it up, check out our locker room the way it's supposed to be—full of shouts and guys whipping their jerseys into their lockers like proud warriors throwing down their weapons after battle. This is what a win's supposed to look like. Doesn't matter if it's us sticking it to Pike or the Pacers knocking off the Thunder. A locker room after a win—a real good win—is the best place on earth.

Even Bolden can't repress his smile when he walks in. Murphy's busting up behind him. Then Murphy makes a crack we can't hear, but Bolden roars in laughter. This we're not used to. And so we simmer down and try to make sense of the crankiest old coach in the state laughing like he's watching some stand-up routine.

"What up, Coach?" Moose asks. He's mid-way through unlacing his kicks, but he just stops, thrown a little by Coach's levity.

"A man can't live a little after a win?" Coach says. "Boys, I'm too old to chase skirts. This is as good as it gets for me."

Most of us shrug and go back to our business, but Moose isn't

Slump 213

fooled. "Nah," he says. He points back and forth between Bolden and Murphy. "You two are up to something."

Bolden acts all mock-innocent, but then he laughs again. He turns to Murphy, who's standing over by the chalkboard erasing halftime instructions. "Coach? You want to tell them the whole story about how you shut down Zack Randolph?"

Every head in the room swivels toward Murphy. He stops erasing. Looks once at Bolden. Then a sly grin creases his face. "All right," he says. "I didn't tell you all Randolph sat out the second with two fouls." He pauses, scratches his head. "Or that he sat out the fourth because they had us whipped by twenty."

Guys groan, realizing we'd been suckered by that in-game speech. But nobody's actually upset, since it helped us put the clamps on Newsome.

"Hey!" Murphy shouts. "Bottom line's the bottom line. When I was a senior, I outscored Randolph, eight to six. Ain't nothing can take that away from me!"

"Shiiiit," Moose says. "I knew you didn't have that kind of game. Telling lies at us."

Murphy loses it then, cracking up at Moose. And the celebration's back on—almost like we're a team that's clicking.

Kevin Waltman

26.

Give Wes this—no matter how much he sighs around and his bottom lip trembles every time he tries to talk, he doesn't cry. Not once. It's probably because we're in Uncle Kid's car, and Wes doesn't want to look like a chump in front of him. But he spills it all to us. Iesha flat-out deaded him. Just stopped returning texts, calls, everything. And on top of that, he saw her leave the gym tonight pressed up on JaQuentin Peggs, the thugged-out guy who hosted that party a few weeks ago. In other words, a total 180 from Wes.

"Is that what she wants?" he asks. He's riding shotgun as Kid cruises the city, whipping us downtown on Capitol. "I mean, am I supposed to start acting like some banger?"

"Little man, you got to *think* now," Kid says. He's slung back in his seat, steering with just the bottom of his left wrist, rocking a full-on chill pose. That's why I chose Kid. At some point Wes has heard all I've got to say. Kid might not be the best role model, but he knows how to make a person relax. "This guy Peggs? Man, there have been guys like him forever. A real bad-ass at eighteen but headed nowhere."

He gestures toward the dark blocks around us as evidence. Another couple minutes and we'll pass under I-65, and suddenly everything will brighten, but right now the view is bleak. "And what can I say? They get their share. It sucks. But your girl will figure him out soon enough and come running back."

"But what if she doesn't?" Wes asks.

"Hey, if that's who she wants, then that's who she wants. And believe me, if she wants him, then you don't want her."

Wes nods, then leans his head against the passenger window. He admits that Kid's right, but his body language shows how dissatisfying Kid's take is. I get it. Hell, everyone gets it. Just because you can't change a girl's mind doesn't stop you from wishing you could.

"Don't sweat it, Wes," I chime. "She'll be begging you to take her back soon enough."

"Yeah," he says, but it's an empty sound.

I lean forward and backhand Kid's shoulder. "Kid, man, hit Wes up with that song," I say. Kid takes his eyes off the road and looks at me quizzically. He doesn't say a thing, just waits on me to explain, and I realize if I don't start talking he's gonna just cruise all the way down Capitol without looking at the road. "The one you played for me, Kid. That 'ex girl' cut."

Kid smiles. "Ahhh, yeah," he says, like he's been reminded about some great exploit of his own back in the day. He digs into the glove box, the car swerving into the neighboring lane as he does. Cars all around us lay on their horns, but Kid doesn't even react. Finally, he finds what he wants and pops in the song. "This is your creed, Wes. Right here," he says, pointing to the stereo.

The song starts. At first Wes isn't feeling it. But as soon as the rhymes start flowing, he perks up. "Hey, I know who this is," he says. Figures. Wes is an encyclopedia of beats, even the ones laid down before we were born. "My dad used to play it."

And just like that, Kid wins. He's changed the whole vibe in the car. He rolls his window down, dead of winter, and raps half a verse to some scared white lady at a stoplight. It's all Wes and I can do not to fall out. It's cruel, sure, but that woman looks like she'd shatter to pieces if she so much as turned her head a centimeter toward Kid.

By the time we roll past the Capitol building, Wes is Wes again. He's straightened back up in his seat. We're all re-hashing the Pike game, cracking jokes and feeling good. Maybe too good, because a police car swoops in behind us, as if it's against the law for us to have some fun. Or maybe that woman Kid rattled called us in when she turned off. Doesn't matter. We cruise past Lucas Oil Stadium, home of the Colts. When Kid kicks a left on McCarty, the cop hangs a right. I don't know if Kid even noticed, he's so busy rapping to Wes about how to "rope females," but I did. Then again, Kid's probably pretty used to police in the rear view. Kid's always been a little more JaQuentin Peggs and a lot less Wes Oakes.

Kid takes the ramp onto 70 and puts down the hammer, as much as his old bucket has one. We rip north on 65 before he eases back into the near Northside. We backtrack east to our neighborhood. Pretty soon there we are on Patton again. Kid throws it into park, letting us know our night's through. "Remember," he tells Wes, "Ex girl to the next girl. Ex to the next."

As soon as we're out the door, Kid speeds away with such urgency

Slump

it's pretty clear that his night's not over. Maybe he really does have the next girl to get to.

"Your uncle's a good guy," Wes says.

"He's that," I tell him. But the end of the ride means my own girl troubles come back to mind. My phone's been lighting up the whole time—texts from Daniella, who, when I told her I was kicking it with the boys instead of coming over, acted like I'd just robbed her mama. I turn to Wes. I knew Kid could shake him out of his funk, but we're too good of friends not to hash it out a little on our own. "You keep your mind off Iesha," I say. "Anyone who treats you that way doesn't deserve you thinking about her."

"I hear you," he says.

I turn to head down to my house, but call back. "But, hey, cool it on Kid's advice. That's all good for a song, but that 'ex to the next' move can backfire."

I chose the bookstore. First, it's my territory. I came to this place every Sunday for who knows how long with my parents, at least before my dad got laid up, so I'm comfortable here. Plus, it wasn't a hard sell to get my mom to drop me off. No parent in the world fusses if their kid wants a ride to the bookstore on a weekend. Plus, when I talked to him about it, Kid hit me up with some advice—if I'm dropping Daniella, I best do it in a public place. Less chance of a scene. Less chance of her getting me off alone and working her spell.

I grab a table over by the coffee stand and crack open a *SLAM*, see what they've got to say about the Pacers' chances of taking the East. But I don't get far. In comes Daniella, and anyone can see the girl *knows.* How could she not? She lowers her eyes as she starts toward me, gazing down like she's walking a tightrope.

The place is crowded. Between the noise of people chatting and placing orders and the whoosh of the espresso machine, I can barely hear Daniella's hello. She sits across from me, looks at me once, then folds her arms across her chest and looks toward the window at people hustling through the cold.

"Hey, Daniella," I say.

No response.

"You want something?" I gesture toward the coffee stand, like maybe one of those pastries in the glass case will make everything okay. A dumb move.

"No, I don't want anything," she snaps. There's a guy standing behind her at the magazine rack. He cocks his head toward us, then moves away. "What do you want, Derrick?" she says.

I hesitate. Part of me just wants to let it slide or—in the most cowardly move possible—just say nothing's wrong, and then ice her out until she gets the picture—but I can't do that.

"Say it!" she says. "Go ahead." She's done looking out the window now, her eyes boring into me.

"Well, if you know what I'm gonna say, then—"

"Say it!" This one's loud and a few more people look, just a quick glance at us before going back to their business.

"It's not gonna work out," I blurt. I keep eye contact with her, so she knows I'm for real. "I mean, us. It's just not clicking."

She leans back, cocking her head and taking me in. "Oh, I see," she says. "Sure seemed to click for you the other night."

"That's different," I say, all defensive. I catch myself looking away, but stop. "I mean, obviously I like that, it's just—"

This time she erupts. "You mean you like fucking me, but you don't want me to be your girlfriend!" It's loud. So loud I bet people up on the second floor heard it. Everyone turns now. While some people are polite enough to go back to their own business, we get a few gawkers. I remind myself that at least the crowd at a bookstore doesn't cross over much with the people who are up on their high school point guards. To them, we're just two more teenagers acting the fool. Still, embarrassment surges into my throat and cheeks, choking away anything I might find to say. Maybe the stares get to her too, because when she starts in again she takes it down a few decibels. "You never really gave me a chance, you know," she says. "I mean, I'd try talking to you. I'd try being something more than a hook-up. But the only way I could get your attention was—" She drifts off then, disgusted at the whole thing. Then she decides to go on the attack once more. "Am I not as proper as Jasmine? Is that it? I don't have my nose far enough in the air like that uppity bitch?"

"Easy," I say, my embarrassment getting flooded out by a surge of anger. "This isn't about her."

"Right," she says. "Right." Then we sit in silence for a little while. I don't know what else I'm supposed to say. Maybe I'm supposed to just get up and leave, but I have this awful feeling that she'd grab at me if I did. I realize I don't really know her that well. And I realize too that she's right. I don't know her because I didn't give us a chance to be anything else. Still, it's over, and she knows it. But she doesn't want to let me off that easy. Then she does something pathetic. She leans across the table, her face contorted in some cross between pain and that expression of seduction she'll give me. "Fine," she says. "We can just do what you want. No strings attached, okay?"

If you'd have told me a few years ago that some girl as stacked as Daniella would just offer herself up like that, no strings attached, I'd have jumped at it. That's the way Jayson still thinks about girls, and I don't blame him. It's just part of the game you've got to figure out—there's no such thing as no strings attached. But besides that, it makes me kind of recoil. The way Daniella all but begs makes me almost hate her a little bit. It's wrong to feel that way, I know, but I can't help it. Then I look at her again, her eyes watery with desperation, and I can see things play out for her—one guy after another just using her up because she lets them, and they won't say no.

"I can't do that," I say. "It's not right. I mean, it's not right for you."

And that sends her over the edge. She stands up from the table and throws her hands in the air. She looks around like maybe she wants something to throw at me, but nothing's there. So she rips the magazine away from my side of the table and flings it down on the floor like a child in full tantrum. "Don't you tell me what's good for me!" she screams. "You don't get to say that!"

Then she storms off, but after only about three steps she wheels back at me. "You think you're so good. But let me tell you, Derrick—" she scans me up and down—"you're no different than any other guy."

Then she makes her exit, leaving me to deal with all the stares. I can hear a couple people laughing. The only thing I can do is pick up the magazine, go pay for it, and leave. I don't even feel angry at her. After all, if I think about it from her perspective what she said at the end is right. For her, I'm just another guy who did her wrong.

Slump 221

27.

We're all just kicking it in the hall after lunch. Just messing. We've scratched out a few wins and things are starting to feel better. The sun streams in through the windows. The teachers seem to go easier on us. All the honeys smile when they pass us. Devin's limp seems a little less severe, like he might make one more run at it yet. I mean, food even tastes better when you win.

Right now, Moose is ragging on Reynolds. He's spinning some story about how Reynolds blocked him out of hooking up at a party on Saturday after the game. Everyone gives us room as we all shuffle down the hall, like we've got some celebrity status. They stand to the side and eye the team while we do our thing. Moose gives Reynolds a good shove, so hard he bumps into a bay of lockers, his shoulder rumbling against it like someone pounding a bass drum. Out of her door comes Mrs. Hulsey, her eyes all squinched up in concern like she thinks this is a real fight. She's been extra crabby this semester. Last time she handed back an exam she smacked me with a D+. She even added a little note that she expected more out of me. Somehow the + made it worse, like she thought she was encouraging me no matter how bad I bombed. I keep that up and Dad won't be the only one walking around our house with a limp.

Now, Moose smiles at her. "No worries, Mrs. H. I'm just teaching this pup he can't be hanging around like some stalker when I'm chatting up a female."

The explanation doesn't seem to please Mrs. Hulsey, but she doesn't say anything. She just gives a quick roll of her eyes like she's disappointed in herself for expecting better from her day. She hangs in her doorway, maybe just to let us know we're still being watched.

"You know," Fuller pops up, "I've been thinking about this thing the football team at my old school did." He straightens his back up real stiff like he's giving some formal speech in class, then nods his head real seriously.

You can just see everyone's shoulders slump down. Here we are, clowning, and Fuller wants to kill it by giving us yet one more talk about his old school. Moose, already worked up from messing with Reynolds, is the first one to turn on Fuller. "Man, you got all this talk about your old school. You're like some seventy-year-old telling stories about how it was back in the day."

Guys laugh, but Fuller plows ahead. It's just how he gets on the court sometimes—makes up his mind he's going to the rim even if every damn body on the floor is standing in his way. "No, I'm serious," he says. "It was cool. The whole team would get up early and go out to breakfast before school. They'd all wear their jerseys on game days. It was pretty dope."

"Yeah," Moose says, flat and sarcastic. "That sounds awesome."

Slump 223

"It was!" Fuller shouts, getting too worked up for his own good. The guys laugh at him again. He's as eager and earnest as he was the first day he showed up. He's just never learned to dial it back, even a little.

"Where the hell did you transfer from anyway?" Stanford asks. He gets his chest puffed out some, knowing Fuller's one guy he can lord over a little. "I've heard so much about it, I figure I ought to know."

Fuller glances down at the floor now, knowing he's just being set up for more. "Columbus," he mutters.

"Columbus where?" Reynolds asks, happy to have everyone piling on someone—anyone—instead of him. Fuller mutters something again, but we can't hear him. "What?" Reynolds asks.

Fuller raises his head and puffs out his chest, refusing to be ashamed now. "Columbus, Mississippi," he barks.

That sends the team into even more laughter. I mean, *Mississippi?* Moose voices what we're all thinking. "What? We supposed to take lessons from some country-ass place where they can't even read?"

Fuller blushes and hangs his head, accepting all the abuse he knew would come his way. And that's when I do something that surprises even myself. "I think we ought to do what Fuller says," I pipe up. I mean, you'd have thought I'd fired a gun in the hallway. Everyone just stops. Looks at me. I've been pretty cold to Fuller all season. We're never going to be tight. He's so straightlaced, it's like he's begging for people to crack on him. But maybe that's why I feel like I need to bail him out now. Besides, the truth is, I kind of like the idea. "I mean, why not? We could wear our practice shirts or something. Be kind of nice to all get together. A show of force."

Moose shakes his head. I can tell he's about to turn on me now, give me all he's got about how stupid an idea this is. But before he can get started, Fuller jumps in again. "Moose, one more thing—where I transferred from, all the cheerleaders came too."

That stops Moose cold. You can practically see the images flashing through his brain—our cheerleaders still sleepy-eyed, only minutes removed from their warm beds, cozying up to him on a gameday morning. He cocks his head, then glances around at all of us. Even Devin, his fellow senior, knows that what Moose says next is the verdict for the team.

"I feel you, Fuller," he says. "Let's do it. Just don't expect me to be eating grits or any of that other Southern stuff."

"Cool," Fuller says, again too eager. I can see Moose kind of grimace at Fuller's enthusiasm, but it's too late to backtrack now.

Mrs. Hulsey, who's been eyeing us the whole time, gives us a reminder—a quick cough and a glance at her watch—that next period's about to start. We start to scatter, like we're breaking huddle, and merge into the rest of the students doing their school thing. But I shout back over my shoulder to everyone, "Hey! I know the place."

The Donut Shop. North Keystone. Used to be part of our weekend ritual before Dad's accident, and I've been missing it. So I insist and insist until this becomes the gameday breakfast place for us.

I get there first on Friday morning, day of the Warren Central game. I bring my boys Wes and Jayson with me. Well, the truth is Wes had to drive, but I want to get him back among the living again so he'll quit moping about Iesha. Sitting next to some cheerleaders might help. And Jay—well, I know I've been neglecting my little

Slump 225

brother. As soon as I suggested it to him, my parents all but made it mandatory. I think they're just happy to have him under someone else's watch for one morning.

It's early, still dark out. School starts at 7:45, so if everyone's going to eat and get back down to Marion East in time, we had to make it this early. I rub my eyes and yawn, and just for a second start to re-think my support for Fuller's idea. The restaurant feels cold too, like they keep their prices low by refusing to turn on the heat. Then that glass door swings open and in comes Moose with two cheerleaders, Marianne Marks and Kelle Burke, and the whole vibe changes.

"D-Bow!" Moose shouts, loud as if we were in the middle of the game. Everyone else turns to look, wondering what the hell the ruckus is about, but Moose just eats it up. The more eyes on him, the more he can show out for Marianne and Kelle. "And my boy Wes," he hollers and walks over to give Wes a fist bump. You can almost see Wes' shoulders lift, like he's infected by Moose's confidence. I start to introduce Moose to Jayson but he cuts me off, telling me he knows who the little man is, how he hears him heckling the other team every night. Then he turns back to his girls. "You two just do your thing and go order. Whatever you want, I got it."

He drags a couple chairs over to our booth and then flat hooks Wes up. Jayson sits on my side, but when Marianne and Kelle come over, he motions for Wes to stand so they can slide into the booth. Then he says, "Girls, let my boy Wes squeeze in. I'ma sit on the end and save this chair—" he pats the other one he pulled over— "for Devin. You three just get cozy. It's a cold morning, you know."

Wes blushes and swallows hard, like he's about to panic he's so sprung. I know the kid's out of practice talking to girls so I just mouth to him when nobody sees: *Be cool*. That silence he's worried about filling up evaporates quick though. The glass door swings open again, and there's Fuller, followed by Reynolds and Stanford. Then it's a parade over the next few minutes. Devin and a couple more cheerleaders. Jones and a couple sophomores who never get minutes. A couple more cheerleaders and their friends. Pretty soon the whole Donut Shop is transformed into a mini-Marion East, buzzing with chatter, our school colors—our jerseys pulled over long sleeves, the cheerleaders all in school sweatshirts, everyone else just rocking our red and green—filling the whole front of the restaurant. It's noisy. A few customers kind of make faces over their coffee and newspapers, like they didn't expect a bunch of teenagers to be kicking it in this place at quarter till seven. But the manager seems happy to see us. Maybe he senses a ritual in the making because he comes over three different times to make sure everyone's taken care of.

It's all good. I mean, this is the kind of thing I had in mind for this season. This, plus about 20 more points a game for us, but there's no room to complain.

Then the door opens one more time, and I get a chill all the way down my spine. It's not from the cold outside, but from who comes in—Daniella Cole.

She's got her hair pulled back tight in braids, and she's not wearing any make-up. Her eyes are puffy too, like she just woke up. She seems dazed. For a second, I think maybe she's just there by coincidence. A few other people see her, but they don't say a word. Moose shifts in his chair so she can't see his face. I lower my head like

Slump

I'm studying something real fascinating on the table. Otherwise, the Donut Shop keeps on humming—people yapping away, the manager instructing a worker on keeping things organized, the hiss and pop of hash browns in oil. Part of me gets a wild feeling, because just the sight of her brings back all those other scenes—at JaQuentin's party, in her car, at her mom's apartment—scenes I've played over and over in my head in weaker moments when I've been tempted to text her. But I don't give in. Not at night when I can't sleep and certainly not now. *Just go on*, I think to myself, willing Daniella to move along almost like I'm praying. *Just let me be.*

Then I feel a presence at the side of our table. I know what's up, but I wait an extra second, like maybe she'll get the picture and go away. No luck. She taps her foot on the linoleum floor a couple times. There's no more ignoring her. When I look up, she squeezes in between Devin and Moose so she can stand right against the table. I'm 6'3" and used to looking down on folks everywhere I go, but now I see what it's like from someone else's angle. With me seated, Daniella looms over me, staring down in judgment. I should know by now that you can't just wish things—or people—to go away. You have to deal.

Every once in a while you get caught on the court—you're the only one back against a break, and you're off balance. There's nothing you can do but just take the hit that's coming. That's how I feel with Daniella standing there, with what feels like the whole restaurant waiting to hear what she'll say. And considering how she gave me that parting shot at the bookstore last week, it's not going to be pretty. She cocks her head to the side like she's sizing me up. She folds her arms. But then instead she looks to Marianne and Kelle. "They're not worth it," she tells them. "These boys who think they're *ballers*. You'd be better off trying to make a man out of *him*," she says and jerks her hand toward Jayson.

Then, point made, she struts off. Not even a look over her shoulder as she heads for the counter. There's a second of silence, and then Moose looks at me. "Oooooooh, D-Bow. You must have done a number. Girl can't let it go." He laughs, and Devin immediately joins in. Wes grabs me by the shoulder and shakes me a little, like I'm some champ who just needs encouragement in between rounds. Even Marianne and Kelle snipe about how trashy Daniella is, how she never learns.

Daniella is still at the counter. She hasn't turned around, but I know she can hear some of this. I see her glance, just once, toward the door, like maybe she should just bail since this hasn't really gone the way she hoped. As angry as I am at her for trying to blow up the morning, I know she's not the one in the wrong. I think back about what she said that night under the interstate, how she just wanted out. If I'd have been paying attention, I would have known she meant more than just out of this city. "Let it go," I tell the table. "Daniella's got a legit gripe. Maybe she wouldn't act like she does if guys like me would act a little better."

This hushes the table again. Marianne and Kelle recoil a little bit. They're not used to guys saying that they're wrong. Not ever. So I guess if I ever had any plan to make a move on them, that's gone too. Jayson, though, sees an opening. "See!" he blurts, in essence to Kelle and Marianne, but loud enough so the whole damn place can hear. "Forget about these basketball players." Then he points with his fork alternately to Wes and himself. "Give *these players* a try. We'll treat you right."

Slump 229

Kelle shakes her head, says, "Uh uh. You did *not* just say that."

Even Jayson can't keep a straight face on that. Then everyone's laughing again. Order restored. Still, as things return to normal, I watch Daniella make her exit back to her car. I feel regret for so many things. It gives me this sneaking suspicion that even when things work out—when we win, when I do the right thing, when things break my way—that it's never going to be as smooth and pure as the way I'd imagined. It's not ever going to be a nice tidy ending the way the movies make you think.

28.

Balance. As a player, you need it. Come up for a shot off-balance and you're doomed. Float an off-balance pass and it's an easy pick and push for the other team.

But you need balance as a team too. You can't just feast on outside shots, even if they're open looks. Just like you can't just rely on one scorer to take over possession after possession, no matter how good he is. That's the way it is with any good team—yeah, they might have their man come crunch time, but over the course of a game you need all kinds of options to keep the opponent jumping. I mean, the Thunder don't just iso Kevin Durant every time.

We're not the Thunder. Not a soul in the world would make that mistake. But up at Warren Central—a team that's ranked in the top 15—we start to figure some things out, even with Devin still sidelined. One trip down we work forever to get Moose a look in the lane. Next time, I drive and kick to Fuller on the shallow wing for a deuce off the glass. Later, I get my own, muscling one in over a couple guys. Then it's Moose again, free when his man helps on Fuller's cut. And when they

Slump 231

finally pack it way in, sick of me slicing and Moose posting, I drop a bomb on them from three.

For all that, it's not like we're breezing. We still hit those dry spells. And a six-possession drought in the third quarter opens the door for Warren Central to come roaring back. They do. They got a shooter named Rory Upchurch and the kid can flat fill it. No hops to speak of, but he gets it cranked up just as we go cold. A contested three from the corner. Then a free look at the top of the key when Reynolds gets lost. Then he comes flying off a ball-screen and buries a seventeen-footer. Zip, zip, zip, and we go from a 32-26 lead to a 34-32 deficit.

Their crowd is up and loud. There's a reason it's so tough to win on the road at any level—you can just see the Warren Central players breathe in that energy from their people, who get a new jolt after seeing Upchurch get loose. Fuller inbounds to me and I come flying into the frontcourt, but Bolden wants a timeout. There's only 30 ticks left in the quarter, so their fans take that as a sign we're rattled, with a coach who can't even wait half a minute to settle us. I almost laugh. These people *don't know.* I mean, Warren Central might go on and whip our asses, but not because we're shook. After all the stuff we've been through, a little noise isn't going to bother us.

"We okay out there?" Coach asks.

"We good," Moose shouts. "Just gotta get that bitch Upchurch bottled up again." Bolden raises his eyebrows and gives a long look at Moose. As the season's gone on, Bolden's rules about language have become more and more like suggestions, but you never know when the old man is gonna crack back down. "Sorry, Coach," Moose tacks on, just to be safe.

Coach plunges into tactics as a way of dismissing that brief showdown with Moose. We're just down a deuce, he reminds us, and we're not going to give them a chance to add to that lead before the fourth. We'll burn clock and then flatten out for me to go to work. We break, but Coach gives me a quick look to stay behind. "If Reynolds has some space, put it on him," he says. "He misses, we're just down two. But if he can get one to drop, it'll open things up for us."

It seems reasonable enough, so I do as I'm told. I dribble down the clock, shaking my man each time he comes out to challenge—just quick moves to back him off and re-set the five count.

Finally, with about five seconds to go, I bust past him for real. The whole defense jumps, and I've got my choice—a forced runner in traffic or kicks to the corners. Fuller's the easier pass, but Reynolds is wide open on the far side if I can get it to him, so I rifle one cross-court to give the kid a chance. He catches with two ticks left and hurries it. The shot comes off flat and hard, like he's trying to rifle in a pool shot. I can see Reynolds grimace as soon as it leaves his hands.

And then the ball finds the bucket. I mean, it defies the laws of physics, because I swear that thing never gets above ten feet. But the thing thumps home, giving us a one-point lead. Reynolds actually pops his head back in surprise, but then starts nodding his head on the way to the huddle, getting more exaggerated all the time. "They can't check me," he says when he gets to our sideline.

I'm about to tell him to shut his mouth, but Bolden beats me to it. He gets about an inch from Reynolds. "How about you quit clowning and figure out how to stick Upchurch!" Then, to nobody in particular, he grumbles, "God, this team will be the death of me."

Fuller, who always looks like he's about to have a breakdown

Slump   233

when people start sniping at each other, claps his hands in the huddle. "Come on, guys! Let's stick with it now." Stanford rolls his eyes at Fuller's rah-rah act, but nobody says anything about it.

"Who's ball first?" Bolden asks to Murphy. Murphy looks down at his notepad but doesn't answer right away. He starts to say something but then stops and looks at his notepad again. "Jesus, man!" Bolden pops. "I'm not asking you for a scouting report on the Bulls. I just want to know who gets the ball first."

"We do, Coach," Murphy offers meekly.

"Are you sure?"

Finally Murphy straightens up. "Yes, Coach. I'm sure."

Bolden claps his hands. "Then let's just run the same damn thing at 'em. Derrick, burn a little time to make them jumpy and then see if we can find Reynolds in the corner again." He turns to our freshman. "You want to puff your chest out like a big man? Then see if you got the stones to make another."

Reynolds shrugs his shoulders like, why not? And the rest of us just laugh. Sure. *Why not?*

We check it in and the edge is taken off of Warren Central's crowd. They're still stomping and clapping, but there's a world of difference between a two-point lead and a one-point deficit. I idle out top for a while like Coach said, just taking my time. I make eye contact with all my guys, one by one, make sure they're ready. Then I take a deep breath and attack. My man's sitting on my right, so I spin back left to the elbow. They all jump again, and there's Reynolds, hands out. I put it right on the money and he steps into it, full of confidence— and sails the thing a good solid two feet over the rim. Lucky for us,

Stanford's quickest to react. He gathers in the air ball and scoops it up for a deuce. Three-point lead just like that.

Their crowd sits, and I see Upchurch shaking his head. Breaks like that can fill a team with doubt. As we hustle back on D, I arc out toward Reynolds. "Atta boy," I shout. "Perfect pass to Stanford." He shakes his head at me, then smiles, my little crack letting him off the hook. But then I remember my conversation that night with Dad, about how maybe I haven't been helping people as much as I could be. "Just sit on Upchurch's shooting hand," I shout. "He gets past you, that's on the rest of us to cut off his drive. Just no easy Js. Got it?" Reynolds nods and then hurries to hunt down Upchurch.

That balance we had early comes undone. Reynolds does his best on Upchurch, but he's got the yips on the other end now. Fuller gets a head of steam to the rim only to get called for a charge. Stanford misses a J from the short corner. And Moose is bottled up and getting frustrated. I drive a couple times and draw fouls, my four three throws like a life preserver for us.

Still, we grind like hell on the defensive end. Upchurch gets free for a couple buckets, but aside from that we just give up two free throws to their forward. So we milk a one-point lead into the final minute. Our ball, after a Warren Central turnover.

"Good shot here," Bolden shouts. "Just get a good one."

Or none at all, I think. A couple weeks ago, I'd have all but spit on a win where we only score one field goal in the fourth, but those were different times. Now, when I circle out top to get it from Fuller, I don't care if we never put it up again. Just get out of this gym with a W.

Slump

My man comes out to challenge and I blow past him, but I'm in no hurry. Sure, the D jumps again, and there's Reynolds in the corner with his hands out like he's got a wild notion, but I just back it out. No way I'm getting in a rush and no way I'm giving it up to Reynolds at this point. Only way this thing's going up is if I get a run at the rim or if I find Moose with position down low.

The more I kill the clock, the more the Warren Central crowd starts to jeer, all indignant like we're breaking the rules or something. *Let 'em.* I dribble out top again, and check Coach—he circles his index finger in a motion to keep running clock. Soon, those boos from the crowd start to change in pitch. When the clock hits 30 seconds, they get nervous. *Foul,* they start shouting. *Foul him!* But good luck catching me. I break down my man and get past him to the lane, then back it out to the wing when help comes, then turn my man around again when he races over. Twenty-five left. The crowd gets on their feet, anxious that they're actually going to see a kid dribble out a full two minutes on them. My man finally gets the picture though. He stays low, but motions for the guy guarding Reynolds to double with him. Then they come at me for the trap. Their problem is, I've got all the space in the world—a hard dribble right and then a cross-over and I split the double. I push it into the lane, playing keepaway. Two more rush at me. This time there's no choice but to give it up—right to Fuller who's cutting free to the rim. He catches it in stride and plants his feet, only to get hammered by the one defender left.

I look up, see there are ten seconds left. We're up one. Fuller at the line for two. Looking damn good.

Then I hear Bolden and Murphy go ballistic: "What!?" they shout. Bolden almost races onto the floor, but Murphy catches him.

Kevin Waltman

"He was shooting!" Bolden shouts at the ref. "My God! How is that not in the act of shooting?"

But the ref just shakes his head at Coach, then raises his palm up to tell him to cool it. "He never got off the floor, Coach," he says. Then he raises both index fingers, making the signal again—one-and-one.

It's a garbage call. The only reason Fuller didn't get the thing up to the rim was because he got tackled, but anyone with a brain knew he was going up with that thing. Now their crowd feels it, feeding off of Coach's frustration. We all go over to Fuller and encourage him, tell him to just bury these anyway, but when he gets the ball from the official, he takes a deep, nervous breath. I might have thought there was no rattling us, but a clutch free throw with the crowd hollering and jumping up and down behind the basket is a different beast.

"Shut 'em up!" I shout at Fuller, but I don't know if he can hear me above the noise.

He takes his time, going through his routine. He slaps the ball with his right hand, then pounds it on the hardwood three times, so hard it's like he's trying to dent the floor. But when he lets go, all that confidence is gone, and it pops off the front rim.

Warren Central rips it and runs. They outlet to Upchurch, who hustles into the frontcourt. Reynolds is into him pretty good, so Upchurch glances over at the bench, like he's wondering what to do. Call time? Push on? It's just a veteran baiting a freshman. Reynolds relaxes for just a second, and Upchurch whips past him. Even before he sets his feet, you can hear the crowd buzzing. And they come to their feet as he rises. Then, when he drops a fifteen-footer on us, the place just explodes.

Reynolds looks so distraught, I think he's going to just lay down on the court and bawl. There's no time for consolation. We got four ticks. An eternity. Fuller hesitates on the inbounds, looking toward our bench and then toward the ref like he should call timeout, but I know better.

"Ball!" I shout, so loud the people in the last row can here. Fuller finally snaps out of his daze and gets it to me. And from here, I fall back on the advice I got from Uncle Kid the first time he took me to the playground for a pick-up game: When in doubt, *go to the hole.*

I get the leather in my hands and just go. I'm past my man in a flash, past Upchurch trying to pick me up, into the lane among their bigs. I get smacked once across the forehead, but I know I'm not getting a whistle at this point so I push on through. Up to the rim. Their center's there, challenging, so I have to arch back to create some space. I float one high off the glass and hear the buzzer sound just after it leaves my hand.

It kisses. Then drops through.

Moose is the first one on top of me, all but burying me on the baseline. "Yeah, boy!" he screams in my ear. He grabs my head with both hands and shakes it. I'm as helpless as a child beneath him, but I don't care. "That's what I'm talking about, D!" Pinned underneath him, I just see kicks from my teammates—jumping, sprinting back and forth in celebration—and then the casual shoes of the Warren Central fans as they shuffle for the exits. Moose finally lets me up. By that time, Bolden and Murphy are busy trying to calm us down to some kind of dignified state, ushering us back to the locker room.

That doesn't stop the party. In fact, we hit that locker room and we really make some noise. Reynolds jumps around like he's just won the lottery. Stanford goes from teammate to teammate for chest bumps. He's got that baby face bobbing up and down in rhythm. But he's worked himself up pretty good, so those chest bumps knock a few people back a few steps. I know they can hear us down the hall in Warren Central's locker room, but that's not our problem. Only Fuller seems a little subdued, and Coach Murphy catches it. "Hey, Fuller," he says, "don't sweat missing that freebie. You know why guys miss shots like that? Just because they want to win so bad. If it didn't matter to you, you wouldn't get nervous."

Moose doesn't miss a beat. "What, Coach? You saying that guys like me who hit shots don't care?"

Murphy starts to defend himself, but then he sees Moose cracking up. It's all good. Even Stanford gets his digs in, shouting at everyone that he made half our fourth quarter field goals. Granted, that just means one out of two—his put-back on our first possession, and my game-winner on our last. Not long ago, a quarter like that would have had me losing sleep. Now, I figure, let Warren Central stay up all night wondering how they lost to a team that only scored two buckets in the fourth.

We're not about to let that mo swing back. Fresh off our Warren Central win we go up to Bishop Chatard and knock them off. They're just .500. It's another grinder—39-33—and it's hard to feel like we're getting on the kind of roll we were on last year. I mean, our margin for error is razor thin. Still, back-to-back road wins in February? I'll take that in a heartbeat.

It's a short bus ride back to Marion East, but everyone's living it up. Bolden's in such a good mood even he starts jumping in the conversation. When Moose and Murphy start debating the best-

Slump

ever—like always, an argument between LeBron and Jordan—Bolden stirs them both up. "Forget those two," he growls. "Winning is what matters. And the guy with the most championships is still Bill Russell."

That draws a chorus of shouts from the whole bus, everyone protesting Coach's claim. "Oh, please, Coach," Moose begs. "They still shooting underhanded back when he played?"

"You go ahead and laugh," Bolden snaps back. "He won eleven in thirteen years. And if little LeBrat would've played back then, he'd have never gotten to the rim against Russell."

"Oh, come on!" Moose shouts. It's all in fun, but the big man's getting worked up. "You just talking crazy now. James is 6'8"! With hops!"

Bolden gives an exaggerated frown and shakes his head back and forth. "If he's so good, then how come he had to team up with all those All-Stars down in Miami to get a ring?"

Again the bus erupts in protest. When Murphy and Moose were arguing Jordan-LeBron, it was pretty much split down the middle, but now everyone's united against Coach. I keep quiet, just enjoying the noise—good noise, the kind teams are supposed to make, rather than static and sniping or a brooding silence. Stanford pats Moose on the shoulder from the seat behind him. "He's just messing with you, Moose," he says. "He's just doing his Coach thing."

"Coach thing my eye!" Bolden says. "Answer the question. Anyone." He challenges the whole bus, and I even see the driver checking us in his rear view, smiling at Bolden getting us all worked up. "Why couldn't LeBrat win in Cleveland? The great ones don't run off to get help. Jordan didn't do it. Magic didn't do it. Bird didn't do it."

That tears it. Now even Murphy—who'd been arguing against LeBron earlier—practically leaps out of his seat. "Larry *Bird?*" he screams. "Larry *Bird?* I swear I want to move out of this state so I don't have to hear about Larry Bird anymore. And you acting like LeBron copped out when he went to Miami. I mean *poor Larry Bird* having that *terrible* burden of teaming up with Robert Parrish and Kevin freaking McHale."

Even Bolden can't keep a straight face anymore. He holds his hands up in a defensive pose and laughs. "Easy there, Murph. Didn't mean to strike a nerve. You just better not go saying that kind of stuff if we ever go play one of those Terre Haute schools. People there hear that, they'd just about shoot you dead."

"Well, it's the truth!" Murphy shouts, still a little worked up. Then he mutters to himself more about *Larry freaking Legend.*

Bolden stares at him for a few seconds. I watch a wry little smile crease his face. We're almost back to Marion East, the driver slowing for the turn in. Guys begin gathering up their stuff to unload, and Bolden waits until we come to a stop to stand up. "Good one tonight, boys," he says. "Let's keep it rolling. One more thing though." He turns to Murphy, stares at him with that crazy smile again. "If anything, Larry Bird is underrated."

He turns and exits before Murphy can say anything back, but I can see Coach's back rising and falling with a little laughter. The man just loves to stay after people. Murphy flops back in his seat, like he's been staggered by a shot, then howls, "I work for a crazy man! I work for an absolute crazy man!"

That sends all into the night laughing, feeling pretty damn full of ourselves.

Slump 241

29.

We go up to Chicago and clip Lincoln. Then come home and squeeze
out a win against Ben Davis. And, now, Broad Ripple—last game of the
regular season. Last year we turned these fools in circles up in their place.
And in the first half, we get cracking pretty good. A run to put us up 5.
Another little spurt to stretch it to 10. And by half it's a 14-point lead.

Bring on Sectionals.

Thing is, we blink. We lose sight of a cutter and they get a
bucket out of the locker room. We miss an open shot, and their off-
guard gets loose for a three. Fuller gets a wild notion and turns it over
on a drive, leading to another break—and another three. We're still
up seven, and you'd think it's no sweat, but the whole vibe's changed.
Quick as that.

Basketball's brutal that way. Here we are on a four-game roll, and
Broad Ripple's just playing out the string on another sub-.500 season.
But the floodgates have opened for them. For the rest of the night, it
goes like that. They make everything they put up, knocking in shots
from out of their range, getting ridiculous rolls.

Coach burns timeout after timeout, but we can't seem to get them back under control. It's like one possession we over-extend and get beat to the rim, and the next we're too passive and they drop in another J. We get a bucket here and there, just enough to keep them from catching us, but soon it's late in the game and they've shaved the lead all the way down to one. It's our ball under our bucket, and we need a deuce something desperate. Our crowd has gone from a confident roar in the first half to nervous buzz in the second. You can hear individual voices piercing through the quiet. Each of them try to encourage us, but there's always some undertow of dread in their tone—*You guys still got this* or *They can't keep this up*. Things like that.

I lob out top to Reynolds, then circle up to get it. All I'm thinking is get a good look. Doesn't matter who. I dribble, wait for Fuller to empty out the right wing, then head there while Stanford cross-screens for Moose. He pops free, and I zip him the rock right at the rim. It slips right between his hands and out of bounds. The crowd's silent as a stone. Hell, you can hear the official's footsteps as he jogs to retrieve the ball. I mean, the day Moose—the most sure-handed big I've ever played with—mishandles a pinpoint pass, you know we're cursed.

Jogging back on D, we chatter a little. "My bad," Moose says. And I tell him it's all good, that we still have these guys. Then Fuller reminds us that all we need is one stop. But it's all hollow talk.

At least Broad Ripple doesn't prolong the misery. They make one ball reversal and find their three-man slashing to the rim. Stanford hacks him for good measure, and that's that. Yeah, there's more than a minute left and we're only down two, but the whole place knows we're cooked.

Slump 243

Afterward—after we miss a few desperate threes and they pad the final at the line—I lean back in my locker in disbelief. I mean, Broad Ripple? Shit. Just when it seemed like we were piecing things together, getting ready for a run like last year, we lose—at home—to Broad Ripple.

But here's the bigger shocker—Bolden doesn't seem too upset. He comes in frowning, but when he addresses us that usual demeanor of disgust is gone. "Rough one, boys," he says. "But now, listen. We missed some shots we usually make. Some nights it just goes that way." I can barely believe what I'm hearing. Here's Coach Bolden blowing out sunshine like he's okay with it all. Then he claps his hands, loud and sharp. "I'll forgive us missing shots. They were good ones and they'll drop. But! On defense? They kicked in a few from the cheap seats and all of a sudden we stopped working." He puts his hands on his hips. There's some fire in his voice now, enough for us to know he means business, but he's not unleashing hell like I figured. "We've come too far for me to go nuclear because of one loss," he says. "But remember—we're good, but only if we get after it every single possession. We do that, we can beat anyone. We let up, well—" he just points back out toward the floor, since what just happened out there is evidence of his point.

It takes the sting out a little, but I still just shake my head. You blink, and it's gone. One night you're all laughing it up on the bus, feeling good. Then—bang—you get tripped up by a squad you should crush. It's enough to give you whiplash.

I shower up, then hit the floor again to find my people. Dad's still not here. He's insistent he won't go out until he's walking without a limp.

"By Sectionals," he keeps promising, but he's got exactly one week left until that starts.

Everyone else is out in force though. Jayson's clowning over by Moose, trying to chat up those cheerleaders from the other week. I can tell they're humoring him. I know I'll have to hear him yap about how he gets more action with females than I do. Then, on the far end under the bucket, I see Wes kicking it with some older guys—nothing but trouble. Each one of them is on their way to being another JaQuentin Peggs. Or worse. Why Wes is hanging there is beyond me, because he looks ridiculously out of place. In fact, they're all chilling in this circle, and he's kind of clinging to the outside, like some planet in orbit. He sees me watching him and nods, like nothing's up. Then he pulls out his phone, points to it and then to me. *Text you later*, he mouths, then tries saying something to the biggest guy in that circle of badness. The guy looks at Wes, kind of puzzled, shrugs, then goes back to what he was saying. I don't know Wes' game, but it looks like one he can't win.

But then I see something that blows that straight out of the water. Standing at mid-court is Uncle Kid, just kind of idling, but beside him I see two people chatting and laughing like they're old friends. Mom's one. No surprise. The other? Jasmine Winters, her winter coat pulled tight around her like she's already out in the February night.

I make my way over, trying not to seem too eager. When I arrive, they just keep on talking. I hover outside their conversation the way Wes does those guys at the far end of the gym.

"Don't take this the wrong way," my mom's telling her, "because Thomas is the best man I've ever known. But you've always got to train a man up a little bit. Even now. I *told* him he needed to get to a doctor. Told him I don't know how many times."

Jasmine smiles and nods. "Everyone knows men need told sometimes," she says. "The other problem is they just won't *listen*." Mom laughs in a high wild sound that splits the relative quiet of the gym and makes people look. I'd be embarrassed, but it's the biggest laugh I've heard from her in months. When she stops, they both look at me like they just noticed me for the first time.

"Derrick," Mom says, suddenly full of pity. "You okay?"

I shrug, try to act like the loss doesn't bother me. "Better to get a game like that out of the way now instead of during Sectionals," I say.

"Hey," Jasmine says to me.

"Hey," I say back. Then we both look at each other, unable to say anything else. I'd take a career of losses like this one just to be able to walk out those doors with her, shuffle into the night with her by my side. And somewhere in her stare there's a glimmer—some little mischief lingering in her eye—that tells me she thinks about it too.

"I was just asking your mom how your dad was doing," Jasmine finally says.

"Aw, shit." This is Uncle Kid, intruding in now. "Ask about an injured man for two seconds and then start running him down." He throws an arm around my shoulder and starts to lead me away. "Women can be cold, D," he says, loud enough for them to hear. "Colder than the winter, colder than losses like the one you got hung on you tonight."

I try to pull away from him. Uncle Kid's great and all, but I need some Jasmine-time. But he pulls me in tighter, forces me toward the door. "Trust me," he whispers. "Just walk. Make her want to chase you." I flinch, look back at Jasmine and Mom over my shoulder, offer them a quick wave. Kid re-directs me again and gets back in my ear. "That's one. Don't look back at her again. Just keep walking, man." And then, to distract me, he starts running down all the things we did wrong during the game. By the time we're to the doors, he's in full lecture mode, rattling off a special list of mistakes that he thinks Bolden made—a reminder that for as far as Kid's come he's never going to forgive Bolden for booting him way back when. Some things never die.

Slump 247

30.

Perfect. That's how I want things to be for Sectionals. And so far, so good. I busted my ass studying for an exam in Hulsey's class. When she handed the tests back Thursday morning she paused near my desk, then floated an A- down my way. She added a little note again: *Impressive turnaround, Derrick. Knew you could do it.* She added a smiley face like she thinks I'm a 3rd grader or something, but I'll take it.

Friday morning, we all hit up the Donut Shop, our new tradition. All smooth, and no sign of Daniella. She still hits me with a text about once a week, trying to lure me back. Tempting, but every time I tell her no. There's only trouble in that direction, and I know it.

Then Friday night we ripped it right past Lawrence Central, cruising to a 52-37 win, setting up a Saturday night showdown with Pike for the Sectional championship. I'm sitting in my room, getting my head ready. It was just a few weeks ago we knocked around Newsome and took them down. And I know from experience that a rematch doesn't necessarily follow the first game's form.

We're not quite back to normal in the Bowen household though.

Instead of everyone amped for a big game, it's like a mortuary. The killer is that my dad's still not coming out to the game. I get it. I do. He's a proud guy, and he can't bear the thought of people staring at him while he limps up those bleacher stairs. He doesn't want the other parents coming over and asking him how he's feeling, all kinds of pity drawn on their faces. Mom's a different story. When Dad said he wasn't going, she went *off*. Launched into him for not listening to her in the first place, then got on him for not sucking it up. "I know you don't think basketball's that important," she wound up, "but it *is* to your son. And you should be there, even if it means you might have some people give you sorry looks. Get *over* it!" Dad didn't even respond. He just pulled a blanket over his legs and looked for the remote in the couch cushions. Not finding it, he sighed and pulled the blanket further up, like he was going to sleep, just done with it all. Since then, the house has seemed to reverberate with Mom's anger. I know it's about more than the game. I know she's had to carry the load for a long time now. She's about to break.

A thaw will come. Jayson and I both know this. It might be in five minutes or it might be in the morning, but it will come. They let their tempers spill over two, maybe three times a year, but it never lasts. Still, it makes it hard to focus on the game.

When I was younger, Jayson's age, I had this belief that there would be these moments of absolute clarity in my life that would fix everything. I'd get my first kiss with a girl like Jasmine, and we'd be happy ever after. An injured person would wake up one morning and declare themselves healthy with no looking back. A basketball team would catch fire and never regress. All fairy tales. Things get messy, and they stay messy. Even Wes, who's always been as constant as the sun coming up, is cracking up on me. He's still my boy, but he's so screwed up from Iesha that he's trying to become someone he isn't. Last time we were hanging he smelled like weed. He denied it. It's not the biggest deal in the world anyway. I mean, it's 2014. Nobody's calling in counselors for someone blazing up once. But it makes me worry about him.

Pike, I think. *Get your head right.* I visualize dropping a dime to Moose. Picture a pull-up J finding bottom. Think about switching onto Newsome and sticking him from line-to-line. Then I hear the front door open. I get up to see who it is, but before I'm into the hallway, Kid announces himself: "Who the hell died here?" he shouts. "Sectional finals tonight, or did everyone here forget?"

I come around the corner of the hallway to see Kid standing by the front door with his hands upturned from his questions. Dad rises from the couch, but doesn't really respond. Mom comes down the hall and around the corner to stare a hole in Kid. There's a lot less static between them since he's been helping out so much, but she's in no mood for jokes. "Sit," she tells him, pointing to the chair. "I'll get you something to drink if you want."

Kid smiles, undeterred. "I'm good," he says. "Just want to talk to my brother for a second." He opens the door again, reaches out onto the porch, and pulls in a long, slender, black case. "About time you made a game, don't you think?" he asks Dad.

That gets Dad moving again. He throws the blanket off and stands, leaning heavily on the couch to push himself up. "Now I've already been through this with Kaylene!" he shouts. "Would you people just let me be? I don't want to go limping around like some cripple."

Mom spins and heads back down the hall, disgusted. Jayson passes her in the opposite direction and stands next to me, but he's just checking on the wreckage in the living room.

Kid keeps after Dad. He pulls that case around front of him and slowly unzips it. "You don't have to limp," he says. "Not if you got this." And he unveils a cane for Dad. Now, I don't know a thing about canes, but I can take one look at this one and know it's not something Kid just scooped up at Wal-Mart. The stalk is a thick, shiny black. Instead of curving up into a simple handle like the shape of a candy cane, it's got a bulb at the top in the shape of an eagle's head. It looks like it might be silver-plated. Pretty dope, really. And exactly *not* my dad's style.

"You've got to be kidding me," he says.

"Not for a second," Kid snaps back. "For once in your life just allow yourself to have something with a little flair to it."

"No way," Dad says.

"Aww, Dad," Jayson says. "Come *on*, man."

Dad looks at him, ready to protest, but then he hangs his head and closes his eyes. Mom must sense him soften even from a distance. "Jayson's right," she calls from down the hall. Then she emerges again, joining us. "Come on."

Then we're all after him, almost chanting—*Come on, come on, c'mon*—and I see it in his face. All that dammed up stress breaks apart, and he smiles. He can't resist. "Should I ask where you got something like that?" he asks Kid.

Kid coughs. "A guy owed me a favor," he says. "Can we just leave it at that?"

"Dear Lord," Dad says, but he reaches out, hand open to receive the cane.

When I get to the gym, I learn that Dad's not the only hobbled man ready to give it a go. There's Devin at his locker, in uniform, getting taped up by Darius. He sees me checking him, and he just winks. "Sectional finals senior year? Man, they'd have to cut this leg off to keep me out."

"Well, let's get after it then," I say.

You can feel the energy pumping in that locker room. Last year we took Sectionals for the first time in forever. Win it back-to-back and it'll prove to people there's a new king. We hit the court for warm-ups, and it's like the crowd knows it too. The gym's almost a full house already, way before tip, and the noise we get when we come racing out is as loud as some places get in the middle of a game. Moose gets so tweaked he starts just shouting up to the rafters when he goes through the layup line. Then he gets up in Fuller's face and starts yapping. Fuller gives as good as he gets, the two of them just amping each other more and more.

I can't wait for tip. It's all I can do to rein myself in during warm-ups and keep back some of that burst for the game. Bolden must sense it, because he strolls all the way out onto the court and goes from player to player. When he gets to me, he reminds me I'm in charge on the floor. "Keep everyone aggressive," he says, "but stay in control. Don't let emotions get us carried away." He's right, I know, but the whole gym feels like it could catch fire with the slightest spark.

At last, the clock ticks down to zeroes and we're ready. We go through the starting lineups. I'm last to be announced. The crowd gets so loud it drowns out the *Bowen* from the P.A. I sprint out to join my teammates on the floor. Moose takes charge, getting in the middle of our circle and shouting at us. "This is the *time*," he says. "Our *time*. Game time! Boys step back and men step up!" Truth.

We get the tip and jump right after it. I kick to Reynolds, who still got the start even with a suited-up Devin. He takes one dribble before feeding Stanford in the high post. Stanford pumps once, then hits me on the wing. Drive left, spin back middle, then a quick shuffle to Moose low. Bucket. And we're off.

Pike isn't fazed. They've been through this kind of noise before. They work a few reversals before they find Newsome on the wing. It's clear he's got a new strategy for us—attack fast before we can run bodies at him. He jabs at Reynolds, then launches a step-back three. Pure.

I race back, trying to catch them before they're set. Get it all the way into the paint before I'm cut off. I kick it back out to Fuller trailing. A clean look at a fifteen footer, but it rattles out. A little quick, I guess, but it's a decent shot. Doesn't matter. What matters is Pike running back. Newsome sets on the wing and catches, but this time he shot fakes and is gone like smoke. Stanford helps, but that just opens up the lane for his man. Another quick bucket and we're in a three-point hole.

This time I know to take our time. The crowd's still buzzing, too amped to let a quick deficit bother them. They're used to us grinding now so they don't go dead when we look and look. Finally, I get a crease and drive. It's a pull-up from about twelve that feels good coming off but ticks back rim and pops out. Again, Pike runs and again, I'm caught behind the action. Reynolds switches onto my man and Fuller covers

Slump

Newsome, but I struggle to find Fuller's man. When I do, it's too late. He catches at the elbow, powers toward the rim and lays one in around Moose's challenge.

This time it does kill our crowd. When I cross mid-court, I look to Bolden to see if he wants time. Nothing doing. So again we work for a shot and, again, we get a decent look that rattles out. At least this time we catch a whistle. Stanford walks to the stripe to split two, breaking up Pike's run. But in about five seconds, Newsome shakes Reynolds again and drains a long three. Whap. Just like that it's 10-3. The way they're dropping shots on us it feels like Broad Ripple all over again. This time Bolden has no choice but to call timeout. We come straggling in. Our slog to the huddle, more than anything else, seems to rile Bolden. "Let's go!" he shouts. "Get on in here!"

When we're finally seated he makes one change, sending Devin in for Fuller so we have an extra shooter. Then he tells us to just calm down, but he senses discouragement on our faces. "Oh, snap out of it!" he screams. Then he composes himself. "You guys are moping like the season's over already. Listen to me. *Listen!* We're going to beat these guys." That gets our attention. Even Murphy pulls back a bit, like lightning might strike. I've never in two years heard Bolden make that kind of statement. He smiles, knowing we're all ears now. "I mean it. I hate talking about slumps because it's hard to know if you're losing because you're in a slump or because you're just no damn good. You can't tell until it's over. And, boys, our slump ended about a month ago. That kind of slump isn't coming back now. We stay after these guys and we'll beat them. You know why?" Nobody responds and Coach smiles again. He speaks low, almost in a whisper: "Because we're better than them."

Kevin Waltman

We break that huddle, so ready to get after it that we'd take on an army if Coach wanted us to. If anything, I've got to get myself calmed back down. Reynolds inbounds it to me. I circle out top, just catching my breath. I scan the crowd for my people. I see Jayson, Kid, Mom, Dad. They return my gaze and then they each stand up, start clapping. Dad even thumps that cane on the bleachers a few times. Jayson waves his arms to the people seated around him, demanding they get to their feet. And they do. As the crowd rises and starts to swell with noise, I dribble right toward the wing. I break down my man with a hard dribble right. Then I cross him over. Pull up at the free throw line when the D jumps. Drop a laser on Reynolds at the opposite wing. And I give him a look as I pass it, like *You bury this and it makes up for all your screw-ups all year long.* He catches in rhythm. Flicks the wrist. *Money.*

Pike doesn't blink. They go right back on the attack, running Newsome through a series of screens. Reynolds does a good job, but with each one he trails just a hair further. I know it won't be long until Newsome gets loose. My man cuts through the lane and then heads back to the wing to set yet another screen for Newsome. It's my chance—Reynolds is lagging, but I time it up, peeling off my man just as Newsome rubs past. A quick jump in front and I snag that pass, turn to start the break the other way.

As I dribble, I hear the crowd start to buzz in anticipation of a throwdown. Newsome is thinking that too, because he just rides my right shoulder the whole way down the floor. Their three man closes in from the other side. Fine by me. I drag them both toward the rim with me. I know I could muscle it up between them, but I turn at the last instant and fire it out to Devin who's spotting on the wing. Bum ankle

Slump 255

and all, that's automatic. He splashes in another three. Newsome signals for a quick timeout before even checking with their bench. Our crowd's loving life right now. It might only be the first quarter but they're letting it rip like it's crunch time. Murphy meets us halfway out on the court, clapping his hands and stomping his feet, so pumped I bet he'd suit up himself if he could.

"Don't get carried away now," Coach warns us. "Remember who you are. Those were good shots, but we don't want to live on threes."

He's right. Our crowd might be delirious, but all the swing means is we're back in it, trailing 10-9. Pike comes out of the huddle and runs what looks like the same set for Newsome. He comes off a baseline screen, then flies up to the wing off a down-screen. My man goes over to set that cross-screen again. I know better than to try the same trick. Sure enough, my man slips the screen and cuts into an emptied lane. He still gets a step on me, but he needs more than that. I catch up in a flash. He's smart enough to stop short and scoop it, just to keep me off the ball, but I still have enough reach to get a piece. The ball deflects off the rim, right into the hands of a crashing Stanford. He rips it out to Devin at the near hash, and starts upcourt. We don't have numbers, so Devin just slows it across mid-court. I'm trailing and call for the ball. As soon as I glimpse at Devin, I can tell he's feeling it. I try to call him off from what he's about to do—basically, just the opposite of what Coach said—but I figure he knows when it's time for a heat check. He takes a rhythm dribble left, crosses back right, then launches from *deep*.

Pure as fresh snow.

That one shakes Pike a little. Their center's eyes go wide. Their point shakes his head in wonder, like *What have we walked into here?*

Their coach isn't about to burn another timeout right away so he just barks out some encouragement, then looks nervously up at the scoreboard, maybe wondering how long he's got until the quarter ends. We're only up two, but it feels like a dozen. And, I mean, we haven't hit back-to-back-to-back threes since the first practice of the year. They work a few reversals, and then Newsome feeds their center. Moose has him pushed off the blocks a good three feet, but they're feeling a little jumpy. He forces up a fade that skips off the back rim. It gets tipped around a few times, and Devin finally corrals it on the opposite wing.

I sprint over like I'm on fire to demand the ball. I'm not one to squash a guy when he's rolling, but I have a feeling Devin's going to launch it as soon as he's past mid-court. I slow us down. We've got the lead, the ball, momentum. I figure let's just cool it for a second. From behind me, I hear Coach shouting approval—"That's right, Derrick. No hurry now."

We settle into our offense, but with that series of threes it feels like the seas have parted. They're scared to sag off Reynolds and Devin now, so Moose finally has some breathing room. He catches it once, but can't lift his man with a shot-fake, so he kicks it back to me and then re-posts. I put the rock in his mitts, but this time my man sinks down to double, flat-out leaving me in the corner. Moose feels the pressure, kicks it back out again. My man comes racing back, but this is clear a look as I've had in a long time. I set my kicks behind the line, catch in rhythm, and fire. It's off clean before my man recovers, but his momentum carries him full-bore into me. I hear the whistle as I fall. Then just listen for the roar. It comes, loud as if a freight train were passing right down the lane. I know I bottomed out the shot.

A three. And one. Men step up, boys step back.

Slump 257

It's not all as smooth as that. Of course not. But our early onslaught puts us in control of Pike. When they nip at the lead, we have just enough juice—Moose down low, me slashing, and everyone else knocking in a J or two when the time comes—to keep them at arm's length.

Still, as we come down the stretch, it's turned into another grinder—fine by us at this point—and the crowd's getting edgy. When Stanford misses a turnaround and Pike controls, I can feel the gym tense up. We're up three with two to go, but everyone knows Newsome can make that lead vanish in a heartbeat.

They work a few reversals. Then my man glances over to their bench. Their coach holds up his right index finger with his left hand beneath it, four fingers spread. I know what that means—give it to Newsome and flatten out. They just make one mistake. To get it to Newsome, they run a dribble exchange. As soon as my man shuffles it off to their boy, I'm on it. "Switch! Switch! Switch!" I shout at Reynolds, even giving him a little nudge with my elbow in case he's confused.

So then there I am, out between the circles, soloed up with Major Newsome. I clap my hands in front of me. *Bring it.* Newsome gives a sly little grin, loving the moment. I get it. He's just like every other baller in this city. We grow up dreaming of it—a clock ticking down, a crowd on its feet, holding its breath to see what you got. It's why we burn through our summer, practicing with a purpose when other kids are killing time. It's why we lift weights until our arms are jelly, run sprints until our calves catch fire. It's why when we get our teeth kicked in by a better team, we just bear down and keep working. *This.*

Kevin Waltman

I hear Stanford over my shoulder, hollering at me that his man's coming up to set a ball-screen, but I see Newsome just wave him away. He wants this one on his own. He bends his knees and starts at me, dribbling left a couple times. Then he crosses between his legs and dips his shoulder, penetrating a little. He could go to the hole, but I know this guy wants that three, so I don't bite. He plants and then steps back. I stay pinned on his left shoulder. He rises up to shoot, and I don't over-reach but I get my hand in his face pretty good, making his look a tough, contested step-back.

When it leaves his hands, I hear him holler, "Bucket!" When I turn, I see it arcing toward the rim, looking as good as Newsome thinks it is. It gets about as down as a ball can be without going through, but that thing spins back out on him. And not a soul gonna get a hand on that ball but Moose. He grabs it with a slap. I hear the crowd react, more relief than anything.

They play us straight for about thirty seconds before they know they've got to foul. I make sure to get it in Devin's hands. He steps up, buries 'em both, and it's done. Well, not entirely. They keep fouling, keep clawing, but the clock's just running down the seconds on their season at this point. We stay smart, not fouling. I force myself to stay focused on this one until we hit triple zeroes. Only when Pike surrenders, their coach waving them off from fouling, and our crowd starts chanting down, do I allow myself to think about what's coming. Regionals. Hinkle Fieldhouse. And, maybe, one more crack at Vasco and Hamilton Academy.

Slump   259

31.

Regionals is another double-header set-up. We came out of the gates first and just put the clamps on an overmatched Martinsville team. It's like our defense was made up of five guys sharing a brain. We cut off drives, challenged every pass, sank back to help in the post and then rotated seamlessly. By mid-second, the Martinsville players were shaking their heads in frustration. And by mid-third, Coach started to rotate in some bench players to keep us fresh for the night game. Final: 44-21. Domination.

That is, I thought it was domination until I came out of the locker room to see Hamilton in action again. Somehow, they've gotten better. They drew Warren Central. Sure, we beat Central earlier, but that's the last time they lost. With Rory Upchurch on a ridiculous tear, there was buzz that maybe Central was the team to finally knock off Hamilton.

No chance.

By the time I'm done with my shower, there are only two minutes left in the first and Hamilton's already up nine with the ball. Then they drop the hammer—a Vasco turnaround. A steal off pressure leading to a Charles three. And then, after Upchurch misses with a few ticks left in the quarter, Vasco rebounds and outlets to Charles, who spots up and then drops it back to Vasco trailing—and he drains one from the next freakin' state.

The buzzer sounds and both teams jog to their benches under the thunderous celebration of the Hamilton fans. I swear it, Vasco spots me walking under the far basket and gives me a quick nod, a look that seems to ask, *You ready for more, Derrick?*

It's an eternity before the eight p.m. championship. Even Coach Bolden knows he's got to give us some free time or we'll go crazy, so he cuts us loose for a couple hours before an early team dinner.

Dad drops me at a record store up in Broad Ripple. Not my hang, but it's where Wes wanted to meet. He's already there, flipping through some stacks of old vinyl, when I come in. We get some stares from the guys behind the counter—twenty-somethings rocking wispy beards and knit caps. "Let us know if we can help you with anything," one of them mutters, but the way he says it makes it sound like *Don't even think about shoplifting that Kanye.* Whatever. I just head back to my boy Wes, give him a quick thump on the chest.

"Where you been keeping yourself, man?" I ask.

He shrugs. "Here and there," he says, trying to be all cool. It's strange. He's the same old Wes, combing through old jazz records nobody else our age has ever hear of, but his face is closed off, his eyes narrowed like he's fighting off a headache.

I wait for him to say more, but the only sound is the *flip, flip, flip* of the record sleeves under his fingers. "That's it, man?" I ask.

Slump 261

He rolls his eyes and slouches back. "What you want me to say?"

My instinct is to reach out and grab him by the shoulders, shake some sense into him. But his body's so tensed it's like it might crack apart if somebody touches him. Instead I just say, "Wes, it's me. It's just me."

He exhales and unclenches a little bit, but just dives back into the records. It's like he's got to keep his hands busy on something else to free his mind up. "I can't shake this Iesha thing," he starts. Then he runs it all down. How he tries chatting up other girls but strikes out. How he'll break down and text Iesha again, then go up a wall waiting for a reply that never comes. He even explains how my little plan of getting him out to those team breakfasts failed. "I mean, I appreciate it," he says, "but those cheerleaders pay more attention to your little brother. I'm invisible. I mean, a middle schooler has more game than me."

"Man, forget that girl," I say. He shakes his head, not wanting to hear it. So I don't press the issue. Instead, I try to address all the changes he's been putting on himself without actually saying it. "You just be you. That's all you gotta do."

With a loud *whap*, he slaps his hand on the cover of the record he's got pulled out. From the corner of my eye, I see those slackers behind the corner pop to attention. "That's not working for me, D," Wes says. "Not with Iesha. Not with anyone." He looks down at the album, picks it up like he's going to whip it across the room like a frisbie. "Besides, who am I anyway? Going through this old shit nobody listens to so I can impress a dad who doesn't even live here? Hell with that."

I don't know what to say. Since we were little, there's always been that unspoken difference between us, forever lurking below the surface. My family's far from easy street, but we're a family. Wes doesn't have that. There are times like this one when I can see how it undermines him. He drops the record back in its bin and walks over to the hip-hop section. I follow him, then watch him search in silence.

Finally, he pulls out a CD with some guy all blinged out. He's got the pit bulls on either side of him, three half-naked women writhing on a bed in the background. It's like every bad cliché come to life. Wes inspects it, then nods. "Think I ought to try this look instead?" he asks me.

I stammer for something to say. I mean everyone—*everyone*—is always trying to make themselves into something, especially if it means they might impress a girl, but Wes is almost scaring me.

"D," he says. "I'm not serious. Damn, man." He laughs then. For the first time, I can relax. I see a glimpse of the old Wes—easy, open, just wanting some fun. He points at those guys at the counter, says, "I mean, I'll try *that* look before I try this." Those guys sneer at him, but Wes just sneers back, daring them to yap. I laugh again, but even this— that quick challenge to the world around him—is a new edge to Wes, like a blast of wind that chills an otherwise sunny day. And I know that the "old Wes" will never really be there for long, that he's in the process of hardening into someone new.

I let it go. Right now, we've got a chance just to relax. We drift into talking nonsense about people in school, speculating about the Pacers' playoff hopes. I even let him run smack about how I got my head messed up with Daniella. It's all good. Because when we leave this store, it'll be all business again.

Hinkle's packed to the rafters. There are three other Regional Finals going on around the state, but wherever Hamilton Academy's playing,

Slump 263

that's where the spotlight is. Press row is as jammed as if LeBron were suiting up. The baseline is strung with cameramen fighting for the best spot. I warm up steadily and think about how sweet it would be if they were all here to document Vasco's last high school game.

I take a break from the layup line and stretch near mid-court. In truth, I just want a chance to soak in the scene. There are no guarantees in basketball, especially in the playoffs, so you might as well enjoy every second you can. I linger to see if Vasco will come over and run smack a little. This time he walks over to me and gives me a standard handshake like he doesn't have time for more. He simply says, "Good luck tonight, Derrick."

That's it. No punch line like *You'll need it.* Nothing. It's kind of disappointing. Like he's too tensed up for his own good or something. When I turn, I see Moose checking me out. "You got your head right?" he asks me.

"Most definitely," I say. "My last chance to take down Vasco. That's all."

Moose rocks back on his heels. "Whoa now, D. It ain't you and Vasco. Don't get caught up in that noise. It's us against Hamilton Academy."

"I hear you," I say, and we start back to the layup line.

"Besides," Moose adds. "I'm the one guarding Vasco."

He's got a good point, so I do him one better. I scoop up a stray basketball and direct Moose down to the post. "Remember, big man," I say. Then I spin a bounce pass toward him. "Vasco's gotta guard you too."

Moose catches, then pauses. He gives me a big, knowing smile, then drops a shudder-shake on an imaginary defender before whipping into the lane for a finger-roll.

Coach calls us in for one last huddle before they announce the starting fives. With every second, the arena buzzes a little more. Over on press row everyone's getting their programs ready. The radio teams are wrapping up their pre-games. I know their voices are getting more and more excited with each sentence. But none of that exists in the huddle. As soon as Coach Bolden takes a knee in front of us, the whole universe shrinks down to the people gathered around him.

"We know what to do," he says. "Remember that. Everyone thinks this game's about Vasco Lorbner and Deon Charles. About all those weapons on that other bench. Wrong. This game's about *us*. If we stay patient, and we guard the way we can guard, we can win this thing." A few guys clap and pump their fists, but Coach holds up his hand. "Now, look. They're gonna make shots. They haven't lost a game in more than two years, so it's not like we're holding them to twenty-one points. But the difference between us and all the teams they've beaten is that when they hit a few shots on us, we're not blinking. We're just gonna come right back at them and guard them harder the next time. Thirty-two minutes, boys. Not a second less."

The first trip down, Hamilton goes right to Vasco. They're so crisp, so quick. Just wing to high post to opposite wing to Vasco on the blocks. A quick baseline turnaround and they're up two before anyone's broken a sweat. I catch the inbounds and get a faceful of Deon Charles, who's picking me up full-court. It's clear pretty quick—the pace for this one is going to be totally different from the morning game.

Slump

But we've learned at least one very important lesson—playing with pace doesn't mean running a race. I bring it up against the pressure and then we just go to work. Reynolds on the wing. Shot fake and then a look to Fuller on the baseline. A quick drive, then back to me on the wing. I circle it out top, then come off a Stanford ball screen. Over to Reynolds on the opposite baseline. A feed into Moose—nothing there. Back out to me, then a ball screen the other way. Our cuts are razor sharp, our screens precise. Always pushing, always making them work.

On and on. There are looks, sure. The kind that we might knock down, but also the kind that got us in a track meet with Hamilton in January. And at last, Stanford catches Vasco on a clean cross-screen and Moose comes free. Fuller finds him and it's a tie game.

Our crowd leaps out of their seats, but we don't even react. Charles is too busy ripping the ball back at us like he's been shot from a cannon. I stay in front of him, and Reynolds gives a little late help to keep him out of the lane. I stay glued to him when he widens back to the wing. Charles finds Vasco trailing, and he's got a step on Moose. The pass hits Lorbner right in stride. He barrels to the rim for another bucket, plus a whistle. Except when we look to the ref, he cuffs his hand behind his head and motions the other way. Charge. And who was it taking that collision? Little Reynolds, who got sent sprawling into one of the cameramen on the baseline. We all rush over to help him up, worried that our freshman's concussed from taking on a full-speed Lorbner, but Reynolds pops up before we can get to him. He juts out his lower lip and shakes his head, trying to convince himself he's not hurt. It might be a tough-guy act, but that sends our crowd into a frenzy. It impresses Coach Bolden too. He stomps his feet and pumps his fist. "That's it!" he screams. "That's how we get it done."

Meanwhile, Lorbner's complaining to the ref, seemingly in disbelief that he'd get that kind of call against him. He's rubbing his elbow too, working on the spot where he collided with Reynolds. It's only one foul. We don't even get free throws for it. But if you ask me, the difference between Reynolds' reaction and Vasco's means quite a bit.

On our end, we work and work again, finally freeing Reynolds on the baseline. He might be full of himself from taking that charge, but it doesn't translate to this end. He rattles it out and Lorbner controls. Fuller, always hustling, digs down on Vasco and swipes at the ball. He's got no chance of stealing it, but he bothers Vasco enough to delay the outlet and we can get back on D before Hamilton can put their fast break in effect.

They're still killers in the half-court though. They find Lorbner in the post, and he draws a double. When he kicks it out, we're left chasing shooters. Finally, Reynolds goes flying past his man, who drives into the lane. When help comes, he finds a cutting Lorbner and—*crack!*—before Vasco can get the shot up, Fuller puts the clamp-down on him. It's not dirty, but it's no love-tap either. Again Vasco appeals to the refs, like he thinks he's owed better treatment or something. Hamilton's coaches go haywire too, begging for a flagrant, and that gets their crowd up. They boo and moan, outraged that some kid from the city dare touch their beloved Vasco. Our crowd isn't going to sit and listen to that. They get up, all but taunting the Hamilton people. On the court the refs step in and tell us all to settle down and have a clean game, but the tone's been set between the lines and in the bleachers—this is war.

Late in the first half, Hamilton finds their off-guard for an open three. He drains it to open a four-point lead. But you wouldn't know it to look at them. I've been tighter than another jersey on Charles. He's lugging a fat zero toward half. Vasco's had his, but those early collisions have him off kilter a little. He's playing with a chip on his shoulder, rather than smoothly schooling everyone like he usually does.

Us? We're fine. This is like every game out. Moose keeps working all beast-mode in the paint. The rest of us get our looks here and there. Reynolds finally got one. Devin came off the bench to bury a couple, and Fuller and Stanford have chipped in four apiece. I've only got three points, but I'm not sweating that anymore.

Still, when Hamilton's crowd gets on their feet as I bring it up, I know we can't let them go to the locker room with momentum. After two ball reversals, I demand the rock and then circle out top to hold for the last one. Our crowd stands now too. They know we've taken their best punch and we're only down four, with a chance to cut it in half. I wait and wait. No matter what, I don't want to give them time for another touch. With about five to go, the crowd voicing its impatience, I start to break down Charles.

I go hard left to turn his hips, then behind my back to get past him. I knife down the lane and get between two defenders with a hopstep. Vasco takes a step to help, leaving Moose. I rise, and then passfake in mid-air, freezing Vasco still as a statue. All he can do is stand there, while I pull the rock back, then rip it through right before the buzzer sounds.

I come down right beside Vasco on the baseline, and I can't help myself. "More of that coming in the second half," I say.

He just starts to their locker room, but tries to walk through me on his way. "Shut up," he says. I love it. Right then, I know—we may be down two, and we may have a long battle in front of us, but all the pressure in this gym is squarely on Vasco's shoulders. And maybe for the first time ever, he's feeling it.

We push through the third and nothing changes, except I can see the Hamilton players get a little tighter with each passing minute. We can never carve further into their lead, but they can't pull away. And it's grating on them. Charles in particular seems worked up. He's broken the ice with two free throws on a cheap call, but he's not the kind of player who's used to just chipping in. He wants to see a three fall. He *needs* it.

On our last possession of the quarter, down four again, we work it forever. Every time we back it out and re-set, I hear their crowd groan. It's like they think we're cheating or something. Let them whine.

With ten to go, I hit Devin baseline and his man over-commits. Devin drives into the lane and tries to shuffle one to Stanford, but it gets tipped out of bounds. Devin hops a couple times, favoring that bad ankle, and I run over to him. "You got this," I say. "Don't give in now." He tells me it's all good, but he can't meet my eye. We both know he's playing on borrowed time. But when I look around, I see that Devin's not the only one who's hurting. The Hamilton players are bent at the waist, gasping for air. Defending for forty-second stretches doesn't agree with these guys. The only exception is Vasco, who's still standing erect. I see his broad chest heaving up and down, an angry expression clouding his face.

Slump 269

We have it out underneath with a few seconds left. I look to the bench and get the in-bound play from Coach. It's one that calls for me taking it out. The first look is to Devin off a screen, but Hamilton's seen that too many times to be caught on it. Then I look for Fuller slicing down the lane, but he takes a bad angle and I can't get it to him. When I pass-fake though, Charles turns his head, eager to help on the play. So I go for a little gamesmanship—I pop the ball off Charles' hip, then scoop it up before anyone can react. I gather for a shot, but Vasco comes flying at me. With him airborne, I dump it to Moose for another easy deuce to end a quarter. Meanwhile, Vasco's momentum carries him right to me. I bend down so I don't take a knee to the head, but all of Vasco's weight comes down on me. He goes somersaulting over, landing in a heap at the baseline as the buzzer sounds. It's a big crash, and even our crowd gasps, reacting more to the fall than to Moose's bucket.

I immediately step to him, hand outstretched to help him up. Instinctively he reaches up, but then sees it's me. Like an animal recoiling, he rips his hand back. He scrambles up and towers over me, bumping me backward. The refs are slow to react, so the players are in first, separating us. At first it seems like everyone's going to keep their cool, but then Vasco, as he's being pulled away, reaches out and gives me a quick shove in the chest. He doesn't get his power behind it, but I can't help but react.

"What the hell, man?" I say.

He's still being pulled back, but he strains at the arms of his teammates. "That's dirty basketball!" he shouts. "You're trying to hurt people!"

I decide to let it go. But our big man has his temper up now.

Moose takes two menacing steps toward Vasco. Lorbner might have three inches on Moose, but nobody in this city who doesn't wear a Colts uniform on Sundays wants to tangle with a riled Moose. "You wanna see someone get hurt, come at me and I'll show you!" he screams.

By now all the refs and coaches are in the mix, all of them telling us to cool it down and take it easy, but it's hard to listen to their advice with every fan in the gym calling for blood. There's a mini-scuffle off to the side between Stanford and one of the Hamilton guys, so attentions turn there for a second. That's when Vasco, with none of the refs looking, gives me another shove. One I'll let go—the guy did take a tumble, after all. But two? "Why don't you back the fuck up!" I shout at him.

And *that's* the thing the refs catch. Their whistles knife through all the noise and they T me up, quick as that. The whistles defuse everyone, but as I make my way back to the bench, it hits me. The technical means two freebies for them, but it also means Coach is going to sit me. I don't know for how long, but even a minute could be a killer against guys this good.

Before I even hit the bench, Coach is telling Reynolds to check in for me. Man. Reynolds at the point against Hamilton? That's instant death. But there's nothing we can do. If there's anything we know by now, it's that with Joe Bolden the rules are the rules. I'm relegated to standing behind Coach while he instructs the guys in the huddle. The look on everyone's faces is bleak. I mean, we are *into* these guys, and now it's all slipping away. Coach stops mid-sentence. "What?" he shouts. "What's wrong with you guys?"

Moose is the one willing to say it. "Coach, we need D out there."

"He'll be back," Bolden says. "But I have to sit him. You know

$Slump$

I have to." He picks the clipboard up again, but this time Devin cuts him off.

"Coach, I'm a senior. This could be my last game. So can I say something?" Bolden pauses, huffs once in frustration, but then nods. "You don't have to," Devin says. "You think we don't know you're a hard-ass? You think we'll suddenly stop paying attention because you let one technical slide?"

Bolden starts to explain, but Moose isn't hearing it. "I escalated it," Moose says. "Might as well sit me too."

Bolden smacks the clipboard down in front of him and shouts. "Really? We're doing this now?" He points to the floor. "Get the hell out there and do as I *say!*"

There's no more argument. Bolden and his rules.

When we break huddle, I hear some fans booing the decision. Even though he's twenty rows back, I can almost feel Uncle Kid rolling his eyes and cursing Bolden. Charles steps up to take the technical free throws. Sinks them. Down four again, and their ball out. They inbound it, and you can almost see Charles licking his chops. He solos up Reynolds, and before anything can get going Reynolds reaches in desperation, draws another foul.

Coach signals time.

Everyone comes back in, a little confused, and when they sit Coach just says, "Bowen for Reynolds." It takes us a second to realize what he's done, but before anyone can react, he just deadpans. "Don't ever let it be said I don't sit kids after technicals."

Murphy looks up at the clock and whistles. "Yeah, Coach. Those three seconds were an eternity."

We can't cut into the four-point lead. They stretch it to six a few times, but we keep coming back—only to run up against that four-point wall. We're running out of options too. Devin's playing half-strength. Reynolds, his early bravado aside, isn't ready for this stage. Stanford and Fuller fight like hell, but they're just not talented enough to get easy buckets. And Moose has gone the distance with Vasco, but you don't get far by going right at the best player in the state every time down.

Hamilton brings it up, still working that four-point lead, with about three minutes to go. A bucket here and things start looking dim for us. Vasco senses it too, because he comes out top and demands the ball. Charles is bristling under my defense more each possession, but he has no choice but to obey. That leaves Vasco and Moose up top, a brutal check for our big man. Vasco makes it quick. A jab step, a rhythm dribble to the left, and then a bomb—from a good twenty-five feet—to put Hamilton up seven. A killer.

Before the weight of it sinks in, I get the inbounds and push, hoping to catch them celebrating. It almost works, but Charles flicks the ball away just before I get into the lane, sending it out of bounds. Now, dead ball, you can feel the energy in the gym. The Hamilton crowd is jumping up and down, knowing that their big man's done it again. In their heads, they're already making plans for next Saturday at Semi-State. Our crowd's not dead, but when I look that way I see lots of folded arms, a few people nervously rubbing the back of their necks. But then I catch my dad. He's looking right at me, face full of fire. He mouths something at me, and when I squint he does it again: *Now!*

Moose makes it even clearer. Before the in-bounds he gets in my ear. "D, I been at you all year about you shooting too much. Well, baby, this is you now. Take this thing over!"

I don't need told again. I get the in-bounds from Devin, size up Charles, and attack. I lose Deon with a spin dribble to my left, then cross at the elbow around Fuller's man. No chance to get to the rim, so I pull up from twelve. It clicks front rim, spins right, but then kicks off the glass and in—the kind of roll that's been going the other way all year. Down to five.

They could take their time, but the chip on Deon's shoulder has grown too large. I can see it in his eyes as he comes up-court. That thing's going up. He tries attacking on the left wing, but I cut him off. He circles out top. He gets Vasco waiting on him again, hands out for the ball, but this time he shakes the big man off. Charles attacks me again. As he does, I can hear Vasco shouting at him: "Easy, Deon. Back it out!" Instead, he crosses it between his legs and fires a step-back three. I'm all kinds of on it. I get a piece, and when I turn to block out I see it's falling about three feet short. Fuller's locked in on it before anyone else, so I turn and go. Fuller knows what's up, gets it out to me in time, and I have a free run. There's no clowning now, just a quick rip through to cut it to three.

Now our crowd's back up and roaring. There might be a few people in the Hamilton section re-thinking their plans for next weekend. That quick shift in momentum—Deon forcing and us taking advantage—is the kind of swing that's gone Hamilton's way for so long, everyone's forgotten that the script could get flipped. Deon shuffles down the court to get the ball again. He has this glaze on his eyes—he won't look at me, his teammates, nothing but some far-off point. He's all out of sorts. I take the moment to flap my arms at our crowd a few times, draw those last few decibels out of them. When I turn to our bench, even Bolden and Murphy are just living in the moment. They're pumping their fists and screaming for a stop, Bolden stomping his foot on the hardwood a few times for emphasis.

This time Hamilton does take their time. With under two to go, why not? But after about thirty seconds, they start their offense in motion. Maybe it's their pride, like they think they're too good to play it safe. Soon enough, they get Vasco on the perimeter again, and Moose is soloed up. They flatten out. I can't leave Charles for a second, so all I can do is shout encouragement at the big man. "You got this, Moose. This is what you worked for," I holler at him. With about a minute to go, Vasco crosses left, then whips back right for a look—but Moose stays pinned on him, straight up with no reach. Vasco pumps once, but gets no space. Pumps again for nothing. Then he spins back the other way and fires a ridiculous leaner. *Bottom.* God, the guy's too good. But there was a whistle lost in the madness, and the ref comes flying at the scoring table to wave it off. A travel on Vasco. Probably a fair call, but you know that's not sitting well on the Hamilton side. While they all go ballistic, I get in Moose's face. "Way to be, big man! Way to be!"

He just huffs angrily, so worked up he can barely think straight. Then he settles and gets right back at me. "Bury these guys, D."

When that leather hits my hands on the in-bounds, everyone in the place knows I'm not giving it up unless I'm held up at gunpoint. I attack Charles on the right wing, but the defense hops and cuts me off. I back it out to the right baseline, Charles following me, but it's just

Slump 275

bait. As the defense recovers back to position, I spin hard baseline—past Charles, underneath a big crashing down—and I rise on the right side of the rim. But there comes Vasco, ready to pin that thing on the glass, so mid-air I duck under, shift the rock to my left, and spin it up from the other side. High off the glass, and straight down through. One-point game. I glance at the clock. Forty seconds left. Hamilton calls time.

In the huddle, Coach lets the first half of the break go by just to let us catch our breath. Then he smiles at us. "Right where we want 'em, boys," he says. "We've been playing on the edge all year long. But they're new to these kinds of games. So let's finish this." He lets Murphy explain how they think Hamilton will set up, then he reminds us before we break: "Play it straight. They've been getting jumpy, so they might shoot. But if it gets down around 10, we've got to foul."

As soon as they check it in, all the drama's gone. They just iso Charles way up top and let the clock drain. They all look broken up about it, like this is some kind of admission of weakness, but it's the smart move. I try to turn Charles, but he's too good to just rip it from him. He shakes me and then re-sets time after time. Finally, with fifteen to go, I know I've got to force the issue. The last thing we want to do is foul Charles, so my only goal is to get him to give it up. I hound him out top, forcing him to drive to beat the five-count. This time when he moves, Fuller's on it. He runs at him to double, I clamp down from behind, and Charles picks it up. We play it clean, wanting him to give it up, but when he finally kicks to Fuller's man, I sprint over and foul. Then I look up. Five seconds left.

The kid's a good shooter. You don't get into a Hamilton Academy uni if you're not, but at least he's not Deon or Vasco. He takes a deep breath, eyes the first one, lets it go—spins in. It gives them a two-point lead, but it was an ugly make. I see the kid shaking his head a little. From the far end, Bolden and Murphy shout at us to block out. We know what to do with it if he misses—no timeouts, just an outlet to me so I can push it, with everyone filling lanes behind. The ref checks it to the kid. As he goes through his routine, the gym is a tornado of noise, and then, just as he readies to shoot, it falls into this eerie hush, everyone holding their breath. He fires, and it's off to the side again, spinning out this time. *Go!*

Moose rips it clean since nobody wants to foul, snaps it to me at the right hash. Deon's in my chest, but I shake him and push it up. Across mid-court, top of the key, into the lane. And it's like a black hole in there, all Hamilton's players squeezing in on me. I don't even have to look to know where Devin is. I spin and put a laser on him at the wing. He has just enough time to get off a three-ball from his favorite spot.

Bucket!

We lose our minds. Jerseys come off, fans pour down from the stands, Coach Murphy jumps on a chair, rips off his tie and starts waving it around. The clock is all zeroes, and all that's left for Hamilton to do is beg the refs to wave it off, hoping against a cruel reality that the shot came too late. They do what they have to do—go to the monitors—and for a minute the celebration is put on hold. Everyone's just standing there, still half-hugging, watching the refs watch the replay. My mom's gripping my dad's arm like she's scared for her life. Jayson just keeps insisting that it's good to everyone around him. "Shot, then buzzer," he keeps saying. "Shot, then buzzer."

Finally, the ref stands up from the monitor. I hear Uncle Kid

Slump

shout, "That's a good bucket," like if it's not, there will be a riot. The ref, cool as if it's just a reach-in in the second quarter, signals to the scorer's table. "Good. Three points," he says.

There's a riot all right, but a good one. The whole damn school's on the floor, bouncing and dancing. Even Coach Bolden breaks out a couple moves, shaking those old bones in celebration—it lasts just about two seconds, but it sends everyone into a fit. I see Wes. I see Jasmine. I see Daniella. Hell, I see JaQuentin Peggs. Right now, we're all one.

And then I see Vasco. The rest of the Hamilton squad just emptied the floor, slumping off in disbelief. It was their first loss in 59 games. But there's Vasco, making his way through the crowd to me. He extends his hand.

"You're a very good player," he says, gripping my hand and pumping it up and down. "If we had to lose to someone, I'm glad it was you guys." All I can think of to say is thanks. Then he puffs out his chest again. That old, cocky Vasco, even in defeat. "Don't get used to beating me, Derrick," he says. "We'll meet on the court again sometime. I'll win."

"You go on thinking that," I say. He just gives me a quick thump on the chest, then heads off the court. He's just starting on his basketball journey, and I'm back in the thick of the celebration, living up the best moment so far in my basketball life.

32.

Everyone swears it won't happen to them. No let downs, everyone says.
We're just taking it one game at a time, everyone insists. But here we
are, mid-fourth, playing catch-up against Evansville Harrison, a trip to
the State Finals on the line. It's like we blinked a couple times and—
bam—it's the fourth quarter just like that.

It's not that we haven't played hard. Or smart. We're into it
possession after possession. But we don't have that edge—that surly
don't-mess-with-us attitude—we had against Hamilton. Even our crowd
seems different. They're loud, sure, but it's like that Hamilton game
drained them. Everyone's just waiting on a spark to get going, but with
four minutes left we better stop waiting.

Worse, our grind-it-out pace doesn't bother Evansville Harrison
a bit. A thirty-second possession was an eternity for Hamilton, but it
was clear from the jump that that's the way these guys roll. Across from
me all game, Dexter Kernantz—that sophomore who jumped me in the
point guard ratings—has kept cool. He directs traffic, stays calm, never
forces a thing. But give him a crease and he's gone. A drive and dish. A

Slump 279

slither to the rim. A pull up. A runner. The kid's got a complete game. He's never had that moment, that kind of defining play that leaves the spectators speechless, but he just makes play after play, one possession after another.

We're down 35-30. When I look over at the bench as I bring it up, Coach Bolden moves his hand in a circle, motioning me just to keep running our normal offense. He's kept poised all game, reminding us we're right in it, but now he looks tight-lipped and almost pale. Beside him, Murphy's seated with his head hanging down and his hands on his knees like he's about to get sick. Some voices cut through the crowd, singling me out to take over again. I throw a cross-over on Kernantz, but he stays with me as I drive. I spin back into the lane, hoping to use my size to get one over him, but I see Devin darting into the corner. The pass doesn't have quite the zip I'd like, but he's still got time—except he mishandles a little bit, throwing off his rhythm. I start to cut toward him to re-set, but then Devin gathers again and, despite his man recovering to challenge, forces up the three. Not the shot we need.

It scrapes off long, and Evansville Harrison gathers. They're in no rush, so instead of pushing for a break, Kernantz walks it up. He looks to the bench, signals in a play. Then he dribbles methodically to the right wing, looking for a post entry. He points at the floor to his left, calling for a ball screen, but I don't hear anyone talking me through it. I turn my head, just for a split second, to see who's coming, and that's all Kernantz needs. He darts away for a step-back three, a move he must have been saving up all game. He buries it. Buries us.

There's time, and we've got some fight in us. I get a pull-up, then muscle one in at the rim, then get Moose on a drop-off. The problem is,

Kevin Waltman

Evansville Harrison never blinks. We foul, and they make two. We foul, and they make two. Eventually, we get into desperation, trying to trade threes against their twos, but all that does is widen the gap, and with 20 seconds left, we're staring at a 48-39 deficit. It's over. It seemed like just yesterday we were sinking Hamilton. Then there was a week—a blur or pep rallies and pep talks and puffing out our chests and feeling good. A blink. Then this.

While I watch Kernantz stride to the line for two more free throws, the buzzer sounds. Jones for Moose. Reynolds for Devin. And a scrub who never sees time coming in for me. Coach is waving the white flag. As we walk off, our crowd stands for an ovation, honoring the seniors and honoring me for the best Marion East season since before I was born, but it's a melancholy sound, like they're waving goodbye to us. Well, it's not *like* that at all. This is goodbye. Basketball's cruel like that. Now we're the ones staring at the void of an off-season, and it seems like there should be something more—some, I don't know, some kind of ceremony or official procedure to help us understand. When we hit the bench, Devin starts to cry, but Coach is there. He grabs a towel from Darius so Devin can hide his face, and then he just sits with our senior guard, rubbing his shoulders as the clock ticks away.

33.

I don't cry. I'll let it pass with Devin, since it was his last game, but I won't give in to tears. I do mope around the house for a week or two. My family takes it easy on me. Mom lets me sulk wordlessly through dinners, Dad doesn't force me to talk about school. Even Jayson doesn't get his feelings all hurt if I turn down a chance to play XBox with him.

Then a Sunday rolls around and Dad insists we all go to church. He's up and about, looking like his old self, smiling and full of life. His limp is all but gone, but he still uses that cane any time he leaves the house. He can protest all he wants, but we all know he's started to enjoy having some style for once. It's a gorgeous day, the early March sun making the stained glass windows bright. I try to let some of the spring's hopefulness into my heart. It doesn't really work. Through the sermon, through the hymns, even through lunch at the Donut Shop, I still feel empty somehow, like part of me is still sitting on that bench watching our season slip away.

Finally, when we hit the bookstore, Dad collars me and tells me to sit with him. Mom and Jayson wander off to browse, and Dad orders a coffee and hot chocolate for us. Dad sits the hot chocolate in front of me, then leans his cane against the table and sits. We're at the same table where, a couple months ago, I dropped Daniella.

"Derrick, it's time," he says.

"For what?"

He smiles, and shakes his head. I know what he means, and he knows that I know, but I just don't want to talk about it. There's no escaping Dad though. "To snap out of this funk," he says. "I'm one to talk, I know. It took me forever to get over myself this winter, but here I am. And Derrick—" he leans forward— "losing a basketball game isn't quite the same as coming a few inches from losing your life in a car wreck."

"I know, but—" I let it trail off. There's no real fitting response to that. He's right.

Dad leans back and looks up at the ceiling, as if trying to remember something. Then he goes into a story about my grandpa, the one on Mom's side. He tells me about how great the guy was, working and working and working just so his family could get a foothold. He tells me one story about my grandpa going for a week eating nothing but bread and butter because they couldn't buy more groceries until his next paycheck. Meanwhile, the kids were still getting full meals. Then Dad leans in. "But it hardened him, Derrick. A life like that will do that. He was a great man, but by the time I met your mother he'd just grown kind of severe. He refused to watch anything but the news. He had doubts about me because sometimes I read *fiction*. He hated music. *Music*, Derrick! And sports? 'Foolishness played by fools,' he'd say."

I look at my dad, wondering what the point is. I mean, is he just trying to show that there was once a man who cared less about sports than he does? Is he embarrassed for having got caught up in that Hamilton game and now he wants to get all serious again?

"He was wrong about that stuff, Derrick," Dad continues. "His life had been all work. He lost sight of the things that can actually bring people joy. I admired him as much as I do my own father, but he'd forgotten how to have fun. In fact, you might say he and my parents—and to some extent me and your mom—bust our humps so you can have fun. And that's what basketball is. It's fun." He smiles then. "God, it's fun, and I'm thankful to you for reminding me of that this year. Everyone who was there will remember you guys beating Hamilton for the rest of their lives."

I can't help but smile now. He's right. It doesn't erase the loss that followed but, man, that Hamilton game was legendary. "Fair enough," I say. But he's not done.

"Look, Derrick. We know what's coming, right? That stack of mail in your room is just the beginning. Basketball could get real serious real fast if we let it. So let's you and me make a pact. Let's both remember it's fun first, okay? I think we both need that."

He holds his hand out, and we shake like men making a business deal. It feels good. For the first time, it lifts me out of my funk. Then Dad waves me to the stacks. "Now go find something to read, for God's sake," he says.

What I really want to find is Jasmine Winters. I've bumped into her here more times than I can count, but not in the last month or so. Time has passed for us. And now, strengthened by Dad, I'm feeling as optimistic as any other sixteen-year-old in springtime. I search and search, but she's not there. So I text her. She's always been more of a face-to-face person, but all of a sudden I just can't wait until I get that chance again.

She hits me back, and I slink down in the store, resting against a shelf full of science fiction while I try to pull any possible meaning out of her texts, searching for any clue that she's willing to give me another chance. It's there—she's flirty, teasing, quick to respond. We joke about Mrs. Hulsey, who flat-out lost it on one of her classes last week. We chat about Spring Break, and I learn that neither of us have plans. So there it is—a wide-open week for both of us. This season has taught me that I'm better with the rock than I am with girls, but one thing is true on both sides—you don't take a shot, you'll never make one.

We need to hang on break, I text.

What's 'hang'? she hits back.

You know.

No. Say it. You mean go out?

I wait. Give it a full five minutes so I don't seem over-eager. Then: *Yeah. Like that.*

It's a quick response. *I don't think so, Derrick.*

It stings, but I know the deal—you take a shot and sometimes you miss. But it's better to have taken a shot. I shove my phone back in my pocket and keep my chin up. Enough sulking. That's for chumps. Next season starts now. That's what Coach Bolden told me before we hit the bus that last time, and I didn't want to hear it then. But, like always, the man was right.

Later, when we pile into the car to head home, I pull my phone back out. There's a text waiting from Jasmine: *Just cuz I said no doesn't mean you shouldn't ask again. Try me in the summer.*

Slump

Mom starts the car, and Jayson reaches up between the front seats to crank on some music. Dad slaps his hand away, but Jayson just keeps on, finally winning their mock fight. Mom laughs at them, then wheels us out of the parking garage and into the light of a perfect spring day.

Kevin Waltman